I0583343

TELL
Me

The Organization-Book Two
M.K. MANSON

One Night Publishing

TELL ME

Copyright © 2024 M.K. Manson

The characters and events portrayed in this book are fictitious. Any similarity to real person, living or dead, or events is coincidental and not intended by the author.

No part of this book may be reproduced in any form or by any electronic or mechanical means. It may not be stored in a retrieval system, or transmitted in any form or by any means, electronic, mechanical, photocopying, recording, or otherwise, without express written permission by the author.

All rights reserved
ISBN: 979-8-9993141-2-3
Libray of Congress Control Number: 2025917529

Edited by: Editing4Indies
Proofread by: Karen at Barren Acres Editing
Formatted by: Bravia Books
Cover photo by: Ellen Christy Intimate Portraits, LLC
Cover model: Anonymous
Cover Design by: Frank Manson and Ellen Christy Intimate Portraits

Printed in the United States of America

Trigger Warnings

Stalking
Voyeurism
Attempted assault
Kidnapping
Sexual situations
Murder
Torture

To every girl out there who feels like they aren't good enough. Can't do anything right. Who thinks they are the troublemaker, the bad seed, the wild child...this book is for you.

Chapter 1
Gilly

I walk into my apartment, turn around, look into his piercing blue eyes, and slam the door in his big, stupid face. Letting out an exasperated sigh, I flop down on the couch and scream, "I can't take it anymore!" I pick up my cell and call my sister-in-law, Lola. When I first met Lola in Milan, I wasn't very nice to her, but she's turned into my third sister.

"Lola, I'm sorry to bother you with the new baby and all, but you're the only one who can make Rocky listen. He *has to* give me a different bodyguard. Nico is a jerk."

"What did he do?" I can tell by her voice she's rolling her eyes at me.

"He's treating me like a child."

"How?"

"I just wanted to go shopping. I wanted to wander around, try on a few clothes, and enjoy myself. But he ruined it." There's a pause, and I think I hear Rocky talking in the background.

"Why did you punch him?" she asks.

"How do you know I punched him?"

"He's on the phone with Ethan."

"That son of a bitch!"

"Calm down and tell me why you punched him."

"He said I looked fat."

"What?" She has her hand over the phone, whispering to Rocky. She comes back to me and says, "Maybe he doesn't know how to talk to women."

"He can talk to my fist."

Lola laughs under her breath. "I'll talk to Ethan."

"Thanks, Lola."

I toss my cell on the kitchen island, open the refrigerator, and take out a bottle of water when I hear a faint tapping on the front door. I jerk the door open to see Nico standing there.

"What do you want?" I snap.

Standing tall with his hands on his hips like Superman, he says, "I need to know if you're going out again tonight. I'd like to go home."

"You can go home and never come back for all I care."

"Look, I'm not sure what I did to you back at the dress shop, but I didn't mean anything by whatever I said to piss you off," he babbles.

Lifting my chin and staring into his ocean-blue eyes, I say, "Oh, so you didn't mean to call me fat, then?"

"I didn't say *you* were fat. I said the dress made you *look* fat."

"What the hell is the difference?"

"It was the dress's fault, not yours. Don't take it so personally."

"Don't you have any women in your life, Nico? Women take shit personally."

"For your information, I've had women in my life, but I've never seen a woman as touchy as you are, Miss Gilly."

"Don't call me that," I snap.

"Call you what?"

"MISS Gilly."

"Why not?"

"Because it makes me sound like my damn grandma. Just call me Guilia." Speaking in my best smart-ass voice, I say, "It's pronounced Joo-lee-ah, or just call me Gilly. It's pronounced Jill-ee." He's looking at me like I just grew a second head.

"I know how to pronounce your name, Gui-li-a," he mimics how I said the syllables. "I've known you for years." *Why does he make me so nervous?* "Besides, I don't think the boss would like it if I just call you by your first name."

"It's my name, Nico." *I'm so exhausted by this conversation.* "You can call me whatever *I* say you can call me."

"Fine, Gui-li-a," he pronounces each syllable slowly.

I give him a half smile and say sweetly, "See, now isn't that better?"

"I guess. I'll leave you to it, then. What time do you want me to pick you up for work tomorrow?"

"I'll be ready to leave by ten."

"I'll let the guard downstairs know you're in for the night. If something changes, text me, and I'll come back. Otherwise, I'll see you at ten… Guilia." His deep and sultry voice makes my panties wet.

"Night," I say a little nicer this time, and close the door with a soft click. Nico Acosta is a major and the head of security for The Martinelli Organization, or The Organization for short. My little brother Rocco Ethan Martinelli is our Don Supreme. Most people call him Ethan or Boss, but my sisters and I call him Rocky. Against my will, my brother chose Nico to be the head of my security team.

Nico is a handsome man. He towers over me at six foot two with 235 pounds of pure muscle. His dark brown hair is cut short and styled neatly, and his eyes are the dreamiest pools of blue. His strong, chiseled jaw is always clean-shaven. He's impeccably styled in true Mafia fashion—usually in dress pants and a button-down shirt with the sleeves rolled up. We attended the same high school, but he's two years older than I am. He was a senior and a linebacker on the football team, and I was a cheerleader.

I'm standing on the sidelines at the football game. I'm dressed in my red-and-white cheerleading uniform, clapping and yelling to the crowd. It's a home game, and the stands are filled with angry fans. Our team is losing by a score of three to six. This game will determine whether we make it to the playoffs.

The girls and I are trying to yell over the crowd, but it isn't working. Between cheers, I turn to face the field and look for Nico Acosta. He's a linebacker on our team, and he's so hot. I find him in the huddle, sweat pouring down his face as the quarterback, Craig Fields, yells out instructions. I think I can see him looking up at me through the metal bars on his helmet, and I get a slight tingle in my stomach.

They clap their hands and line up on the forty-yard line. The quarterback yells out his cadence, and the play begins. Nico slams into the player in front of him and runs past another, headed for their quarterback. He hits him with such force that the ball springs loose. Nico snags it and takes off running. The crowd is on their feet. Everyone is screaming as Nico heads for the end zone. He slams the ball into the ground, and his teammates surround him, bumping chests, slapping him on the helmet, and hugging him. He's smiling from ear to ear when I see him shoot a glance in my direction.

~

I'm ready to go when Nico knocks on my door promptly at ten. When I swing the door open, he says, "Good morning, Miss…" He shakes his head and corrects himself. "I mean, Guilia."

I giggle and nod at him. "Good morning, Nico. Can you help me carry these boxes to the car?"

"Of course." Nico picks up all three boxes and motions for me to go out the door. I'm mesmerized by his taut muscles through his black dress shirt, and my breath hitches. How I would love for him to pick me up in those big, strong arms and throw me over his shoulder. *Oh my God. What am I thinking?*

We take the elevator to the ground floor, and he loads the boxes into the back of the black Escalade. I slide into the back seat, and Nico takes his spot behind the wheel to drive me to my shop downtown.

My sisters and I bought a row of shops in downtown Johnsonville about a year ago. It was our dream to open shops to furnish women with everything they needed for a night out on the town. My shop provides hair, makeup, manicures, and pedicures. My oldest sister, Lillianna, owns a shop that sells clothes, jewelry, perfume, purses, shoes, and accessories. Our middle sister, Maria, has a passion for reading, so she opened a bookstore to cater to her love of mushy romance novels. Only one store is left on the strip, and we hope to purchase it as soon as the lease expires.

When my sisters talked me into buying the shops, I was excited about doing it with them. I was afraid I would feel trapped, but I actually like coming to work most days. I hired an incredible staff who runs the shit out of the place when I don't feel like coming to work.

My life has been quite different from my sisters'. Our father forced Lillianna and Maria to marry perfect strangers as soon as they graduated from high school. If my father had his way, they would've been married off even younger. Mother was a staunch believer in all of her children receiving a proper education. Her dream was for all of us to go to college, but my father had other ideas. So they compromised. Everyone stayed in school until they graduated from high school, and then he could ruin our lives.

Our father began training Rocky to take over The Organization from a young age. He hated every minute of it and swore he would get out from under Father's thumb one way or another.

That just leaves me. The last single Martinelli female. The rebellious one. The one who can never do anything right. The one who is always in trouble. The only one who always seems to find a fight.

I didn't want to be forced into an arranged marriage like my sisters, so I left the day after I graduated from high school—

6 M.K. MANSON

before my father could sink his claws into me and take away my will to live. The day I told Mother I was leaving feels like yesterday.

"Mother, I need to talk to you," I say, coming into the kitchen. "Can we sit?"

"Of course, my darling. What do you need to talk about?" she asks in her thick Italian accent. She brings the kettle to the table while I grab two mugs from the cabinet. We take our seats at the table, and I hold her hand in mine.

"Guilia, what's wrong? You're scaring me," she says, her eyebrows creased in concern.

"I'm leaving."

"What do you mean, you're leaving?"

"I'm leaving town, and I don't know when I'll be back." Mother reaches for a tissue.

"I knew this time was going to come."

"I'm sorry I've always been so much trouble, Mother."

"Oh, Guilia, you have never been any trouble. You know what you want, and you don't let anyone stand in your way. I'm so proud of you, my darling."

Warm feelings wash over me at my mother's words. She has never held me back. "Where are you going to go? What are you going to do?" she asks as she raises her hand to my face and wipes a tear from my cheek.

"I want to see everything this world has to offer. I want to see exotic places and meet interesting people. I want to experience life, good or bad, and I can't do it in this town."

"Your father—"

I cut her off. "Will be furious. I know. But I can't stay here and wait for him to take over my life. I just can't. It will suck all the life out of me."

She grips my hands and stares into my eyes. "If this is what you truly want... I won't stand in your way."

"Oh, do you mean it?" She nods. "Thank you. Thank you, Mother." I fall to my knees and put my head in her lap, then wrap my arms around her waist and hug her tightly.

"But..." I look up into her eyes, which are now wet with tears.

"But?"

"Don't tell your father you're leaving." When I open my mouth to speak, she holds her hand up to stop me this time. "Just pack your bags and leave while he's at work. If he finds out you want to leave, he'll do whatever it takes to keep you here."

"I don't want to hurt him," I hiss. I love my father, even though he has his own deranged plans for my future.

"It will be better for all of us if you just leave, Guilia."

Mother is right. He'll do whatever it takes to keep me here. Even if I could convince him to let me leave, he would have guards following my every move. I don't want that kind of life either. I want to be free.

"You are my baby girl, and I love you so much," Mother says.

"I love you too, and I always will. Thank you for this. I knew you would understand why I needed to leave."

"Of course, my love. I know exactly how you feel. When your father and I left Italy, we left our lives behind and started new ones in America to be free."

"I'm not leaving forever like you did," I say.

"Time goes by so quickly, my love. It will seem like forever to me, yet just moments to you. But I want all of my children to be happy, so go. Just let me know you are safe."

"I will."

I'm brought back to reality when Nico opens my car door. "Guilia, are you okay?" he asks.

"Yes. Yes, I'm fine. Just lost in a daydream." He helps me out of the vehicle, and I start my day at the shop.

Sitting at my desk, I try to work on payroll, but my mind keeps drifting back to those years when I was away from home. I left the morning after graduation, just like Mother told me to. I rented a little flat off the Rue Lecourbe in Paris with the help of my trust fund. I lay low for a few weeks, waiting to see if my father would show up on my doorstep and drag me home, but he never came.

I got a job waiting tables at a small bistro within walking distance of my flat and led a relatively uneventful life at first. It was all mine, and I was free. I began building my social media presence from my small flat, and once I hit one million followers, I made money hand over fist.

I moved to Milan with my assistant-turned-friend, Kara. She was a marketing genius. Companies sent me their products to promote while I was on my adventures, including sunglasses, hats, boots, and other items. As I became more well-known, companies would send me to places. I would stay in their hotels or go on their excursions, and all the expenses were paid.

It was great for the first few years, but after the Guilia train started rolling, we left all the fun back at the station. I wasn't doing what I wanted anymore. It was all for the sponsors and the fans. Kara kept pushing me harder and harder. It became all about money. I tried to walk away, but I knew I was in too deep and couldn't let everyone down. So when I was approached by a man at a posh party in Dubai, I took him up on his offer to add a little excitement to my life.

"All you have to do is carry this package on the plane with you tomorrow," the older man named Lorenzo says.

"What's inside?" I ask.

"Jewels."

"What kinds of jewels?"

He leans over and whispers, *"The stolen kind. We need a woman as beautiful as you are to carry the jewels between countries for us. The world knows who you are. You're famous. No one would ever suspect you of doing anything illegal right in front of the public."*

"What do I get for being your mule?"

"Five thousand American dollars."

"How much are the jewels I'm carrying worth?"

"Millions."

"I want ten grand and a hotel room."

"You're a greedy little thing, aren't you?"

"I am my father's daughter," I snark. *Negotiating comes*

naturally to me. "I'm the one taking all the risks. Why shouldn't I be paid handsomely for it?"

"I'll give you the ten grand, but only two nights in a hotel when you reach your destination."

"Deal."

That first transaction gave me the excitement I was looking for. The adrenaline rush I experienced going through security made me feel like I was high on drugs. Lorenzo became my handler, and over the next two years, we worked well together.

He would text me on a burner phone with the location to meet him. Once there, he would fill me in on all the details and where to pick up the packages. I never had a problem with security lines at airports or train stations. It was so easy. Someone would always recognize me, and once the photos started, security just wanted me out of their hair. They would wave me on through, and I would be home free.

Cassandra, the manager of my shop, knocks on my door, putting an end to my daydreams for today.

Chapter 2
Nico

I dropped Gilly off at the shop and headed to the office for a few hours. I left Jackson, one of our sergeants, in charge of watching over her. Buddy shot Jackson while he was standing guard at the boss's penthouse on the day he kidnapped Lola. He has been on light duty for months and is eager to return to work.

The boss, Ethan, isn't too pleased with me when I walk into his office. "What the hell are you doing here? I thought I told you to take care of my sister," he snaps.

"I've been following her around. But she's a handful, and I had some work I needed to do."

"I know she can be difficult, Nico, but I thought you could handle her," he says, dropping his papers on his desk.

"I *can* handle her."

"Who's with her now?"

"Jackson."

"Fine. So what did you need?" He picks his work back up and focuses his gaze on it.

"First, I was going to try to convince you to take me off Guilia's babysitting detail."

"Nope," Ethan quips, never looking up.

"I'm your major, and you've made me a fucking babysitter. What the hell, man?"

He raises his eyes to me and shoots me a cold, dark stare. "Babysitting my sister is the most important job you will *ever* have," he says through clenched teeth.

"Haven't I been a loyal soldier to you? Haven't I earned your respect?"

He puts down his pen and folds his hands on the desk in front of him. "I do respect you, Nico. I respect you so much that I gave you the most important job in the whole goddamn place." His voice gradually turns into a roar.

"I thought you were punishing me."

"Punishing you? I chose you because I trust you with my sister's life."

"Oh."

"Anything else?" the boss says through gritted teeth.

"No." I turn to leave.

"Nico."

"Yeah?" I say, turning back around.

"I know she's a handful, and she tries to be all tough and independent and shit, but there will come a day when she *will* need you."

"Yes, Boss." I exit the room and shut the door behind me.

I'm sitting at my desk, trying to work, but all I can think about is Gilly. I've watched her from afar for years. Now that we're being forced to spend time together, it's getting harder and harder to suppress my feelings for her.

High school, twelve years ago... I'm on the football field during a big game against St. Bernard. It's the championship game, and we're ahead by twenty-one points. The crowd is going wild. I catch glimpses of Gilly in her short cheerleading uniform on the sidelines. Her blond ponytail has red streaks on the side now, and it flies in the air as she takes her spot at the top of the pyramid. I watch her from a distance, like I always do. Sam smacks me on the back of my helmet and barks, "Hey, man, get your head in the game!"

We won the game, and we're the champs. Now, it's time to celebrate.

It feels like the whole school is in the gym afterward for a celebration dance. The football players take showers and walk down the hallway together. As we enter the room, we're greeted with hoots and hollers, and I feel on top of the world. Tonight's the night. I'm going to ask Guilia Martinelli to slow dance with me.

She's sitting across the room with her friends. They're laughing, and her smile lights up the room. Her hair is out of its tight ponytail and lies in soft waves down her back. She's wearing tight blue jeans and a pink short-sleeved sweater that makes her breasts look round and firm. I feel nervous and sweaty. I want to take her hand, lead her to the dance floor, wrap my arms around her, and hold her body to mine and never let her go. My heart races at the thought of kissing those soft peach lips, and a raging boner presses against my jeans.

The slow songs come on, and all the guys spread out across the gym floor in search of a dance partner. I don't need to search because my eyes haven't moved off Guilia Martinelli since I arrived.

I take slow, tentative steps in her direction. I tell myself I can do this. It's no big deal. I'm ten feet from her, and my heart pounds in my chest. I'm just asking her to dance. Five feet, she's almost within my reach. I'm going to do it this time. I'm going to have my arms wrapped around her in five, four, three...

Ronnie Carpentar's shoulder connects with mine as he brushes past me. He holds out his hand and asks her to dance. Her eyes look from Ronnie to me. I lower my gaze and continue to walk past them, like my heart didn't just explode in my chest. I just missed my chance to be with my angel.

I run my fingers through my hair and consider telling the boss about my feelings for his sister. I'm not sure if he knows what his father enlisted us to do to protect Guilia in Europe. How he rotated teams to watch her every move. How I volunteered for as many tours as Antonio would allow because I needed to know she was safe. Guilia can never find out the things I did to keep her safe.

When her father found out she had left home, he was furious. But when he found out she had left the whole goddamn country, his rage couldn't be contained for days. He killed five men with his bare hands. He searched for her for nine months, and when he finally found her, he had a team tailing her twenty-four seven.

Beckett and I have been in Paris for about a month now, staying in an apartment across the street from hers on the Rue Lecourbe. Our job is to keep out of sight and make sure she's safe. The first team assigned to watch her installed cameras in her apartment and the surrounding areas. We're always aware of what she's doing and who she's with. You wouldn't think that would be too hard now, would you? And it's not, until she heads out to a club with her rowdy friends or to the open-air market to go shopping.

Gilly leaves her apartment at ten every weekday morning like clockwork. She works at a bistro down the street. I watch her until one when Beckett comes to relieve me, and I'm back by four. On this particular day, she waits on a table with two men dressed in all black. When she comes to take their order, the one on the left gets a little handsy with her. Touching her on the arm and then her backside. She swats his hand away and smiles, but you can tell she's uncomfortable. She leaves, brings back their drink order, and stands beside the other man. He makes unwanted advances on her backside also. She was able to walk away before it got too intense, thank fuck.

The men in Paris are a little more forward than in America, but that's no excuse. All this touching is starting to piss me off. Knowing I can't blow my cover for something as small as this, I wait. When it's time to deliver their food, she brings another server with her to help and gets away fast. Smart girl. She checks on them but always gives them a wide berth.

When it's time to collect their check, she approaches hesitantly.

The first guy grabs her by the wrist, pulls her onto his lap, and tries to kiss her. I'm ready to pounce. But before I can cross the street, Gilly slaps his face, jumps off his lap, and punches him in the nose. Blood spurts everywhere, and his hands fly to his face. He's yelling in French as she throws her bar towel over her shoulder and walks away—her gorgeous peach of an ass swinging from side to side as she strides across the bistro.

I'm so proud of her. As a Mafia princess, you're trained to defend yourself, but this was the first time I've ever seen her in action.

I snap out of it with a smile on my face. I try to work on the security plan for Maria's bookstore, but I can't stop thinking about Gilly.

She and her friends make their way to Club Piotr in the city center. Beckett and I are big guys, but we don't want to stand out. We arrive dressed like the other bouncers in black dress pants and long-sleeved black shirts. We walk in the back door like we've done it a hundred times before and keep watch from the balcony above.

They party pretty hard for two hours and stumble out of the bar. Her friends get into a cab, but Guilia waves them off and starts walking in the direction of her flat. She's weaving back and forth in her four-inch red heels. Something spooks her, and she increases her speed. When she walks past the entrance to the alley, two large hands reach out and grab her. Just that fast, my angel is gone.

Beckett and I take off running. As we turn down the alley, we see a man in a black leather jacket hovering above her body in the back of the alley. Her pants are pulled down below her knees, and his hand is between her legs. His other hand is on her throat, pinning her down, and his mouth is on her breast.

Beckett rips him from her body and throws him into the trash bins nearby with a loud crash. It's the first guy who touched her at the bistro.

"Son of a bitch, he must've been following her," Beckett says.

*"Take care of this piece of shit and meet me at her apartment,"
I say as I fix her clothing. I pick up my unconscious angel and
cradle her in my arms.*

*I use my key to let us into the apartment. She's still uncon-
scious when I lay her cold body on the bed. I remove her shoes
and cover her with a blanket.*

*"You're okay, Angel," I whisper, running the back of my
fingers down her bruised cheek. The desire to kiss her sweet
lips is so strong that my body is leaning down for a taste before
I know it. Just before our lips meet, I hear the front door open
and shut. "Sleep tight, Angel," I say.*

I turn to look at Beckett when he enters the room. "Well?"

"I took care of it," he says.

"She's resting. Let's go," I say, motioning toward the door.

*My need to be with her is so intense. I want to cuddle her
into my chest and hold her all night, but since I can't do that,
I stay up all night and keep watch over her on the cameras
instead.*

*The following morning, when she wakes, she looks around
the room. Confusion etched on her face. She looks under the
blanket to see she's still dressed in the same clothes from last
night.*

*"How did I get here?" she mutters. "I can't remember any-
thing after Anna and Kara got in the cab." Her hand rubs her
throat, and she throws back the cover. She takes some clothes
from a drawer, enters the tiny bathroom, and closes the door.*

I shake my head. I can't sit here any longer, thinking about
the past when I could be with my angel in person.

Chapter 3
Gilly

I t's almost five o'clock, and Nico will be here soon to pick me up. He and Jackson take turns defending my honor from the Big, Bad Wolf. I know I can take care of myself, but my brother needs this right now, so I play along. My life in Europe looked like all fun and games to the public, but it was so much more than that.

The bell on the door to the shop jingles, and Nico enters, scanning the room. "Are you about ready to go?" His head is always on a swivel, checking our surroundings.

"Yeah, give me a minute to finish up, and I'll be out," I say as I shut down my computer.

I tell the girls good night and head for the front of the building to climb into the Escalade.

"Where to?" Nico asks.

"I'm hungry. Wanna get a bite to eat somewhere?"

"Sure, where?"

"Can we go to the little Italian place Rocky and Lola are always talking about, Anthony's? I think it's on Rogers Street."

"Be there in fifteen." Nico doesn't talk much. He's all business, all the time.

He parks the car, comes around to my side and helps me climb out. He walks me into the restaurant lobby and says, "I'll wait in the car. Just let me know when you're done."

"What? No. Come and eat with me," I say, pulling on his arm.

"I don't know, Guilia. This isn't a good idea."

"What better way to keep an eye on me than sitting at the same table with me? Come on, I don't want to eat alone." I stick out my lip and give him my best puppy dog eyes.

"Fine," he grumbles. The hostess shows us to a table in the corner, and he holds out my chair for me to sit.

"Lola always says how great this place is," I say, looking around the old-world style room. "I think it's because this is where they met and fell in love." I hold my hands up to my face and look all swoony.

"Yeah. They are mushy, aren't they?"

"Yep. Have you ever been in love?" I ask, and Nico looks like he's going to throw up.

"Nope, sure haven't. Have you?"

"Not that I know of. The way Lola talks, you'll know when it happens because your whole world changes." I roll my eyes.

Nico takes a drink of his water and looks like he would rather be anywhere else but here. The silence is deafening while we sit uncomfortably, Nico always watching our surroundings. The hostess brings a basket of warm bread that makes my mouth water just from the smell, and we place our order. I ordered chicken parmesan, and Nico ordered chicken carbonara. I pick a warm piece of bread from the basket for myself and hand him the basket, continuing to pelt him with questions.

"So what did you do after graduation?" I blurt.

"I came to work for The Organization, remember?" His answer makes me feel stupid. He cuts his piece of bread neatly in half and puts butter on both pieces, making sure to spread the butter all the way to the edges.

"Oh yeah, that's right."

"Why did you leave town?" he asks, taking a bite of his bread.

"I had to. If I didn't leave right after graduation, my father would've taken over my life like he did my sisters'. He would've made me marry some old, fat, hairy mobster and have a bunch of brats."

"How do you know that?"

"Have you not met my sisters?" My smart-ass tone takes him by surprise. I tear off a piece of my bread and pop it in my mouth.

"They're not married to old fat guys," he says confused.

"You know what I mean. They didn't get a say in who they married. Father decided. He didn't care if they were mean or beat them. He just wanted the connection between the two families. Lil and MeMe got lucky because their men aren't abusive, that I know of. They both have actually grown to love their husbands. But I don't want to *grow* to love someone. I want to fall head over heels in love with someone." Nico looks like a deer caught in headlights. "I'm sorry. I didn't mean to get carried away. Tell me about yourself. We're together all the time, and I don't really know that much about you."

"You know me. We've known each other since we were teenagers."

"I know you were two years ahead of me in school, played high school football, worked for my father, and now work for Rocky. You never talked to me. You were *his* friend, and our house wasn't the one the kids flocked to after school."

"I'm thirty-one years old. I work for the mob, and I babysit a Mafia princess. And I wasn't friends with the boss. Freddy was, kinda, I guess." He goes back to eating his bread and looking into his water glass.

"No, I mean things like, do you have any brothers and sisters? What do your parents do for a living? What else do you want to do with your life? Do you like to travel? Where do you want to go? Stuff like that," I say.

"You know Freddy is my brother. My parents are dead. I

enjoy working security for The Organization. Only if I have to. Maybe a cabin in the mountains," he barks his answers out in quick succession.

"Wow, thanks," I deadpan. They bring our food, and we eat for a while in silence.

"I'm sorry," he says quietly.

"For what?"

"For being a dick."

I can feel my cheeks heat, and I chuckle under my breath. "You're not a dick. I just wish you would relax."

"I can't relax, Guilia," he quips.

"Why not?"

"Because it's my job to take care of you. If I relax, bad things happen."

"Why do you say that?"

"Because it's happened to me before."

"Tell me."

"I can't tell you, and I can't let anything bad happen to you either."

"I'll be just fine. I can take care of myself. I've done it for years," I say, waving him off.

"But you shouldn't have to take care of yourself."

"I know who I am, Nico, and I knew what kind of a life I was coming back to when I returned to Johnsonville. The city is much safer than it was when I left all those years ago. Rocky's made sure of that. But he's not my father. Do you think I just walk around willy-nilly? Not paying attention to my surroundings or to what I'm doing? Because I don't. It was instilled in me at a very young age that people take what they want and don't give a fuck who gets hurt." I brush my hair back out of my face, sit up a little straighter, and continue.

"I would just like there to be one day in my life when I don't have to look over my shoulder. Don't have to worry about my family. Don't have to worry something bad is going to happen." I stand with tears rimming my eyes. "I need to use the restroom, if you'll excuse me." Nico stands, and I walk away.

I enter the restroom and check under the stalls to make sure I'm alone, then I allow myself a minute to break down and cry. I don't let myself cry often, but when I do, it comes hard and fast. There's a soft knock on the bathroom door.

"Occupied."

"Angel," someone on the other side of the door says softly. *What the hell did he just call me?*

I walk to the door. "Nico?"

"Can I come in?" he asks. I wipe the tears from my face and take a deep breath, twisting the lock and opening the door a bit.

"What are you doing?" I say, peering through the crack in the door at the glorious man with an uneasy look on his face.

"Can I come in, please?" I step back and open the door. He comes inside and locks the door behind him. He takes my hands in his and looks me in the eye. "You left before I could speak."

"And..."

He clears his throat and steps closer to me. The smell of leather and citrus fills my nose. I look up into his soft eyes, waiting for his words.

"I'm here so you can feel safe. I'm here so you don't have to look over your shoulder. I'm here to take care of you."

"You called me... Angel?"

"Because you look like an angel to me." His hands reach up to cup my face. "Don't cry." He uses his thumbs to wipe the tears from my cheeks. "Do you feel safe with me?"

"Yes." My breath hitches

"I'll never let anything happen to you. I would lay down my life for you."

"Don't say things like that."

"It's true."

"Why would you do that?"

"Be... Because you're special to me." I want him to kiss me

so badly. He looks at me like he can see inside my soul. Like he knows everything I'm thinking. "I'll go pay the check, and we can leave whenever you're ready." I nod, and he leaves the room, shutting the door behind him. I stand there, missing his touch already.

What the hell just happened? We hate each other... don't we?

Chapter 4
Nico

I pay the check and wait for her at the end of the hallway. We walk through the restaurant with my hand on her lower back as I usher her to the SUV. She slides into the back seat, and I settle in behind the wheel. "Where would you like to go now?" I ask.

"Home," she says so quietly I can barely hear it.

I drive to her residence, park the car in the parking garage, and escort her to the elevator. When we reach her apartment door, she uses her key to unlock it and turns to me. Confusion is etched on her face.

"We hate each other, right?" she says.

"Yeah, sure. Whatever you want, Guilia," I say, and she goes inside. I stand there until I hear the lock click. I ride the elevator to the bottom floor and let security know she's in for the night. I slide into my Camaro and drive the five minutes to my house. I bought it so I could be close to Guilia if she ever needed me. Tomorrow is Saturday. She doesn't go to the salon on the weekends. When I pull into my garage, I send her a text.

If you need anything, text me.

GUILIA

Okay, thanks.

This evening has been weird as fuck. Why in the hell did I say those things to her? I was doing just fine with short and sweet answers until I followed her to the ladies' room and almost kissed her. Why the hell did I call her Angel? I used to call her that when I was watching her all those years ago. I never wanted her to know her nickname.

I took a shower and rubbed one out, but it's not helping. I want her so damn bad sometimes I can't see straight. As I lie in my bed, I can't understand why she said we don't know each other. I know everything about Guilia. I know she hates to be cold, hates going out in the rain, and hates jalapeño peppers. She loves to eat ice cream in bed and makes warm milk if she wakes up from a bad dream during the night. She makes a little whiny noise when she's getting hangry and hums to herself when she cooks.

I need to get out of this assignment because it's going to go sideways if I'm not careful.

Chapter 5
Gilly

*T*he street is dark, and not another soul is around. The bag of diamonds weighs down the pocket of my trench coat, and I can hear footsteps behind me as I continue to the meeting place. The faster I walk, the quicker the steps behind me echo. I can't turn my head because I don't want them to know I know they are there, so I speed up. But the footsteps continue. I walk faster and faster until I'm running. My breathing is labored, and my legs are burning. Turning the corner, I run head-on into a man dressed in all black with a ski mask over his face. I scream, and he grabs my shoulders in a tight, pinching hold and shakes me.

I fall to the floor with a thud. My eyes search my surroundings. I'm in my apartment. In my bedroom. On my floor. I try to take some deep breaths and get to my feet—another nightmare. I haven't had one of those in weeks. This one was just like the others—a masked man and a bag of diamonds.

I walk across the room to the large picture of my parents on the wall. It swings to the side, and I remove the loose piece of drywall behind it. I stand there and stare at my little black safe. I type in the combination, and the door pops open with a click. Reaching inside, I pull out a black velvet bag and pour the contents into my open palm. Diamonds. Lots and lots of sparkling diamonds rest in my hand.

Germany, two years ago. I met Lorenzo in our usual spot in the village. He hands me a black bag and gives me my instructions.

"Take these to Walenty Heiderman in Berlin. He'll meet you at Charlottenburg Palace on Tuesday at nine. Walk to the bottom of the stairs in front of the fountain and take a seat on the concrete viewing bench to the left. He will sit to your right and say, 'It's a lovely day to see swans.' Your reply will be, 'I prefer beavers.' Leave the bag of diamonds on the bench beside him and walk away. Don't look back."

"How much does it pay?" I ask.

"Twenty thousand." I smile and take the bag.

I arrived at the location a few minutes early. I stop at the bottom of the stairs to admire the water and take a seat, as instructed. People walk by, but no one ever comes to sit beside me or says the phrase I'm listening for. Lorenzo didn't tell me how long to wait, so I sat there for two hours. I've sent Lorenzo five text messages, but he hasn't answered me.

At eleven thirty, I get the hell out of there. My Uber takes me to the hotel, where I pack my bags and check out of the room as quickly as possible. Something is wrong, but until I find out what the hell happened, I need to hide.

I've never had a problem passing off packages before. Now, I'm stuck with these diamonds that were probably stolen from a member of the international mob, and I don't know who to return them to without Lorenzo.

I tried everything I knew to find Lorenzo, but I never heard from him again. I was hiding and hopping from country to country for weeks before I decided the safest place for me to be was home. I knew Rocky could protect me. But first, I need to tell him what I've done. But I'm not ready to be *Gilly the fuckup* again so soon. I let out the breath I'm holding and dump the diamonds back into the bag, locking them back into the safe until I can figure out what to do next.

Chapter 6
Gilly

This weekend has been a rainy one. When it's gloomy outside, I just want to cuddle under the covers, eat ice cream, and watch sappy movies on Netflix. Lola calls.

"Hey, Lola, what's up?"

"I just wanted to call and see how your first week with Nico went."

"I thought you were going to get Rocky to lay off the security or at least switch him out with someone else."

"I tried, but he said everyone is busy with assignments, so you'll have to keep Nico a bit longer."

"Ugh." I let out an exasperated breath.

"Did something happen?" she asks.

"No... Yes... I'm not sure." My voice is laced with confusion.

"What's that supposed to mean?"

"He called me... Angel."

"Angel? Where the hell did that come from?"

"Hell if I know."

"Tell me."

"I kinda forced him to go to dinner with me at Anthony's on Friday night."

"Anthony's." *I can almost hear her waggling her eyebrows from here.*

"I didn't want to eat alone, so I asked him to join me. He wasn't talking to me, so I started asking him questions. He was giving me short, snippy answers, and I got a little upset. He followed me to the bathroom. That's when he called me... Angel."

"Hmm. What did *you* do?"

"I was so dumbfounded. I didn't know what to do."

"Why were you upset in the first place?" Should I tell Lola how I feel? She knows what living in a Mafia family is really like. Maybe she'll understand. She would understand more if I confided in her about the diamonds, but I can't do that, not yet. She'll run straight to Rocky, and I'm not ready to tell him about this yet.

"Because I told him that just once, I wished I didn't have to worry about my surroundings, my safety, my family."

"Oh, Gilly, I'm so sorry."

"That's why I left in the first place, but now that I'm back, it's just... I feel like I can never truly relax. Like someone is going to jump out of the woodwork to hurt me."

"That's what the security is for, Gilly. You have to trust they'll protect you. It's their job."

"That's basically what Nico said."

"Can I ask you a question?" Lola asks.

"Sure."

"Did you feel this way when you were traveling the world? I mean, did you feel safer back then?"

"In a way, I guess, because I only had myself to worry about. I didn't know what was going on at home, so I didn't worry. Is that selfish?"

"I don't think so. You left here to be on your own and not to be controlled by Antonio. Are the feelings you're having now making you want to leave again?"

"No. I don't want to leave. I think I'm safer here, for now." Especially since there is a bag of diamonds in my safe.

"Do you still want me to try to get Nico taken off your security team?" Lola asks.

"No. Just leave it as is for now." I blow out a breath.

"Keep me posted... Angel," she says with a deep, sexy voice.

"Yeah, yeah. Bye."

I hang up with Lola and get a text from Nico.

NICO

Are you planning on going out today?

> No, it's raining.

What does the rain have to do with it?

> I don't like to go out in the rain.

Afraid you'll melt?

> Ha. Ha.

Why don't you like the rain?

> It's not that I don't like the rain. I want to lie in bed in my jammies, eat ice cream, and watch movies all day when it's gloomy outside.

Do you like to text when it rains?

> I guess, why?

I thought maybe we could do the question thing again.

> Are you sure? You didn't seem to like it very much yesterday.

I don't like to talk about myself. But I could ask you questions.

What do you want to know?

I snuggle down into my bed and wait for the inquisition.

What kind of ice cream are you eating?

Rocky road. What kind do you like?

Chocolate chip. Who did you date in high school after I left?

I went to the prom with Peter Valentine.

Oh my God! You're kidding me, right?

No. What's wrong with Pete?

You mean Sweetie Petey. He's gay.

No, he's not!

Oh yes, he is. He hit on Ethan in the locker room after PE once. I thought Ethan was going to beat the fuck out of him.

That explains a lot.

What exactly?

He didn't kiss me good night or ask me out again. I thought he liked Kimberly because he stared at her all night.

OMG! Maybe he was really staring at her date, Will Bradford!

You know I'm laughing my ass off
right now, right?

> Yeah, so am I. Why didn't you
> date in high school?

I couldn't have the girl I wanted.

> Who did you want?

If I tell you, I'll have to kill you.

> Ah, come on, please.

That was years ago.

> I know, but I'm curious.

Why does it matter?

> Let me see if I can guess.

Okay. You get three guesses, then
we drop it.

> Fine.

> Carol Ann MacMillan.

Your teeny-bopper cheerleader
friend?

> Yeah.

Nope.

> How about Becky?

Fowler?

> Yeah.

Foul-smelling Fowler? No, thank
you. You have one more guess.

Melanie Monroe?

Nope, you lose. Next question.

Dammit. What bad thing happened when you were watching someone?

Next question.

Nico, please.

The three dots appear, and I wait impatiently for his reply.

Let's just say I was on watch, and they were taken. They could've been hurt very badly if I hadn't gotten to them in time.

Did you make it in time?

Yes.

Who was it?

Someone I was watching for Antonio. It was a long time ago.

I'm sure they were glad you were there.

Most embarrassing moment.

Pass.

Oh no. You made me tell you.

Don't laugh.

Me. Laugh at you, Angel? Never.

There's that damn nickname again.

> Once, when I lived in Milan, I got locked out of my apartment in my panties.

Just your panties?

> Yup.

WTF! How, may I ask, did that happen?

> I ordered food, and the delivery service left it at the door across the hall by mistake. I tried to run across and get it, but my door slammed shut and locked. I stood in the hallway, holding a brown paper bag of food while wearing only my panties.

Wow! I'm not laughing, I swear.

> Sure, you aren't.

What did you do?

> I held the bag in front of my tits and marched downstairs to the super's office and asked him to let me back into my apartment.

I bet he loved that.

> He was very polite.

Did he make you walk in front of him?

> Yeah.

He was watching your ass in those little white panties.

How do you know that?

What man in his right mind wouldn't want to look at you in your panties?

No, how did you know they were white?

There is a long pause…

Don't all women wear white panties?

Yeah. Sure. I guess.

I gotta go for now. Can we talk tonight instead of text? My fingers hurt.

LOL. Sure, call me later.

Will do.

Chapter 7
Nico

S hit, shit, shit. That was too close. If I'm going to talk to Guilia, I need to be more careful. White panties. How could I be so stupid as to mention that? I remember the day she came out of her apartment in those white panties, but she didn't tell the whole story though.

I can't help but watch her on the hidden camera when she's walking around her flat, half naked. She has just gotten out of the shower and is wearing white cotton panties and a towel on her head. Call me a perv, I don't care. She's beautiful. Her perky tits on display for the whole world to see. Well, they would be if the whole world could see her. For now, it's just me who gets to see her creamy skin.

Her phone lights up, and she looks down at the screen. She heads for the front door and checks the peephole. She takes the chain off the door and pokes her nose out. Suddenly, she dashes out the door, and it slams shut behind her. What the fuck! I know for a fact her door locks when it shuts because I set it up that way.

Switching to the camera in the hall, I see her standing in front of her door, just staring at it in disbelief. She's holding the brown bag by her side and stamps her foot in frustration. After trying the knob several times, she slaps the door. She pauses, squares her shoulders, raises the bag to her chest, and stomps down the hall to the elevator.

I switch the camera again to see her exit the elevator with her head held high, as she crosses the lobby as if it's the most normal thing in the world to walk around half naked in public. Some people point and snigger, and two old ladies' mouths fly open.

Standing in front of the superintendent's office, she knocks on the door several times before he finally opens it a crack. His eyes grow wide, and he opens the door farther. A dirty smile crosses his lips as he looks my angel up and down. Holding her paper bag against her chest, she gestures toward the elevator. He leans back inside, grabs his keys, and follows her to the elevator. They board the elevator, and he stands behind her, eyeing her body up and down. My blood boils at him ogling her like that. His gaze narrows in on her tight ass in those white panties. I'll break his fucking neck if he tries to touch her.

She leads him down her corridor to her door. He uses the master key to unlock it, and she rushes inside. His foot jets out and blocks her from closing the door. There's confusion on her face as they talk. She shakes her head. He pushes on the door, but she pushes back. In one swift movement, she uses the heel of her hand to hit him in the chin and shove his head backward, causing him to lose his balance, just enough so she can slam the door closed on him.

The hallway camera shows him walking off, rubbing his neck in defeat. My angel had to fight her own battle again. I hate this "watching from afar" shit. I want to be the one to protect her and keep her safe. I'm so proud of her. And I'm so glad she remembers her training.

I turn on my computer and zoom in on her lying on her bed. She's lying on her side, facing the camera, and her eyes are closed. She's cuddled up in a fluffy blanket as her chest rises and falls with each breath. The television plays in the background, and her empty ice cream container sits on the nightstand. I go for a run, shower, and eat while she sleeps.

At seven o'clock, I dial her number and watch her on the camera as she picks up her cell. She smiles when she looks down at the screen, and I think my heart misses a beat.

"Hey there," she chimes.

"Hey. Are you still in bed watching movies?"

"Yep."

"What are you watching now?"

"*Nice Girl Like You*. You have to watch this. It's hilarious."

"Okay, give me a sec." I pull up my Netflix account and find the movie. "Okay, I got it."

"Wait, I'll start mine over, and we can watch it together."

"Isn't that a little weird?" I ask.

"You've never watched a movie with someone before?"

"Not like this. Usually, we're in the *same* room."

"You need to broaden your horizons, sir." Sir… Oh my fucking God. I want to hear her call me sir when she asks permission to suck my cock. *Down, boy.*

"What if I have to pee?" I ask.

"We can take a potty break. Oh, and snack breaks too. You'll have exactly five minutes to do your business and get what you need, then get back to your spot."

"Five minutes? Why only five minutes?"

"Because, silly, it's a race." *Sure, like I would know it's a race.*

"I think you're making up the rules as you go, Miss Martinelli."

"Aw, come on, it'll be fun."

Laughter erupts from us as the girl in the movie is trying to say the word cock in the mirror. Guilia's laughter makes me want to pull her into my arms and kiss her. I'm watching her on the camera as she wipes happy tears from her cheeks. *What the fuck am I doing?*

After about thirty minutes, out of nowhere, she yells, "Potty break!" She drops the phone on the bed, and I can see her scampering across the floor to the bathroom. This woman is driving me crazy. I take this time to grab some chips and a soda.

"Whew! That was close," she says, flopping back on the bed.

"You know it's not really a race, right?"

"I know, but it makes it more fun."

I toss a few chips into my mouth and crunch them.

"What are you eating?" she asks curiously.

With my mouth full, I say, "Potato chips."

"What kind?"

"Lays. Why?"

"I'm out of chips."

"Oh, I won't eat anymore. I'm sorry." I place the bowl on the coffee table.

"No. No. It's okay. Enjoy." I stare at the bowl. Just one more. I reach over and pop one in my mouth, trying to chew it quietly.

"You know you can eat them, right?"

"That's all I'm going to eat. I'll stop." I can hear her chuckling under her breath.

A few minutes pass, and all I can do is stare at those stupid chips. I'm not even watching the movie anymore.

"You're looking at the bowl of chips, aren't you?" she asks. *How in the hell did she know that?*

"Yes," I confess.

"Would you just eat them already?"

"If you insist." Grabbing the bowl, I start stuffing the chips into my mouth. I wolf them down to get it over with. With a sigh, I pop the last one into my mouth and lick my fingers clean.

"Okay. There. I'm done," I say.

"Are you good?"

"Yeah."

"Let's finish the movie, then."

We can't contain our laughter when the girl in the movie is in the sex shop and her lips grow huge. Gilly is rolling on the bed, tears streaming from her eyes, and she lets out a snort.

"Oh my God! My stomach muscles are killing me!" She laughs.

"I know, mine too. She's hilarious."

When the movie ends, I see her stretch across the bed and turn off the TV.

"I've kept you long enough. What are you going to do tomorrow?"

"I don't know."

"Let me know if you're going out somewhere."

"Nico."

"Yeah."

"I'm sorry you have to babysit me."

"It's okay, Angel. I like spending time with you. Besides, the boss says keeping an eye on you is the most important job there is."

"That's sweet."

"Night, Angel."

"Night, Nico."

Chapter 8
Gilly

I crack my eyes open, and again, the room is dark as the rain pelts the windows. I take a shower and work on the computer for a while, but I'm bored. Picking up the phone, I call Nico.

"Guilia. Is everything okay?" His voice sounds on edge.

"Yeah, I called to see what you're up to on this dark and gloomy Sunday?"

"Just doing a little paperwork. What do you need?"

"Nothing. I'm just bored."

"Because of the rain?"

"I guess."

"You're not watching movies and eating ice cream?" His voice sounds more relaxed today.

"Maybe later. Sorry I bothered you."

"You didn't bother me, Guilia."

"I think I'll take a nap."

"Okay, I'll talk to you later then," he says.

At seven, there's a knock on my door.

"Who is it?" I say, trying to lower my voice to sound like a man. When I look out the peephole, it's dark.

"It's me, Nico," he says. *What's he doing here?* I smooth my hair and blow on my hand to see if my breath smells.

"What are you doing here?" I say, opening the door with a smile.

He removes his finger from the peephole and holds up a paper bag. "I come bearing ice cream and potato chips." I just stare at him as he stands in my doorway with a crooked smile on his face. "Can I come in?" he asks hesitantly.

Snapping out of it, I say, "Yeah, come in, come in." I wave my hand to usher him inside.

"What are you doing here?" I ask as he makes a beeline for my kitchen.

"You know you just asked me that, right?" he says, setting the bag on the counter.

"I'm sorry. It's just we don't normally *hang out*. I mean, it's okay, but you caught me off guard."

"I can leave if you want me to. I'm sorry if I'm interrupting." He turns to head for the door, but I stop him with my hand on his forearm.

"No, don't go. Stay."

"Okay." He smiles as he starts pulling pints of ice cream out of the brown paper bag. "You said you liked rocky road, right?" he asks.

"Yes. Did you bring chocolate chip for y…" I stop talking when he holds up a pint of his favorite flavor. My face can't stop smiling. "What do you want to watch tonight?" I ask, pulling out spoons from the drawer and poking one down in each container after he opens them.

"Something funny, like last night." We both sit down on opposite ends of the couch. I pick up the remote control and start searching through Netflix for something to watch.

He digs the spoon into his ice cream and takes a bite. "Are you okay? I was worried about you," he says with his mouth full.

"Yeah, I'm good. What did you do today?"

"I went for a run, did some work, took a shower…normal stuff. What did you do?"

"I called my friend Kara in Italy, and we got caught up. Then I took a shower and a short nap."

"Do you miss Europe?" he asks.

"I do, sometimes. Mostly because all my *real* friends are there."

"Why do you say it like that? 'All my *real* friends are there.'"

"Because they didn't know I was Antonio Martinelli's daughter. I could just be myself and have fun."

"I understand that, but I'm glad you're back home."

"Why?"

"I… um… I know your family missed you while you were gone."

"Here, let's watch this. It's called *The Hating Game*," I say, starting the movie.

"You really like Lucy Hale movies, don't you?"

"I can relate to her a lot. You know, on the dating front." *More like on the awkward front.*

"You don't have any trouble finding dates."

"I guess not, but it doesn't mean I don't feel awkward. I never know what to say, and they always want more than I want to give. I didn't have a lot of second dates while I lived overseas."

"You haven't been back in town very long. I'm sure you'll start dating again," he says, licking his spoon with his long, thick tongue. I bet he could put it to good use between my legs. *Where the hell did that come from?*

Pulling my stare away from his mouth, I say, "What if I don't want to *date*? Why can't I find someone to just have sex with? You know. No strings attached. No feelings. Just sex."

"Just sex?" He stares at me in disbelief.

"Sure, why not? Guys do it all the time, and they're studs. Girls do it and we're sluts."

"No, no, I'm not calling you a slut. I don't want you to get hurt, that's all."

"Why would I get hurt if it's my idea?" I dig to the bottom of my pint for one more scoopful.

"Because women have all these *feelings*. Men can fuck you once and never think of you again."

"I could do that."

"Sure, you could," he says, rolling his eyes at me.

"I could! You don't believe me?"

He shakes his head. "I don't want to find out. Can't you just date?"

"No! I want to have a fuck buddy."

He spits his ice cream all down the front of his shirt.

"A fuck buddy?" He grabs a napkin and wipes his shirt. "Your brother would kill the guy, then he would kill me because I'm supposed to be watching out for you."

"My brother has no say over my sex life." I square my shoulders and sit up taller.

"He's the head of the family."

"So what? It's *my* body. If I want to give it to someone for pleasure, I will."

"Oh my God. I'm going to die right here on this couch." He flops dramatically back on the cushions.

"I never should've said anything to you." I sit back against the couch beside him and fold my arms over my chest.

"No. No. I'm glad you told me what you were thinking about doing."

"Why?"

"Because now I know what I'm dealing with on this assignment."

"Will you help me find a fuck buddy?"

"Oh, hell no!" He jumps up from the couch and starts pacing the room. He runs his fingers through his hair while he mutters to himself and starts to break out in a sweat.

He stops in front of me. "Let me be your fuck buddy."

Chapter 9
Nico

can't believe I heard those words come out of my mouth. I'll be the one the boss kills.

"You?" she asks with a blatant laugh.

"Sure, I can be just as unfeeling as the next guy." *What the fuck am I saying?*

"You want to be my fuck buddy?" Confusion is written all over her face.

"Well… I… I don't want it to be some random guy. You know me. You trust me not to rape and murder you, right?"

"I think so," she says.

"I can fuck you. I mean… I can do this for you."

"You're crazy. You know that? Rocky *would* kill you."

"He gave me this assignment."

"He said for you to *watch me*, not fuck me."

"You're right. Let's forget the whole fuck-buddy thing and watch the movie." We resume our spots on opposite ends of the couch and stare at the screen. I'm not paying attention to it because now all I can think about is being Guilia's fuck buddy. Could I really do that? Could I have sex with the woman of my dreams and not catch feelings for her?

Halfway through the movie, she yells, "Potty break!" She pauses the TV and runs for the bathroom. I run to the kitchen and search her cabinets for a big bowl. I pour the chips into it and grab two bottles of water. We spot each other from across the room and race back to the couch.

"I win!" she shouts.

"Oh no, I win!" I yell back, and we both burst out laughing.

"I got the drinks and snacks. You just peed," I say, holding them out like an idiot. We're sitting side by side on the couch now, so we can both reach the bowl of chips. I can feel her thigh touching mine, and electricity shoots through me. *How can I fuck her for fun if I can't even sit beside her on the couch?*

She resumes the movie, and we crunch away on our potato chips. I can't concentrate on the movie. Her berry scent fills my nose, and I keep thinking about what it would be like to be inside her. I laugh when she laughs, so I don't look like a complete idiot, but I can't stop thinking about being my angel's fuck buddy.

When the movie is over, I head for the door. "I'd better get going. Glad you're going to forget all about the whole fuck-buddy thing," I say nonchalantly.

"Who said I was forgetting about it?" I stop dead in my tracks. *Fuck.*

"Well, I just assumed…"

"You assumed wrong. Can you pick me up at ten in the morning? I have some calls to make."

"Calls to make?"

"Possible fuck buddies, of course." I think I'm going to throw up as she closes the door in my face again.

At eight the next morning, I'm sitting in Freddy's office.

"I need to talk to you about something." I'm wringing my hands in my lap.

"Dude, what the fuck is wrong with you?" he asks in his deep rumbling voice.

Freddy is my brother, but he's also the head of illegal operations for The Organization and the boss's second-in-command. We've always been close. He's the only family I have left.

"I need to talk to you as my brother and not as my boss for a minute, okay?"

He puts down his pen and leans forward. "What did you do?" he snarks.

"Nothing... yet."

"Tell me."

"You know Ethan is making me babysit Guilia, right?"

"Yeah, and I know you hate it and you've been trying to get out of it like a little pussy."

"Maybe this was a bad idea." I stand, shaking my head.

"Sit! I'm listening. Go on."

I blow out a breath and sit back down. "You can never tell Ethan. He'll shit."

"Good God, man! Tell me already." His deep voice booms through the room.

"She wants a fuck buddy."

He lets out a loud cough.

"See, that's what I did. I about choked on my ice cream when she said it last night."

"Last night? Where were you last night?" he croaks.

"Watching a movie in her apartment."

"Watching a movie?"

"I was protecting her. Well, keeping her company and protecting her."

He stares at me for a long moment. "What in the fucking hell is a fuck buddy?"

"It's someone you have sex with, but it's just for fun. No relationship. No feelings."

"Why does she need one of *those*?"

"She feels uncomfortable dating. She needs to build her confidence. She thinks if she has a fuck buddy, then she can have her sexual needs met with no baggage."

"Why the fuck are we talking about Guilia's sexual needs?" Freddy groans. "I'm gonna die."

"Because you're my brother and you're going to help me," I say.

"Ethan is going to kill them. You know that, right?"

"I told her the same thing. But you can't tell Ethan. Ever."

"You're there to protect her. You kill them."

"I can't."

"Why the fuck not?"

He stares at me for a second, and then it hits him. His eyes grow wide, and he says, "No fuckin' way! You're her fuck buddy! Are you stupid?" he shoots forward in his chair and yells in my face. "Ethan... Oh my God... he'll..."

I hold my hands out to stop him from spiraling. "I only offered to be her fuck buddy, and before you kill me, don't worry, she didn't accept."

"Why the hell would you offer something like that?" He jumps up from the desk and goes over to the window and leans his forehead on the cool glass.

"Think about it. I don't want to see her with the other guys on my watch. I would always have to be on the lookout for the person who was going to take advantage of her or, worse, hurt her. And then I'd have to kill them. This way, we know who it is. I won't do anything to hurt her, and..."

"And what?"

"I've always had a crush on her, Freddy. Even when we were in high school. Why do you think I always volunteered to watch her in Europe?"

"Oh. My. God! How did I not know this?" Freddy is freaking out again.

"Because I never told anyone, until you, right now." He's pacing the room, mumbling under his breath and shaking his head. I've never seen him like this before. "What are you thinking?" I ask.

"I'm trying to think of a way to keep Ethan from killing my only brother." He plops down in his leather chair, puts his elbows on his desk, his face in his hands, and stares at me through his fingers.

"Do you really think you can just be her fuck buddy?"

"I don't want her to be with some stranger. Someone who doesn't know how to treat her like she deserves."

"I hear you, bro, you like her. But can you fuck her and not catch deep feelings for her?"

"I've gotta try."

"Do what you think is best." He lets out a sigh. "I'll try to run interference with Ethan."

"Thanks, Freddy."

"But you better not hurt her," he says, pointing a finger at me.

"I would never hurt her."

I knock on my angel's door at ten.

"Good morning. Are you ready to go? I have a meeting this morning," I say.

"Sure, let me get my bag." She grabs not one but four bags and heads toward the door.

"Here, let me help you," I say, taking them from her.

"My hero," she says sarcastically.

I load all of her shit into the car and pull out of the garage, headed for the shop. I can hear her on the phone with someone.

"What are you doing tonight?

"About eight.

"How about you come to my place?

"Do you think you can handle it?

"Okay, see you then."

"So you have somebody coming over tonight. That's great," I say. *Just fucking great.*

"It's my first candidate."

"Candidate?"

"Yeah, for fuck buddy." I pull the car over as fast as I can and turn around in the seat to look at her.

"Are you fucking serious right now?" I snap.

"I told you I thought it was a great idea."

"I know what you said, but I thought you gave up on the idea last night."

"You wanted me to give up the idea, but I didn't say I would," she says.

"I can't let you do this, Guilia."

"You don't have a say in this, Nico. It's my body," she snips. *Again, with the crossed arms and the pouty face. How I'd like to spank the brat right out of her.*

"From a safety perspective, this is not a good idea."

"Safety shmafety."

"What's your brother and sisters going to say?"

"First of all, I already told my sisters, and they're proud of me for taking control of my body. Second, it's not Rocky's business as either my Don or my brother who I give my body to."

"What if someone tells?"

"My sisters have my back. You're the only other person who knows. Are *you* going to tell Rocky?"

"Fuck no!"

"Well then, I think we're all good here."

"I… uh…" Knowing she's right, I say, defeated, "I'll get you to work." I turn back around and feel like I've been slapped in the face. She just totally put me in my place. Why didn't I just say, *I'll be your fuck buddy*?

I let her out at work, and confirm I'll be picking her up at four today. I check in with Jackson and head to work at The Organization. I can't concentrate on anything other than Gilly fucking some rando guy tonight.

I pull in front of the shop a little before four, and she's already waiting in the doorway for me. I exit the car and hold the door open for her. I slide back behind the wheel and ask, "Home?"

"Yep, I gotta get ready." She looks like she just had a day at the spa. Her nails are freshly painted. Her hair is styled, and her makeup is a little darker.

"You're really going through with this?" I ask.

"Yes, Mr. Security Man, I think I am. I got a manicure, a pedicure, a facial, and got my hair done. Oh, and I got a new dress to wear," she says, holding up her bag.

"You look amazing," I croon.

"Thank you." I almost think I see her blush in the rearview mirror.

"But I still don't think this is a good idea. You know, from a safety standpoint," I say.

"We're just going to talk. He's going to pick me up, and we're going to Lowell's for dinner. We'll talk about the details of the arrangement, and I'll see if he's the right fit. If he isn't, then it'll just be a nice evening out."

"Jackson and Marco will be your security team tonight. They'll be following you in the SUV. If you need to get out of the date, text them or get their attention."

"I will, *Dad*. But I'll be just fine. I'm a grown-ass woman."

"I know you are. But I need you to be safe."

"You *need* me to be safe. What does that mean?"

"You know what I mean, or Ethan will kill me. You're my responsibility."

"Yeah, right. Your responsibility." She doesn't say another word for the remainder of the ride to her apartment and the walk to her door.

"Remember what I said about Jackson and Marco."

"I will," she says with a huff as she goes inside and shuts the door in my face, for the third time. I want to be on the other side of that door. I want to be her fuck buddy. But I know I have to respect her decision and trust she won't do anything stupid tonight.

Chapter 10
Gilly

"Are you sure you want to do this?" my oldest sister, Lilliana, asks over the phone.

"Yes. Now, stop worrying. I won't be alone. Jackson and Marco will be close by if I need them. Besides, I've met Josh before."

"But you said it's been a long time since you saw him last." She whispers into the phone, "Are you planning on having sex with him tonight?"

"I don't know. Maybe," I whisper my words back to her, being the smart-ass I am."We need to talk about all the details first."

"You make it sound like it's a business deal." She chuffs.

"It is, in a way. He may not even be interested in doing it with me anyway," I say.

"What guy in their right mind wouldn't want to fuck you, Gilly? You're an intelligent, gorgeous woman, with a great sense of humor."

"Whose brother is the head of the Mafia," I deadpan.

"Yeah, well, then there's that."

"I'll be fine. I won't do anything stupid."

"I'm not worried about you, honey, I'm worried about him."

"I'll call you tomorrow."

"Be safe."

"I will. Good night."

There's a knock on my door promptly at eight. Promptness is a good quality to have, right? It means he's interested, but when I open the door, it's not Josh.

"Nico, what are you doing here?"

"I just wanted to check on you before your date arrives and see if I can talk you out of doing this," he says.

"No, you can't. Now, would you please leave?"

The elevator dings. Josh steps off and swaggers in our direction. Nico takes a step back as Josh stops in front of me. He leans in, kisses my cheek, and says, "Guilia. You look stunning."

"Thank you. Josh." My face feels hot at his words. Nico raises an eyebrow at me. "Oh sorry. Josh, this is Nico. He's the head of security. Nico, this is Josh."

They are both the same height so they shake hands and stare at each other for a moment. "Have a nice time, and don't stay out too late," Nico says flatly, eyeballing Josh.

Josh knows who I am and all about my family. Me having a security team doesn't surprise him at all. I grab my purse, and we head out. Josh drives us in his BMW M4 coupe as if we were just a normal couple going out to dinner. All the while, the black SUV carrying Jackson and Marco tails our every move.

"It's been a long time since we've seen each other. How have you been?" I ask.

"I've been busy with work. I'm a stockbroker now with Hendrix and Roswell."

"That's a high-pressure job, I'm sure."

"It has its moments. How was backpacking across Europe?" he asks.

"I wasn't exactly *backpacking* across Europe. I was a content creator on TikTok, Instagram, and YouTube. It's hard work to keep an internet presence up and running." *Not to mention being a diamond runner for the mob.*

He actually laughs. "Yeah, all the free stuff doesn't hurt, does it?" I'm not sure I like his snide comment, but I brush it off and keep going.

"Have you thought about my proposal?"

"About being my girlfriend? It kind of came out of nowhere, don't you think?"

"I didn't ask you to be my boyfriend. I asked you if you wanted to be my fuck buddy."

"What exactly is the difference? I mean, I get the fuck part. What does the buddy part have to do with it?"

"No commitment, no feelings, no romance, just fucking."

"Like friends with benefits?" he asks.

"I guess, but we don't have to hang out or anything. We just call each other up when we want to fuck." It's not a hard concept to grasp, Josh. *What the hell?*

"Can I fuck other people?" he asks. *What the fuck?*

"How many other people do you want to have sex with, Josh?"

"Well, you said we wouldn't be exclusive, so I should be able to be with whoever I want." I guess I didn't think this through. I don't want to catch any diseases because Josh can't keep his dick in his pants.

"You wear condoms, right? I mean, we would need to stay clean for one another."

"I don't like condoms."

"How many girls do you sleep with, Josh?"

"It depends on whether I go out or not. I usually bring one back to my place whenever I go out."

"A different girl every time you go out?"

"Yeah."

I'm having serious reservations about Josh. He sounds like a slut. He pulls into the restaurant parking lot and leans over, kissing me on the lips. He plunges his tongue into my mouth. His hand lands on my breast, and I give him a shove.

"What the hell are you doing?" I clip.

"I thought you wanted to fuck?"

"I wanted to have a grown-up conversation with you and see if you were the right fit for a partnership."

"We talked. Let's fuck," he says, brushing my hair back and attacking my neck with his lips. I shove him again.

"I'm not fucking you in this car, Josh!"

"Oh, I know. I need to feed you first. I got it. You're gonna make me earn it." He waggles his brows at me. "Cool. I can play your game as long as I get to fuck you tonight." I think I've heard just about enough from Josh. He's a pig.

He gets out of the car and moves to stand by the trunk and lights a cigarette. I step out of the car and slam the door. I smooth down my dress, whistle, and wave to Jackson and Marco. The blacked-out SUV pulls in beside us.

"Well, this has been a real blast, Josh. Have a nice life," I say, walking toward the SUV.

"But what about being your fuck buddy?" he asks.

"How about you just fuck off!" Jackson looks between us and offers his hand to me. "Now that's an actual gentleman." I take Jackson's hand, and he helps me into the back of the car.

"Take me home, please." I lean my head back on the headrest and let out an exasperated breath, feeling like I just dodged a bullet.

I should've known Jackson would've snitched and told Nico they were taking me back home. Because he's standing in the hall in front of my apartment door when I exit the elevator.

"Fuck," I groan.

"Thank you, Jackson. I'm in for the night," I say, leaving him on the elevator.

"Why are you here?" I ask in disgust as I unlock my door.

"Jackson said your night didn't go as planned, so I thought I'd come by and check on you."

"I'm fine," I grumble as I walk in the door and leave it open for Nico to follow.

"What happened?" he asks, shutting the door behind him.

"He was a selfish asshole who had no manners and sleeps with any woman he comes into contact with," I say a little too loudly. I drop my purse on the island and grab the handle of the refrigerator, pulling it hard enough to make everything on the door rattle.

"That's half the men in the city, Gilly."

I kick off my shoes and let out a harrumph as I flop down onto the couch.

"He's not the right guy for the job. He's a player," Nico says.

"I know that now, but where do I find the kind of guy I'm looking for?"

"What traits does he need to have?"

"He can't be a disgusting pig like Josh."

"Okay, what else?" He chuckles. "What do you really want?" He sits down on the couch beside me.

"He needs to have manners and understand this arrange-ment is for *both* of us. I don't want to be just a piece of meat. I want to be treated with respect." I sit crisscross applesauce on the couch and put a pillow in my lap. "I want to have fun and laugh, as well as have great sex. I just don't want the relationship part. Why can't I find someone I trust to do this for me?"

"You'll find the right person if you're sure you really want to do this."

"I'm very sure. I'm not giving up. I have more people in my arsenal I can try." I get up and walk over to my desk, where I pull out my address book.

"What are you doing?" he asks.

"I'm not giving up this easily. I want to try again." He rolls his eyes at me and stands.

"I'll let you get to it, then," he says.

Chapter 11
Gilly

I t's Friday night, and I have another cross-examination to perform. That's what all this is starting to feel like. Tonight's contender is Maurice Packard. He's thirty-four years old with brown hair, brown eyes, glasses, and a mustache. He's roughly six feet tall and weighs a lean 200 pounds. I met him at a party at Maria's house when I moved back to town. I think he was her husband's friend.

I cross the room and open the door. I half expected Nico to be standing there, but he wasn't. Maurice stands in my doorway all cleaned, pressed, and looking fine. He's a business executive, not a mobster, so he has a different air about him.

"Maurice, won't you come in?" I say with a smile.

"I was surprised when you called, Guiliana. It's been a long time."

"It's Guilia," I clarify. "It has been a while, but you know what it's like getting a new business off the ground."

"Business?"

"I opened a row of shops on Market Street with my sisters last year."

"That's great. How's that going for you?"

"It's been a real learning experience, but I enjoy working with my sisters. Would you like to sit down, or would you like to go on to dinner?"

"Can we sit down for a minute?"

"Sure." I extend my hand for him to have a seat. "Would you like a drink?"

"No thanks. I'm good." I sit down on the couch beside him. He's toying with the cuff of his jacket.

"Are you okay?" I ask.

"Actually, I thought maybe we could talk more about the proposition you suggested on the phone. I need to be sure I understand what you're asking."

"Of course."

"You're looking for a *fuck boy*?" he asks tentatively. Hearing him say those two words makes me almost laugh out loud.

"No, silly, I said a fuck *buddy*." I chuckle, but he doesn't look at all amused.

"I still don't understand."

"We wouldn't be in a relationship. There would be no commitment, and no clinging allowed. We call each other when you need a little... sexual fulfillment. That's all."

"How often does this take place?" He speaks very professionally, as if we're discussing a merger or something.

"As often as we want, I guess. We both must use protection when we have *relations* with other partners and be tested periodically for STDs." I added the testing part since Josh was such a hoe bag.

"I-I-I'm not sure I'm interested in a relationship like that."

"That's the beauty of it. It's not a relationship at all."

"But it kind of is. You call each other when you need sexual fulfillment. But then what happens when it's over? Do you just leave? No aftercare, no cuddling, no nothing?"

"Well, no."

He shakes his head and stands. "I'm sorry, Guilia, but I don't think this is going to work for me. I'm thirty-four years old. I'm tired of one-night stands and blind dates. I want more in my life now. Besides, I don't think I could fuck you and just *leave*." All the oxygen leaves my lungs at his comment.

"What's that supposed to mean?" I'm not sure if it was a compliment or an insult.

"You're a beautiful woman, Guilia. A woman I could fall for. I can't just fuck you and leave. I would want to stay and care for you, hold you, and... love you." *Love me? Clingy much? Holy shit! Yeah, he needs to go.*

"I'm sorry, Maurice, but that's not what I'm looking for." He walks toward the door and turns back.

"If you have a change of heart, give me a call."

"Sure," I say as I close the door behind him. I lean my back on the door and bang my head against it. I was just turned down. I never dreamed this would be so hard. I growl in anger as I walk down the hallway to my bedroom.

~

Nico

I watch as douchebag Maurice leaves. No kiss, no hug, nothing.

"Yes!" I shout to myself as I fist pump the air. He must've been a dud for her to turn him down so fast. I watch as Guilia walks into her closet, and a few moments later, she comes out dressed in lavender sleep shorts and a pink tank top. She leaves the room again, coming back with a bowl of ice cream and turning on the TV. I wait until she's almost done with her ice cream before I text her.

> How was your date? Jackson said you never left.

GILLY

> Oh shit. I forgot to tell them to go home. I'm not going out after all.

I'll let them know.

I already sent Jackson a text and told him the night was a bust and to go home when I saw Maurice leave.

What happened? Was he boring?

GILLY

No, he wasn't interested.

Wasn't interested in you?

Nope.

Is he gay? You know this wouldn't be the first guy you dated who was gay.

No, he's not gay! He just doesn't want a fuck buddy. He wants an actual relationship.

Ah. Not your type.

Nope.

Sorry.

He was nice about it. He even said I was the kind of girl he could love.

Love! What the fuck? Who says the L-word on the first date?

I thought it was sweet.

Too needy. He's gotta go.

Yeah, I know. I guess I'll have to keep looking.

Of course, I'm watching her on the cameras in her apartment. I see her get up and grab a book from her dresser. She climbs back on her bed and starts flipping through it. She points at the page, her finger landing on a name.

Do you remember Nathan Reed?

Nathan Reed from high school?

Yeah, do you know him?

You don't want him.

Why not?

Because he's worse than Joshie boy.

How do you know that?

Let's just say we partied in high school, and he wasn't a nice guy.

Maybe he's changed.

Guys like him don't change. They just learn to hide it better.

What did he do?

He attacked Cindy Cook.

Attacked her?

You know...

No, I don't know. Be more specific.

Damn her. She's just going to make me say it.

The rumor was he put drugs in her drink at the homecoming dance and had his way with her when she passed out in his car on the way home.

He had his way with her?

Gilly, you're killing me.

He raped her.

I never heard that before. I looked him up on the computer, and he has never been arrested. Not even a speeding ticket.

Like I said, they learn to hide it better.

And like I said, maybe he's changed.

I doubt it, but you do whatever you want.

You know I will.

Why is she so fucking stubborn?

See you Monday morning.

Night.

Chapter 12
Gilly

Five days later, I'm on another date. I guess Nico doesn't approve of Nathan because he didn't show up on my doorstep tonight. I haven't broached the subject with Nathan yet, so at least we made it inside the restaurant this time. So far, he's been a perfect gentleman. I guess Nico was wrong, after all. We're tucked away in the back of the room, having a pleasant conversation.

"I followed you on Instagram while you were gone," he says, swirling his spaghetti with his fork and spoon. "Your trip to Krakow looked fun."

"Thanks. I enjoyed touring Wawel Castle. Poland is such a beautiful country."

"Why did you move back to Johnsonville? Your life was so exciting over there."

"It was exciting. But I missed my family." *And I'm on the run from the international mob for taking off with a big bag of diamonds.*

"I understand that."

"What about you? What have you been doing the past few years?" I ask.

"You know, I recently made partner at Smith, Wilcox, Johnson, and now *Reed*."

"No, I didn't know. That's amazing. What type of law do you practice?"

"Corporate. Let me know if you ever need anything. Maybe I can help you out."

"I will. Thanks." Taking a sip of my wine, I replace the glass and say, "Look, I wanted to talk to you about something. You can say no if you want to. There's absolutely *no* pressure."

"Sure, sweetheart. What is it?"

I inhale a deep breath and begin, "Have you ever heard of fuck buddies?"

He chokes on his spaghetti. His face turns red, and he gasps for air.

"Oh my God! Are you all right?" There's more coughing as tears roll down his cheeks. The server comes over and asks if he's okay.

"Yeah, yeah, I'll be fine," Nathan sputters.

I suppose I need to make sure people don't have anything in their mouths when I ask that question.

"If I had known it was going to kill you, I wouldn't have asked."

"No. No. You caught me off guard, that's all." He wipes his mouth with his napkin. "Go ahead. Ask your question again. I'll be ready this time."

"Have you ever heard of fuck buddies?" I hush my voice across the table this time.

"No, I haven't. What is that exactly?"

"A fuck buddy is a person you call whenever you just want to have sex. No relationship, no feelings."

"Why are you asking me this, Guilia?"

"Because I'm looking for one."

"A fuck buddy?" His voice is higher now.

"Yeah, and I thought maybe since you're so busy being a high-powered attorney, you might not be interested in a relationship and everything that comes with it. Maybe you would want to be my buddy."

"You don't even know me," he says, rubbing the back of his neck and shaking his head.

"We've known each other for years."

"In passing. We never dated in school or even had the same friends."

"Weren't you friends with Nico Acosta?" I ask.

"I wouldn't exactly say we were friends. What do I have to do?"

"We stay available to one another. When you want to have sex, you call me and vice versa."

"That's it?" he asks.

"We have to use protection if we have sex with other people and get tested periodically. Are you a hoe bag, Nathan?" I ask. His eyes grow wide, and he's looking at me like I've lost my mind.

"I don't know, Guilia, am I?" he asks, raising a curious eyebrow at me.

"No feelings, no stalking, no relationship, just sex. And you can't tell *anyone*. You know who my brother is, right?"

"Oh, I know who Rocco Martinelli is, all right."

"It has to stay between us," I say.

"I can do that, but…" I don't hear him rejecting me, so I continue my selling points, as if I'm in a television commercial trying to convince him to buy my laundry detergent.

"Aren't there some nights you just need a good fuck? You don't feel like dealing with all the other bullshit that comes with it?"

"Yeah, I guess so."

"It's the perfect solution," I say.

"I get it. You're making the offer sound sweet, but…"

"But what? You don't find me attractive?"

"Oh my God, Guilia. You're an amazing woman." He grabs my hands and whisper-shouts at me. "It's just."

"What?" I'm getting frustrated, fearing I'll be rejected again.

"What if we're not sexually…compatible?" he asks.

"There's only one way to find out," I say, staring into his eyes and standing my ground.

"Why are you doing this?"

"Because I'm tired, Nathan. I'm tired of all the bullshit relationship stuff. I'm not good at it. I don't want to do it anymore. Sometimes a girl just needs to get fucked and fucked good." His eyes widen, and a smirk spreads across his lips.

"We *are* two consenting adults," he points out.

"That's right. No one needs to know our business."

He sits up straighter, squares his shoulders, and looks me in the eye. "When do we start?"

"Really?" I can't believe my ears. "Tonight, if you want."

"Of course." He raises two fingers to our server. "Check, please."

The security detail is hot on our tail as Nathan drives us back to my apartment. He parks, and we head for the elevator. Neither one of us says a word when we step inside. My hands are sweaty, and I think my armpits are leaking. I wonder if he's as nervous as I am.

We stop in front of my apartment door, and Nathan places his hands on my waist.

"Are you sure about this?" he confirms once more.

"Yes." I place a chaste kiss on his lips, and I slide the key into the lock.

Chapter 13
Nico

D aniel's voice booms through my earpiece as I fly through the streets of Johnsonville toward Gilly's apartment.

"They're entering her apartment, Boss."

"I heard you the first time you said it, Daniel. I'm driving as fast as I can."

What the fuck is she thinking? I told her what a piece of shit Nathan Reed was in high school and how he attacked Cindy Cook. She didn't hear one word I said. Her one-tracked mind is set on *fuck buddy*. Why didn't she take me up on my offer? At least I'd know she wasn't going to be physically hurt if I was doing the fucking.

"Boss, they're standing by the door kissing." Christ, how am I going to get through this night listening to my angel getting fucked by this maniac?

"Where's the van parked? I'm almost there."

"We're behind her building in the alley."

"Copy that." I park on the street, run down the alley, and enter the van. "What's happening? Is she all right?"

"Yeah. But I don't like this asshole. There's just something about him, ya know."

"Yeah, I know. Turn the speakers on and turn the volume up." Daniel takes off his headset, and their voices come through the speakers.

"Would you like to sit down?" she asks, gesturing to the couch. They sit side by side on the edge of their seats. He reaches out and takes a strand of her hair between his fingers and twists it around his finger, leaning forward, trying to get her to look at him.

"Are you nervous?" he asks smoothly, brushing her hair back over her shoulder.

"Maybe a little. Shouldn't we get to know each other better before we...?" He doesn't give her a chance to finish before he's pulling her mouth to his and kissing her hard and deep. His hand moves to the back of her head and grabs a handful of her hair. He pulls her head back roughly and stares into her eyes—no doubt trying to gauge her reaction.

"I *am* getting to know you, baby." She winces at the tug of her hair before his mouth crashes back down on hers.

I'm pacing around this tin can, and I want to break every-thing in here. I put my hands in my hair and pull hard, trying to take my mind off what I'm being forced to watch as her head of security. *Yeah, keep telling yourself that's why you're watching every move he makes, dumbass.*

He eases her back on the couch, and his hands start to roam over her body. I concentrate on my angel's eyes, looking for any signs of hesitation in them. When his hand reaches for the hem of her dress, she jerks back to consciousness and bolts upright. She pushes her dress down and asks nervously, "Um, would you like some wine?"

"No wine, thanks," Nathan says sharply, pushing her back into the couch and scooting in closer. This time, he's more aggressive in the way he touches her. Squeezing her breast in one hand while he grips her chin with his other, he holds her exactly where he wants her.

"She's still kissing him back," Daniel says quietly, trying not to anger the beast fighting desperately to break out of my chest.

"I can see that, Daniel," I say with clenched teeth. One of her hands comes around his back from behind, and the other reaches up and strokes his hair. She pulls him closer to her while his head moves down her neck with kisses and licks. He pulls back to unbutton her collar, and when his hand dips inside her dress, she pushes him off and leaps from the couch.

"Maybe we should stop for tonight."

"Stop? You started this fuck-buddy shit," he barks.

"I know, but I thought we could get to know each other a little more and go a little slower before we—"

He cuts her off as he stands. "You wanted to be *fucked*. No strings, no commitments, no relationships, that's what *you* said."

She's backing away from him, but he matches her step by step. "I do. I mean, I want to. I just need to go slower."

"I don't do slow. I don't do soft. I don't do...gentle, Guilia."

In two strides, he has her twisted in his arms once again, shoving his tongue down her throat and lifting her dress. She pushes back on his chest.

"Maybe you're right. Maybe we aren't compatible," she nervously says, trying to wiggle free.

"You haven't given me a chance to show you just how compatible we are yet, beautiful."

"I-I-I think you should leave." She shudders.

"No. You don't mean that. All this was your idea. You were basically begging me to fuck you at the restaurant."

"I know and I'm sorry, but I think I've changed my mind."

"Changed your mind?" He shakes his head and laughs. "You fucking changed your mind."

"I don't think my brother would like this."

He roughly grabs her by both shoulders and holds her away from him. She winces at his grasp.

"You bitch! How dare you threaten me with your brother!"

"I didn't threaten you. I don't think Rocky would like me doing this, that's all." Good girl, playing the mob card.

He shoves her away from him. "You're just a little cocktease, aren't you?"

"I didn't mean to be, but you're scaring me," she says quietly.

His eyes grow wide with rage while his fists clench at his sides.

"Scaring you. Scaring you! I'll fucking scare you, bitch!" he yells as he lunges for her again. This time, he throws her over his shoulder. She's kicking and beating her fists on his back as he carries her down the hall to the bedroom.

"I'm going in," I yell as I open the door to the van. I start running toward the apartment building, and say into the earpiece, "Jackson. Marco. Let's go."

Adrenaline is pumping through my veins as I sprint up the stairs instead of waiting for the elevator. I kick in the front door to her apartment and barrel down the hall. Her bedroom door is locked, so I slam my shoulder into it and burst inside.

My eyes scan the room, finding my angel pinned beneath Nathan on the bed. Her dress is bunched up around her waist, her panties are down to her knees, and his hand is between her legs, just like the night in the alley in Paris. He has both of her hands pinned above her head in one of his while she bucks and struggles. *He's fucking touching what's mine.*

"Get the fuck off her!" I roar as I grab him by the back of his shirt and throw him to the floor. He springs to his feet, and I punch him in the face. His head snaps back, and he throws his body at me, but I shove him away, hitting him in the face again with my clenched fists. Right, left, right, left until he falls to the floor. He tries to get up again but can only get to his knees. I use my boot to kick him in the side, and his spent body falls to the floor. Blood runs from his bruised, unrecognizable face when Jackson and Marco enter the room.

"Get this piece of shit out of here," I instruct them. When I turn back around, I find my angel huddled in a heap at the head of the bed. Her knees are pulled in tight, and her head is buried inside them. The sound of her whimpers fills the room.

"Angel," I say cautiously. Her head is shaking wildly. I sit on the edge of the bed and push her blond hair away from her face.

"You were right. I should've listened to you," she cries.

"Angel, it's over," I say as I pull her onto my lap and wrap her in my arms. I pull the duvet over her shaking body.

"Get him the fuck out of here!" I yell at the guys again, but they're looking at me with their mouths hanging open. "What the fuck are you looking at? I said to get him out of here!"

"Yes, Boss," Marco says, finally snapping out of it. They pull Nathan up from the ground. His head hangs low from his beating, and unrecognizable groans leave his chest. They haul his body out of the apartment, and I hear the door slam shut. Guilia stays on my lap while I rock her like a child who had a nightmare.

"He's gone. Shh. It's okay, Angel." She grips my shirt in her fist, and her whimpers have turned into full-on sobs.

"Hey." I try to soothe her tears. "I've got you. You're safe now."

"I'm sorry," she mumbles. I take her face in my hands, brushing tear-soaked strands of hair from her face, and try to get her to look at me.

"You have nothing to be sorry for."

"I shouldn't have started all this fuck buddy stuff. It was reckless and irresponsible to think I could find someone I could trust to do this with me. I should've stayed away from Nathan like you told me to. I just wanted... I just...."

"I know what you wanted. But he wasn't the right person for the job." We sit here until her sobs slow, and she's wiping the tears from her eyes.

"Come on, let's get you a drink."

I get her to stand and guide her to the couch in the living room. I cover her with the throw from the back of the couch, then cross to the kitchen. I take down two highball glasses from the cabinet and place a generous pour of bourbon into each. After handing her a glass, I sit down beside her.

"How did you know to save me?" she asks, swallowing a drink of the amber liquid.

"What?" I try to look clueless. *How am I going to get the hell out of this one?*

"How did you know he was hurting me?"

"Hunch." Even I wouldn't believe that one. I turn my eyes away from her gaze.

"Nico?"

"Fine, but don't get mad," I say, taking a big swig from my glass and setting it on the coffee table.

"I'll do my best. Now go on."

"There are cameras out in the hall and in your living room. When I saw him pick you up and carry you out of sight, I took off running to get to you."

"Running? From where?" *Oh man, she's going to go ballistic.*

"The surveillance van in the alley. I know you're mad, but I—" My words are cut off by her lips on mine. They're warm and sweet. The taste of tears is still on her lips. Is this really happening? Are my angel's lips really pressed against mine? She pulls away, but I don't want to open my eyes. If it's a dream, I don't ever want to wake up.

"Nico," she says sweetly. I force my eyes open, and her gaze is on me. "Thank you."

"For what?"

"For saving me."

"You're not mad?"

"Well, I'm not thrilled the entire security team was watching me in my home, but I know it comes with Mafia life. Thanks to those cameras, you saved me from the unthinkable."

After a moment of awkward silence, I say quietly, "I'll do it."

"Do what?"

"I'll be your fuck buddy."

"Yeah, right? Don't tease me," she says, lowering her face into her hands.

"I'm not teasing you, Guilia. I'll be your fuck buddy." Her head lifts, and her eyes are filled with confusion.

"I've given this a lot of thought. I'm the perfect person for the job. You've known me since we were teenagers. You trust me. Ethan is already making us spend time together, so he'll never suspect a thing. And I'm not all that bad-looking, am I?" I waggle my eyebrows at her and she giggles.

"You're not interested in me, so this might work," she says, turning her body toward mine. "You won't get attached?"

"Have you ever seen me in a relationship?" I declare.

"No. You're not gay, are you?"

"No. I'm not gay," I laugh awkwardly.

"Everybody already thinks we hate each other," she says. I can hear the wheels in her brain turning.

"That's the beauty of it. No one will ever suspect we're doing *it*."

"You do make some strong points, Mr. Acosta."

"Thank you, Ms. Martinelli." We burst out laughing.

"So what do you say? Am I your new fuck buddy?"

She thinks about it for a second and then reaches her hand out to shake. "Yes, I think you are."

Guilia writes a list of rules on a napkin and hangs it on the refrigerator.

FUCK BUDDY RULES
No feelings
No relationship
No clinging
No romance
No telling anyone
No hard feelings if the other can't meet up
No unprotected sex with others
Either party can initiate an encounter
Periodic STD testing

Chapter 14
Gilly

I spent the next day with my sisters. After a morning of shopping, we stop for lunch at a new restaurant in town called The Flower Patch.

"This place is so cute," MeMe croons. "Maybe when we buy the fourth unit, we should turn it into a restaurant."

"The space is too small for a restaurant," Lil says matter-of-factly. "So what's everyone been up to?"

I might as well start the conversation off with a bang. "I found a fuck buddy."

"You found a what now?" MeMe yells.

"Oh yeah, you don't know about that. I decided I'm tired of dating and just want somebody I can call whenever I want a good fuck."

"And you knew about this?" MeMe points at Lil.

"Yeah, but I didn't think she would find one so fast. Did you choose Nathan?"

"No, he was an asshole."

"Who is it then?"

"I'm not ready to share his name quite yet."

"Please be careful," MeMe says, grabbing my hand across

the table. "There are a bunch of crazies out there."

"I'm being careful. Don't worry. He's a nice guy."

"So what exactly is a fuck buddy?" she questions.

"No dating, no commitment, just fucking."

"Girl, you come up with the craziest ideas."

"It's the perfect arrangement."

MeMe lowers her voice. "I know you think it is right now, but what about the first time they come, they fuck, and they leave? Won't you feel…bad on the inside?"

"I don't think so. We both know the deal."

"If you're sure," she says, shaking her head.

"I'll be fine. It'll be fun."

We finish our lunch, and Jackson drives me home. He helps me carry all of my packages to the apartment.

"I'm in for the night. You can go home, Jackson. Have a good night."

"Yes, Miss Gilly."

I flop down on the couch, kick off my shoes, and text Nico.

> Hey, Fuck Buddy. What's up?

NICO

> How was shopping with your sisters?

> It was fun. I told them I have a fuck buddy now.

> Please God, tell me you didn't tell them it's me.

> I didn't tell them. Besides, we haven't even done anything yet.

> So speaking of yet. When does this arrangement commence?

> Want to come over tonight?

> Sure. What time?

How about eight? I have some
things to do around here first.

Okay, see you at eight.

I take a shower, change the sheets, and tidy up the apartment. I'm wearing a baggy baby-blue sweatshirt and matching
sweatpants. Nothing special. There's a knock on my door.

"Who is it?" I say in a singsong voice.

"Me, silly, open up." I unlocked the door and swing it open
to find Nico standing in my doorway with a bottle of wine and
flowers.

"We agreed, no romance. You've already violated our
contract in the first five seconds," I say with my hands on my
hips.

"I know, but it felt weird coming empty-handed." I motion
for him to come inside, taking the flowers and walking over to
the island.

"Did you turn the cameras off?" I ask, removing a vase from
the cabinet. "How did you know I love irises?"

"Lucky guess. And yes, I turned the cameras off. No one
will know I'm here," he says as he watches me lay the flowers
out, cut the stems, and arrange them in the vase.

"Did you know the iris is the flower of France?" I say.

"Really? How interesting."

"Thank you for these. They're beautiful."

"You're welcome. So how do we do this? I mean, I know
how to have sex, but how do we start this?" he asks, pointing
back and forth between us.

"Well, I've never done it before, either. Not sex. Dang it,
you know what I mean."

"I think we're both a little nervous. Let's have some wine,"
he suggests.

I take the corkscrew out of the drawer and hand it to him.
He opens the bottle of wine while I take down the glasses. He
pours us both a glass, and we retire to the living room.

We sit in awkward silence, sipping our wine as the uncomfortable minutes tick by. I guess I started this whole thing, so I should make the first move. Setting my glass down on the coffee table, I tuck one leg underneath me and scoot a little closer.

"Maybe we should start by kissing," I say, wiggling my eyebrows at him playfully.

"Okay, that sounds like a good idea. Kissing. Sure. We can do that," he babbles.

"Nico Acosta, are you nervous?"

"Me. Nervous? No. Scared to death the boss is going to find out I'm his sister's new fuck buddy. Hell yes!"

"He'll never find out."

"How do you know that?"

"I'm not going to tell him. Are you?"

"Fuck no!" He regains his composure and says, "I mean… no."

"Okay then." I scoot as close to him as I can, rest my hand on his chest, place a soft kiss to his lips, then lean back and wait for a reaction.

Chapter 15
Nico

Guilia fucking Martinelli just kissed me, again. The girl, I mean, *the woman*, I've been in love with since we were teenagers is sitting so close to me our thighs are touching. I feel like I'm fourteen again. I turn my body toward hers and kiss her back, sweet and slow.

"Are you good?" I whisper.

"Yeah. I'm good," she says. A sweet smile crosses her lips, and I'm overcome by the need to touch her. I place a hand on her thigh, and I can feel her leg quiver beneath my touch. I need her closer to me. I lean back onto the couch and pull her onto my lap.

"Nico!" she squeals.

"I need better access to these lips," I croon, cupping her cheeks with my hands. I pull her mouth to mine for a real kiss. Our tongues intertwine as we explore one another, and I can taste the wine on her tongue, and her lips are plump and full.

"Do you want me to stop?" I ask.

"No," she purrs.

Her tongue playfully swipes over my top lip before she pulls my bottom lip into her mouth and sucks. My brain can't take any more. With one hand on the back of her neck and the other across her lower back, I pull her body tightly against mine and crush my mouth to hers. Our kisses are frenzied and heated. I can't get enough of her mouth when she rocks her hips on my lap, and I realize I made a huge mistake by placing her there.

Her pussy sits directly atop my hard dick. The same dick I've been trying to talk down all day. I can feel her heat through my jeans as she rocks and sways. My dick gets harder and harder with each sensual motion of those hips.

"Angel," I say as I grasp her hips and stop her from rocking. "If you keep moving your hips on my dick like that, we're going to have a very sad ending tonight."

"Sorry. I can't help it. My body just… moves. I'm not doing it on purpose."

"It's okay." I readjust her on my lap and rub my hands up and down her thighs. Her fingers find their way to my neck and slide into my hair. When her nails gently scratch my scalp, a low moan escapes my throat.

"Oh, you like that, do you?" she purrs.

"Mm-hmm."

"Do you want to go to the bedroom?" she asks. Her hot breath sends shivers down my spine, and I can't speak, so I nod like a schoolboy. My mind is saying, *Stop! You're making the biggest mistake of your life,* but my dick is screaming, *Go! Bedroom! Now!*

She stands and takes my hand, guiding me down the hall. I'm mesmerized by her confidence and the way her hips sway from side to side. I follow her like a lost puppy as she leads me to her bedroom.

We stand beside the bed, and I'm content to stand here in awe of her beauty. This is so much better than watching her on the cameras. She takes the hem of my black T-shirt and pulls it over my head. I run my hands across her shoulders, down her arms, and to the bottom of her sweatshirt.

"Are you sure you want to do this?"

She looks up at me with hooded eyes and nods. I lift it from her body and deposit it on the floor. No fuckin' bra. My heart is in my throat when I see my angel standing before me with her bare breasts on display. My hands instinctively cup them and knead them gently. They're plump and round and more than one hand can hold. She reaches for my pants, and I stop her. This girl is running on overdrive, and my mind can't keep up.

"Gilly, can we go a little slower? I know we're *just fucking,* but I need to take my time."

"I'm sorry. I thought you would want to get it over with."

"Get it over with?" *What the fuck is she thinking?* "I want to memorize every inch of your body before we do this." How could she think I just wanted to breeze through this whole experience? That I wouldn't want to take my time and enjoy every glorious minute of it.

"Oh... okay," she says innocently as a blush falls over her skin. She takes a deep breath and lowers her hands from my pants. I pull her into me once more and kiss her sweet lips, her cheeks, and trail kisses down to the crook of her neck and drown in her sweet berry scent. Our naked chests are touching, and I think the air-conditioning has stopped working because the temperature in this room just rose ten degrees.

I lower myself to my knees in front of her and slide my tongue over her nipples. First, the left and then the right, learning every freckle on her soft skin. She closes her eyes, and her head falls back. I roll her nipples between my fingers and thumbs, giving each a little tug, and she rubs her legs together. I think my girl is needy for a release. She giggles as I place kisses down her stomach and stop at the waistband of her sweatpants.

"Are you ready?" I ask. She nods and gives me a sweet smile. I slide my fingers into the waistband of her pants and feel her warm lower belly on the backs of them. I push them over her ass and down her velvety smooth legs. She steps out of them, and I glide my hands up the outsides of her legs until I'm squeezing her ass cheeks over her panties.

Her pussy is within my grasp, and I can smell her arousal. My God, this woman is going to kill me. Just the thin scrap of fabric is between me and heaven. I trace the fabric with a single finger, feeling a wet patch seeping through the center.

"Somebody is already wet for me, aren't they?" My voice is deep and hungry.

"Yes." Her voice is shaky.

I move my nose to her pussy and take a deep breath. Her sweet smell takes over my senses, and I want to see her, taste her, feel her, smell her, and hear her moan my fucking name while she begs me to make her come. I slide her panties down her legs until my angel stands before me, totally bare. Her voice sweetly chimes my name, and I look into those beautiful green eyes and wait for more words to fall from her mouth.

"Do you wanna get on the bed?" she asks.

"If you'd be more comfortable. Whatever you need," I say as I stand and take her hand. "Lie down in the middle." She does as I instruct, and I climb on the bed between her legs. I gently push them apart and almost come in my pants at the sight of my angel spread wide for me.

"You're so goddamn beautiful, lying here open for me."

"Nico." A little nervous energy seeps through this time.

"Shh… I told you. I've got you."

The need to taste her is so overwhelming, I can't hold myself back any longer. My tongue slides between her wet folds, and she moans. I need to rearrange my cock in my pants to relieve some of the pressure on my zipper. I watch her face from the sweet spot between her legs as I lick and flick her clit. Her eyes are closed, her mouth opens slightly, while little gasps escape her throat.

"I'm going to make you come all over my tongue, Angel."

"Yes, please." She sighs.

I explore her pussy with my tongue. Sucking her pink lips into my mouth, I give a teasing suck to her clit. Her body jerks, and it makes me smile. I flatten my tongue and lick her center in long, languid motions, and she gasps.

"I like that," she moans as she rocks her hips in a circular motion.

"What my angel wants, my angel gets." I lap at her pussy over and over, and her thighs shake beneath my touch.

"No coming until I tell you to, sweetheart," I say as she whimpers at my withdrawal. I use my thumbs to hold her open wide for me as I dart my tongue into her core and taste her sweet cream.

I slide one finger into her center, and she lifts her hips to me. I add another and match her rhythm. I want to learn everything that makes my angel moan and jerk under my touch. I follow the cues her body gives me as I devour her sweetness. When I suck her clit into my mouth, she grinds against my face. Knowing I've found something else she likes; I suck the sweet nub harder. Her hands find my hair and pull. I know she's close.

"Come for me, baby," I say. At the same time, I lift my fingers upward on her G-spot, suck her into my mouth, and rub my tongue over the right side of her clit. She explodes in my mouth. Her core contracts around my fingers, and her abs clench, pulling her torso up off the bed. A smile crosses my lips as her mouth flies open, but no sound comes out.

"Breathe, Angel," I purr.

I gently run my tongue over her sex until she pushes on my head. I know the sensations are too much for her sensitive clit, but I can't resist a few more little flicks to make her flinch.

Her eyes flutter open, and she looks me square in the eye. Without any hesitation, she says, "I'm going to need you to fuck me now, Nico." My angel always surprises me.

I rise from the bed and remove the rest of my clothes. My cock stands at attention, and I'm one step away from blue balls. Sliding over her body, I hover above her.

"Birth control?" I ask.

"Yes, I'm on the pill."

"Condom?"

"No. I haven't been with anyone for months. Have you?"

"No." I want to tell her she's the only one I've ever wanted. That no other woman could ever compare to her. But she only wants a fuck buddy. I'll need to be satisfied with giving her what she wants for now.

I place a kiss on her soft lips and slide my hand over my cock, tugging once, twice. I trace my hard tip over her vulva, running it up and down, back and forth, and in a circle. Her hips arch up for more.

"Are you going to come just from my tip, Angel?" I ask while I lick and suck her neck.

"Nico, please. I need more." Not wanting to make my girl wait any longer, I notch my crown at her entrance, and she flinches.

"Oh God, Nico, you feel so big." Worry is etched on her face.

"I'll go slow. I got you," I say as I push in a little farther, waiting, allowing her body to adjust to my size.

"I've never had a dick this big before. How are you going to fi…"

"Shh…" I push in farther.

"Oh God, Nico," she moans.

"Relax your muscles, Angel. You're clenching me so tight I'll never get in." She takes a deep breath and gradually, the clenching lessens.

"That's my good girl," I praise. Breathing deeply myself, I push in a little farther. "Are you okay?"

"Yes… I feel so full… but keep going."

"Just a little more. You can take all of me." She nods her head, and I push myself to the hilt and wait. Her hips shift beneath me as her body makes room for my cock. Her pussy flutters around me, and I try not to lose control.

"You can move now," she says softly. I start thrusting into my girl with slow, even strokes. It's all I can do not to come after the first one. I've waited so long for this moment. To be inside my angel. It feels like a dream, and it's all I can do not to come from the feeling.

"I'm not going to last long, baby."

"Me neither." In and out, I thrust as Guilia wraps her legs

around my waist and pulls my body deeper into hers, and I groan.

Feeling my balls tighten, I pant, "Come for me, Guilia." We're both holding on to the other for dear life as her pussy tightens around my cock, and we fall into our bliss together.

When the sensations subside, I lie beside her and pull her into my arms. I could lie here forever. The scent of our sex surrounds us as relaxation takes over.

"Thank you, Nico," she says sweetly.

"For what?"

"For being a good man. I trust you. This means the world to me."

"I'll always have your back, Angel." She leans up on her elbow and places a light kiss on my lips.

"Come on, I'll fix you something to eat before you go." And just like that, her bed is cold, and I'm all alone. *Go? Fuck.* I can't forget the rules. No feelings. No relationship. No romance.

⌒

The next evening, I drive her home from the shop, and as she's opening the door, she asks over her shoulder, "Would you like to come inside for a little while?"

"Is this a fuck buddy thing?" I whisper discreetly over her shoulder.

"It could be," she says with a giggle.

As soon as we close the door, we're all over each other. Her lips suck mine in, and the need to fuck her flows through my body. In a blink, our clothes are off and strewn across the floor. We move to the couch this time, kissing and touching. She gestures for me to lie down, and she straddles my lap.

"I haven't been able to stop thinking about you all day. What we did last night was so hot. I want to ride you like a stallion tonight," she says. I can't speak. I just let her take control and do whatever the hell she wants.

She rubs her pussy over my hard length. Her juices coat my

cock as she slides herself up and down. She takes my dick in her tight fist and raises her body above it. Slowly, painfully slowly, she lowers her body down my shaft. I moan with pleasure as her body melts over mine until I'm fully seated inside her.

"Fuck, Nico," she groans. She rolls her hips, and my eyes fall back into my skull.

"Angel." That's the only word I get out before she begins to ride my cock. She pulls her body off my cock and slams down on me. Our moans fill the apartment. No woman has ever fucked me like this before.

Her face is flushed, and a glimmer of sweat shines on her upper lip as her body takes over mine. I would toss her onto her back and pound into her myself if we weren't on this damn couch, so for now, she runs the show. That familiar feeling surges at the base of my spine, and I know I'm close.

She flips the script on me and says, "Come for me, baby." I can't hold back any longer. My release shoots into her sweet pussy, filling her with ribbons of my cum. Her head falls forward, and her pussy grips me so tight it sends spasms through me.

Our cum floods from her pussy, and I can feel it sliding down the crack of my ass. She collapses onto my chest, and my arms wrap around her. Our panting and heaving breaths sound like a chorus of angels to me.

Her lips meet mine, and she lifts from my cock, heading to the bathroom to clean up. What the fuck do I do now? Leave like last night? That's all she wants, but is it all I want? Fuck no. But I promised her. No feelings. No relationship. No clinging.

Chapter 16
Gilly

It's been five long days, and Nico has driven me back and forth to work without mentioning our time together once. It's Friday night, and I'm going out with my sisters. They all need a little time away from their husbands and kids, and I need to have some fun. When we're away from the grumpy Mafia men in our lives, we always have fun. We're sisters. That's what we do. Nico drops me off at the apartment, just as he does every day.

"You remember that Lil, MeMe, Lola, and I are going out tonight, right?" I ask Nico as we exit the Escalade in the parking garage. Lil is my oldest sister; it's short for Lillianna. She's married and has three children. MeMe is the nickname for our middle sister, Maria. She's married and has a baby boy, and Lola is Rocky's wife. That leaves me, the last single Martinelli woman, and I'm enjoying every minute of it.

"I'm the head of security, Guilia. How would I forget that? Do you know how much time and planning goes into making sure it's safe for the four of you to be out on the town together?" My eyebrow lifts at him, waiting for him to tell me a number. "A lot." *So much for specifics.*

"You men are out on the town all the time, with *meetings*. We need to let off some steam and have fun, too."

He huffs out a breath. "The car will be here to pick you up in two hours," he says, depositing me at my front door.

"I'll be ready." I let myself in and shut the door behind me. It's only been twenty seconds, and I hear a light tapping on my door.

"What?" I say without opening it.

"You didn't lock the door."

"Oh my God! Give me a second to put my crap down and I'll lock it!" I turn the lock roughly, and it makes a loud clunk sound.

"Thank you."

"Whatever."

I spend the next two hours getting dolled up for our night on the town. If I know my sisters, they'll be dressed to the nines and ready to get drunk. I'm wearing my black Louis Vuitton heels, black leather pants, and an off-the-shoulder red sweater. My hair is down in waves, and I have smoky eye makeup on with layer after layer of mascara. There's a knock on the door. When I open it, I'm surprised to see Jackson standing there.

"Where's Nico?" I ask.

"He had something to take care of. He sent me instead," he says.

"Oh. Okay. I'm ready."

When he opens the door to the black limousine, chaos floods my ears.

"Gilly! Get your ass in here, girl!" Lil yells. That's my sister—loud and crazy. I laugh and climb into the car. A glass of champagne is thrust into my hand.

"Where did you decide we're going tonight?" I ask Lil, drinking down the bubbly goodness. I just let them all duke it out. I don't care where we go as long as there's booze and dancing.

"Scarlett's," MeMe says with a naughty giggle.

"Scarlett's, holy shit! How did you get Rocky to let us go there?" I ask Lola.

"I told Ethan if he would let us go to Scarlett's, we wouldn't ask to go anywhere else. That it would be less work for security, and he can have all the control he wants, and we can do whatever we want." She playfully winks.

"You mean...sex stuff?" I whisper. Scarlett's is a dance club Freddy runs for The Organization. In the back, there are rooms you can rent to live out your wildest sexual fantasies or just have a quick fuck, or do whatever you prefer.

MeMe laughs, shaking her head. "I'm not doing that." She's definitely the prude out of the four of us.

"You don't have to do anything you don't want to do." I chuckle. "I'm just surprised your husbands are allowing their sweet wives to go to a place like that."

"Sweet wives!" they yell in unison.

"Girl, don't you know who you're talking to?" Lil barks. She raises her glass. "The Martinelli women rule this fuckin' town." She's met with cheers from the group.

Ten minutes later, we're walking into Scarlett's like the bad bitches we are. Vinny, the bartender, watches us with his mouth agape as we walk toward the VIP section.

"Vinny, bring us some shots, please," I say as we walk past him, waving my hand in the air. He scurries around the bar and follows us with a tray full of shots a moment later. I can only imagine what Giovanni, Lil's husband; Alessandro, Maria's husband; and Rocky are thinking at this very moment. I'm sure they're all up in the office watching their wives on the monitors. They like to let us think we're on our own, but we all know they're watching us. Our devoted protectors.

Vinny sets the shots of bourbon on the table in front of us. We all take one and lift it into the air. I yell above the music, "To us!"

"To us," they all chime back. We all shoot back the amber liquid and slam the glasses on the table. MeMe is such a lightweight in her pink Chanel ensemble. She tries to keep up with the rest of us, but she can't. I'm sure she'll be the first one to drop out tonight, as usual.

Lil yells, "Again!" Poor Vinny needs a big tip for all the trips to the bar he's going to make tonight.

Four shots later, the music starts pumping up, and we all head to the dance floor. I finally feel my buzz kicking in as we laugh and dance around the floor. We aren't dancing very long before four big guys approach our little dance circle. A guy slides in behind each one of us, and we don't need to say a word because the same thing is going through all of our minds. *Oh shit. What are the guys going to do to these men if they touch us?* We try to wave them off and leave the dance floor, but they make a barrier with their bodies around us.

I try to reason with them first. "Look, fellas, we're just here to have some fun. We're not looking to get fucked tonight. So please let us go."

"Now, why would we want to do that?" the bald man behind me says.

Lil pushes me aside and bounces her chest off his stomach and yells, "Because we're Rocco Martinelli's sisters, that's why." Their eyes pop out of their heads, and they give us a wide berth as we head back to the VIP area.

We all sit down, check our surroundings, and burst out laughing.

"You are one bad bitch tonight, Lil," Lola says as Lil throws back another shot.

"I needed that," Lil says, slamming her shot glass on the table. I'm glad they backed off. If shit goes down, the fun stops and we have to go home, and I'm not done yet.

Another hour goes by, and we're all getting pretty wasted. The lights dim, and slow music fills the speakers. It's very strange for there to be slow songs playing at Scarlett's. It's not a romantic place. It's a place to get fucked, plain and simple.

We all look around, wondering what in the hell is happening. Out of nowhere, Ethan, Giovanni, and Alessandro stride across the room toward their women. Right before my eyes, my bad bitches melt into ooey-gooey messes for their men. The guys hold out their hands and lead them to the dance floor.

Now I feel like the wallflower of the group, left sitting at the table all alone. *This sucks.* I stand and head for the bathroom and lock myself inside. After a quick second, there's a knock on the door.

"Occupied," I yell out.

"It's me, Angel, open up." That familiar voice echoes through the door.

"Nico?"

"Yeah."

I unlock the door, and he slides inside, locking us in a bathroom once again.

"Why do we always meet in the bathroom?" I ask.

"It's quieter in here," he says. "Why are you *hiding*?"

"I'm not *hiding*."

"Oh really?"

"Well... maybe a little." I look away from him. "I thought you were working tonight?"

"I am working. Who do you think is running all the security?" With his hands on my hips, he pulls me closer to him. "Why aren't you dancing?" he croons, running his nose along mine.

"There's nobody out there I want to dance with." I pout.

"Did you change your mind about our little arrangement?" he asks.

"No... I thought maybe you changed yours though."

"No. I still want to be your buddy, if you want me to."

"Well, I think we've established we both want to continue our partnership, so now what do we do?" I ask.

"We can't do anything here, not with your whole family out there."

"You're right. We need a plan."

"I'll come over tonight after the limo takes you home. How does that sound?"

"Good, but I have a question?"

"What?"

"Can everyone see us on the cameras at the apartment?" I ask.

"I'll turn them off."

"Can we go to your house instead? You don't have any cameras, right?"

"Nope, no cameras at my house."

"Okay, how about I take an Uber to your house instead of the limo? Let the happy couples use it to go home."

"I guess that's as good a plan as any. I'll text you my address," he says.

"Are we really going to do this?" I ask. My insides are fluttering around like I swallowed a hive of bees.

"I think so," he says, nodding in agreement. "I'll go out first, and you follow in a few minutes."

"See you later."

He places a quick kiss on my lips, and he's gone.

I make my way back to the girls, and they're out on the dance floor. The music is thumping throughout the club, and they left my shot on the table. I shoot it back and join them. The husbands are all gone again, and we're back to acting like wild women. It doesn't take long, and the bald man comes in behind me once more.

"Hey, pretty lady. Wanna come in a back room with me?" He puts his hands on my hips and turns me to look at him. My feet tangle around each other as I stumble into him.

"No thanks. I told you before, I'm here with my girls tonight. Thanks anyway." I wave him away and turn back to the group.

"Come on, baby, let me show you a good time." This time, he grabs me by the wrist and pulls me in the direction of the back rooms. The girls start yelling and pulling me back to them by my other wrist. I'm being pulled in both directions like a wishbone, and all the alcohol I've drunk is starting to make me dizzy. Before I can think straight, Nico is there, prying the bald guy's hand off my wrist.

"The lady said she doesn't want to go with you," he growls.

"No one was talking to you, asshole," the bald man shouts above the music. He tries to reach for me again, but the girls pull me away and use their bodies to shield me from him. We back out of the way as Nico takes my place in front of him.

"It's time for you to leave," Nico says.

"Like hell it is. She's coming with me."

"Like fuck she is!" Nico yells back. The man reaches for me again, but Nico's had enough. He punches the man in the face with such force he falls to one knee. Nico raises his fist to strike again, but the guy holds up his hands for Nico to stop. He wipes his lips with the side of his arm and stands to his feet. Two bouncers step forward and haul him out of the club.

The girls step to the side and let Nico through. "Are you okay?"

"Yeah, I'm fine. Just a little dizzy." As the words leave my mouth, my knees give out, and I start to drop to the floor. Nico swoops me up into his arms.

"I gotcha," he says, and my head rests on his shoulder.

By now, Rocky, Giovanni, and Alessandro have emerged from the office to protect their women.

Nico whispers into my ear, "Change of plans." Nodding, I close my eyes and melt into my protector.

"I'm taking her home," he announces in a strong, loud voice. He turns to Ethan. "You guys take the girls home in the limo. I'll take Gilly home." Ethan nods. He knows this is the protocol for the head of security. Take charge of the situation and get me out safely.

With that, Nico carries me from the club and sets me in the front seat of his black pickup truck. Both of us have big smiles on our faces because we know what's coming next.

Chapter 17
Gilly

We pull into Nico's garage, and he shuts off the truck. I let myself out and look around at all the cars and motorcycles.

"This garage is a lot bigger on the inside than it looks on the outside. You have a lot of vehicles in here."

"Come on, let's go inside." Nico takes my hand and pulls me through the door to the kitchen.

The kitchen is bright and open. It has cornflower-blue cabinets, marble countertops, and silver pendant lights hanging above the island. Not at all what I pictured his home would look like. In contrast to the kitchen, the living room has a large chocolate-brown leather couch, with heavily carved wooden end tables on either side and a large coffee table in front of it. The wood-burning fireplace takes up the center of the wall across from the couch, with shelves on both sides filled with books. A large television is mounted on the wall above the fireplace.

"I love this room. It's so masculine but cozy."

"Thanks. Would you like a drink?"

"Just water, please. I had a lot to drink tonight."

"Yeah, I know." He chuckles.

"Were you watching us?" I whine.

"You know I was in the security office with the boss." He sets the water down on the oversized coffee table and sits on the couch beside me. My eyes scan the room when I spot some pictures on the mantel. I walk over and take a frame down.

"Is this your family?" I ask.

He comes to stand behind me. Wrapping his arms around my waist, he rests his chin on my shoulder. "Yeah, that's Freddy, me, Momma, and our little sister, Laura," he says, pointing out each one.

"You are so cute." He has on a red baseball cap, with the biggest smile on his face. His sister holds pink cotton candy in one hand and a teddy bear in the other. Freddy has his arms around both of their shoulders, while their mother looks down on them all with a sweet smile.

"How old were you in this picture?"

"I was seven, so that would make Freddy ten and Laura five. Momma took us to the fair, and we were on our way out when one of her friends stopped us and took our picture. Freddy won Laura that teddy bear playing the dart game."

"I didn't know you had a sister. Can I meet her?"

His body stills. "She died a few weeks after this picture was taken."

"Oh my God. Nico, I'm so sorry. I didn't know." His finger runs over the little girl's face, and his face fills with sadness. He takes the picture from me and places it back on the mantel and picks up another one.

"This is my mom. Her name was Calliope. It means beautiful voice in Greek."

"You're Greek?" That's where he gets his gorgeous skin color. He always looks kissed by the sun.

"Partially."

"Did she have a beautiful voice?"

"She would sing us songs at night when we went to bed. Lullabies mostly."

"That's a lovely memory to have."

"She was a great mom."

"What happened to them?" I ask as he places the picture back on the mantel beside the other.

"She was driving Laura to dance class. It was raining hard, and a Mack truck crossed the center line and hit them head-on." My hand flies to my mouth, and I gasp. "The police said they died on impact."

"Nico." I put my hand on his arm. "I'm so sorry."

"I'm okay. It's been a lot of years ago." Walking back around and sitting on the couch, he says, "Sometimes I wonder what Laura would be like today. What kind of woman she would have grown up to be. She wanted to be a teacher, but who knows?"

"I'm sure she would've been a great teacher."

Shaking us out of the silence, he asks, "Are you hungry?"

"Huh?"

"I don't think I saw you eat anything all evening," he says.

"I...um, sure. I can eat."

"Let's order pizza and watch a movie," he suggests.

"You know it's like midnight, right?"

"Are we in some kind of hurry?"

"No, but..."

"You do know they deliver pizza until like three in the morning, right? I'll grab my phone."

I wish he would hurry up and kiss me already. I've been waiting all evening to feel his lips on mine again.

"What do you want on your pizza?" he asks, flopping down on the couch and tapping his phone.

"I like anything."

"Pepperoni?"

"Sure. That sounds good." He orders the pizza and grabs the remote. He kicks off his shoes and props his feet on the coffee table. I follow his lead and do the same. He covers our legs with a plaid throw, and I cuddle into his side.

"What movie did you have in mind?" I ask.

"Got another Lucy Hale movie we can watch?"

"Yeah, there's a new one out. It's called *Which Brings Me to You*."

"Perfect."

Chapter 18
Nico

We watched the first part of the movie in silence, but a knock on the door finally sets us free from the uncomfortable feeling in the room.

"That's the pizza. I'll get it," I say, pausing the movie. I place a chaste kiss on the top of her head and retrieve our mouthwatering goodness from the driver. After I place it on the coffee table with some napkins, she opens the box.

"Could you have sex in a coat closet?" she asks casually. I'm sure she's asking because of the scene in the movie we're watching.

"I don't know, maybe. I could probably be persuaded to try it." I waggle my brows at her.

"Does Scarlett's have a coat closet?" she continues.

"Not that I know of, but I think Lowell's does." We both break into laughter. The thought of fucking this woman in a coat closet has my cock swelling in my pants. I turn the movie back on, and we devour the pizza.

"I can't believe I ate so much. I was hungrier than I thought,"

she says. We both slump back on the couch and rub our bellies. I've laughed more with Gilly these past few weeks than I've laughed in the past few years.

"Me too," I say, sliding my arm around my angel. I sit, not watching the movie, but watching her. I lean in close, and her berry scent envelops me. My thumb draws circles on her arm as I place a kiss on the side of her head. She turns to look at me with hooded eyes.

"Nico."

"Yes, Angel."

"Can you kiss me?"

"I thought you'd never ask," I say and pull her in close for a kiss.

All those nights I watched her on the cameras in Italy, Germany, and Russia, never being allowed to talk to her, let alone touch her. I want to soak up every minute of her now. Our foreheads touch, and I watch those pouty pink lips of hers. She bites her bottom lip when she's nervous.

"Are you all right, Angel?"

"I need you." The words come out so quietly, I almost miss them.

My tongue swipes her lips, and hers calls me inside. Our tongues are licking and tangling. The movie continues to play, but neither of us is watching it anymore. I can't get enough of this woman. I toss the blanket off to the side and lift her onto my lap. She takes my face in her hands and controls the kiss. She sucks my bottom lip into her mouth, and I pull her body closer to mine. Brushing her hair behind her ear, I kiss her neck and the top of her shoulder. I want so much more, but I hold myself back. She rushed me out the door after we had sex at her apartment. But tonight, she's staying all night with me, and I'm going to enjoy every moment of her being in my arms.

Her hands are warm as they glide over my arms and chest, landing in the hair at the base of my neck. I love the way she touches me. The way she tugs on my hair sends shivers down my spine, and I moan a little in her mouth.

"I like that sound," she coos.

"You do?" I say playfully. "I want to hear all the sounds you make when I make you come on my cock." The smiles are gone now, and we stare into each other's eyes.

"I'm ready,"

I won't make her tell me twice. I lift her from the couch in one swift movement. Her legs lock around my waist as I carry her to my bed. I place her at the foot, and she reaches for the buttons on my black shirt. Looking up at me with those big green eyes, she unbuttons them one by one and slides the shirt off my shoulders. I toss it on the chair.

I reach for the hem of her red sweater and lift it over her head. Her blond hair falls around her shoulders, and I bury my nose in the crook of her neck.

"I want to get lost in you. Every inch of you," I say. My cock twitches in my pants when her hands roam over my back, and she scratches me lightly.

"You're giving me chills, baby girl."

"I'm sorry."

"No. It feels amazing." I can see her nipples standing erect under the lace of her red bra. I want them in my mouth. Her hand lands on the button of my jeans, and my eyes shoot to hers. I take her hands in mine and stop her.

"Nico, please. You're always giving me pleasure. I want to give it back to you. Let me touch you," she says.

"I want to take our time tonight. We don't have to be rushed like we have been. We have all night to explore one another. I want to make you come over and over until you pass out from the pleasure." She drops her hands in disappointment, but I'll make it up to her. *Am I a bad person because I want to make her feel special?* I'll give her all of me soon enough. We can get down and dirty later.

I reach around and release her bra, sliding it down her arms and dropping it to the floor. I kiss her deeply, letting my hands roam over her body. A small sigh slips from her throat as I pull her hard nipple into my mouth—licking, sucking, and nibbling my way from one to the other. I pinch them, and she squeals, goose bumps covering her flesh.

I undo the side zipper on her leather pants and ease them down her legs. She steps out of them and stands before me in only her red lace panties.

"Oh my God, Angel. You take my breath away." Her eyes are trained on my every move as I use my hands to explore her body.

"I want to kiss every freckle," I say, and goose bumps fill her arms. "And every goose bump," I say, and she giggles.

"Oh, Nico."

The anticipation is going to kill me, but I stifle it down and continue. When I reach the waistband of her panties, I loop my thumbs through them and ease the thin piece of lace down her legs. I raise them to my nose and inhale the sweet smell of her arousal before tucking them into my pocket and continuing my descent to her delicate pussy.

Chapter 19
Gilly

Nico is driving me insane with this sensual treatment. Tonight feels different. It's not the spontaneous, passionate sex we've been having. This is slow and intense. He's making me feel so wanted and special. He took my panties and motioned for me to lie on the bed. The sight of his colossal form between my legs causes my arousal to flood my core. When his fingers make circles on my skin, coming closer and closer to my hot sex, I can't help but raise my hips, hoping he'll touch my aching slit.

His wicked eyes shine up at me from between my thighs. His dark stare never leaves me as he sticks out his tongue and lowers to my pussy. Flattening his tongue the way he knows I like, he laps up my juices.

"Fuck, Angel, you taste so sweet," he croons.

"Nico, yes, that's it."

The things he does to my body send me into sensory overload. I close my eyes and relish his treatment. But when he lands on my swollen clit, a jolt of electricity explodes through my body.

"Please," I beg.

"Please, what, Angel?"

"Please, make me come."

He lets out a hum of approval, and I can feel the vibrations on my clit. A thick finger slides into my center and then another. He pulses them in and out, turning his hand from side to side.

"I'm close, Nico. Don't stop." My hands move to his head, and I hold him right where I need him to be. He doesn't stop. Instead, he doubles down on my clit, sucking it hard while flicking it with his tongue. I swear I feel him nibble on my clit when my climax cascades through me. My body bears down on his fingers buried deep inside me.

"Fuck… Oh, Ni—" I cry out as my whole body quakes.

While my body comes down from its high, he licks my pussy clean. I open my eyes and see his dark hair hanging in his eyes. I brush it to the side, and that shit-eating grin is looking up at me once more. His mouth and chin are covered in my release as he rises above me and kisses my lips. I taste myself on his tongue and devour him.

"Can I taste *you* now?" I ask.

"If you put my cock between those lips tonight, I'm going to come down your throat." The thought of his hot cum sliding down my throat causes the wetness to return to my pussy.

"Would that be so wrong?"

"Just being near you gets me excited. I'm afraid I won't be able to control myself, and I'll come like a teenage boy as soon as you put me in your mouth."

"That's the chance I'm willing to take. I want you in my mouth."

He rises and removes his jeans and boxer briefs, then comes to stand beside the bed. I finally get a close look at his cock, which is on its way to being as hard as stone. His shaft is long and thick. There is a tiny freckle on his thick tip and it makes me smile. I lick my lips at the thought of having him in my mouth and him coming down my throat.

"I want you so much," I gasp. "Please, Nico. Let me taste you," I whine, sticking out my bottom lip. I watch as a drop of precum escapes his tip, and it glistens, asking me to taste it. "Just one teensy, weensy taste?" I tease, fluttering my eyelashes at him. He closes his eyes as if praying to God to hold on. "I won't torture you tonight. I just need a taste."

He motions with a nod, and I scoot to the side of the bed. I stick out my tongue and ever so slowly lick the tip of his cock. A guttural moan comes from his chest. I wrap my lips around the head, and Nico's back stiffens. When my tongue circles his slit, his hands come to my head, pulling me away. His eyes are black, and his face is stern.

"Guilia." My name comes out of his mouth like he means business.

I climb onto my knees in front of him and kiss his lips softly. "Fuck me, Nico."

My back is on the mattress in one swift movement, and he hovers above me. He lines the crown of his cock up to my entrance and notches it just inside me, and I gasp. He's a big man, and his cock reflects that, but I need every last inch of him inside me now.

"I need you, please," I beg.

Hearing those four words, he begins to move inside my slick channel. He pushes deeper with each thrust until he's fully seated inside me. He pulls almost all the way out and pauses. All at once, he thrusts back into me, circling his hips while his cock is buried deep inside me. His pubic bone brushes over my clit as he rocks in and out of my core. I raise my legs around his waist and pull him in even closer.

When I open my eyes, he's staring deep into my soul as he lowers his lips to mine. "You make me so fucking crazy." He peppers me with kisses as he increases his pace. He rails into me over and over, exactly how I like it.

"Harder," I cry.

"Deeper," I moan.

When he's close to his release, he says those words I need to hear to push me over the edge. "Come on my cock, Angel." My body erupts into the most mind-blowing orgasm I've ever had. My eyes roll back in my head, and my hips bear down on his dick as his body tightens, and his cock pulses as his hot seed fills my pussy.

"Damn, baby, you're still gripping me so tight," he says as he lays his body over mine. Our bodies twitch as our pleasure quells. After a short while, he leans up on his elbows to pull out of me, but I clamp my legs around him tighter.

"Don't go. Not yet. I need to feel you inside me a little longer." He doesn't say a word, just lowers himself back down to my chest and wraps me in his arms. His weight is heavy, but the way we're wrapped around each other makes it feel like I'm in a cocoon. I run my fingers gently through his hair. I never want this night to end.

When I finally release him, he settles beside me and hugs me close. I wrap my body around his, and we lie there entangled in each other in the darkness.

"Let's play a game," I say.

"A game. Right now? Really?"

"Yeah."

"What kind of game?" he asks.

"I want to know more about you. We shared the most intimate thing a man and a woman can share, and we hardly know each other."

He pushes me back to look into my eyes. "How can you say that?"

"I don't know much about your childhood. You were older than me, and besides, you were Rocky's friend."

"You keep saying that."

"Keep saying what?"

"I was Rocky's friend. We weren't friends. We didn't hang out. You act like we were besties or something. We weren't."

"Tell me about your dad. I don't remember him at all."

"He's not a subject I usually find myself compelled to talk about."

"Why not?"

"Because I hate him."

"Oh."

"Freddy was more of a father to me than he ever was." Nico pushes back the duvet and sits on the side of the bed. He drags his hands through his hair and down his face. His back is toward me, and his body sits rigid.

"I'm sorry. I didn't realize talking about your father would upset you."

⤸

Nico

Why the fuck does she want to know about my dad? I don't remember much about him, except he was mean to us. He was never there, and when he was home, he was drunk.

"My dad didn't handle losing Momma and Laura very well."

"What do you mean?"

"He shut us out. We were just kids grieving for the two most important people in our lives, but he didn't care about us."

"What kind of dad was he before the accident?" she asks.

"Okay, I guess. He held down a job and provided for his family. We never heard them argue. Life was good. We were happy kids."

"And after the accident."

"He would leave us alone for days at a time. I should be thankful he left us money for food. He could've left us to starve. Freddy was the one who made sure I got to school on time, had clean clothes to wear, and food in my stomach. Not my dad."

"Where would your dad go?" Guilia asks, her hand stroking gently over my back.

"Who knows? When he was home, he was yelling at us, drunk, or both. Freddy took the brunt of everything because he was the oldest. He would tell me to hide or to run outside and play whenever Dad was around. When it was safe for me to come home, Freddy would find me and bring me back. He always had bruises or cuts on his body."

"I'm so sorry," she says. She started this conversation, and now I can't stop my damn mouth from talking.

"One night when I was fourteen, Freddy had walked to the store to get some groceries to make dinner. Dad came stumbling in the front door. I tried to retreat to my bedroom, but he wasn't having it. He started calling me names and telling me I was a loser and stupid. He said I was going to grow up and be a worthless piece of shit. When I tried to back away, he punched me in the stomach and threw me across the living room.

"I remember hearing Freddy burst through the back door. I guess when he saw me crumpled on the floor, he lost his shit. He said he was tired of Dad taking what happened to Momma and Laura out on us. That the accident wasn't our fault, but he's made it feel like it was every day since it happened. He wasn't the only one who lost someone. We lost our mother and sister too. There's not a day that goes by I don't think about them."

"Then what happened?" she asks.

"Dad kept egging Freddy on, telling him he didn't have it in him to hit him back and he was weak. When he called him a little pussy, Freddy punched him in the face. I remember the look on Dad's face. It was like he couldn't believe Freddy actually hit him."

"Dad shoved Freddy back into the wall and grabbed him by the throat. He was squeezing so tight that Freddy couldn't breathe. Before I could move to try to pull him off, Freddy picked up the lamp from the side table and hit Dad in the head with it. He fell forward into the fireplace and hit his head on the brick hearth. I can still hear the thud sound in my head. His body dropped to the floor, lifeless."

"Oh my God, Nico. What did you do?"

"Freddy helped me up off the floor, and we walked over to Dad. He was lying slumped over. When we rolled him onto his back, there was a big gash on the side of his head. Blood had poured out of the wound onto the carpet, and it made a red circle under his head. We didn't know what to do. We stood there for what seemed like forever and just stared at him. We knew he could never hurt us again, but we didn't know what to do next."

"Is that the night you came to my house?" she asks.

"Yes. We knew your dad could help us."

"Help you? How?"

I know my angel is confused, but she needs to know at least this bit of truth about our families.

"Your dad had so much power in this town, and everyone was afraid of him. We knew he would know what to do, so we went to your house and begged to speak to him."

"I remember that. I was supposed to be in bed, but I heard someone pounding on the front door and peeked out my door to see what was happening," she says. "You and Freddy were there. You were drenched from the storm, begging our butler to let you speak to my father."

"Your father agreed to speak to us. He didn't have to do that, Gilly. But he took pity on two stupid boys."

"What happened in his office?"

"Freddy told Antonio what happened and asked him to help us. If social services found out our dad was dead, they would split us up and send me to God knows where. Freddy was going to turn eighteen in just a few months, so we made a deal with Antonio."

"What kind of deal?"

"Antonio said he would take care of the body as long as we laid low and acted normal until Freddy turned eighteen. He would have his lawyers draw up papers to make Freddy my legal guardian, provided Freddy would come to work for him after graduation. Our horrible father was out of our lives forever. I got to stay out of the system with my brother, and Freddy wouldn't go to jail for murder."

"I don't know what to say." Gilly sighs.

"Everyone always talks about how ruthless your father was, Guilia, but he *helped* us. I don't know if it was because he thought we were Ethan's friends, or he wanted our loyalty forever. But he helped us."

"What happened to you while Freddy worked for my father?"

"I went to high school, played football, hung out with my friends, and led a pretty normal life. When I graduated, I came on board with The Organization as well. We were always loyal to Antonio. He groomed us and taught us the Mafia ways, and in turn, we did everything he said, no questions asked."

Guilia pulls me down into her arms again. My head is on her chest while she gently strokes my temples.

"Thank you for telling me," she says softly. "I had no idea my father took care of you like that."

"I've never told another soul about what happened to my father, and you can't tell anyone either, Guilia. Freddy holds a powerful position in this city. He can't show any weakness. I'm a major in your brother's army, and I have a reputation to uphold to my men as well."

"I won't say a word, Nico, I swear."

We fell asleep in each other's arms for the first time.

Chapter 20
Gilly

*I*t's dark, and I'm walking toward a streetlight when I realize I'm on the sidewalk beside the club in Paris. I try to flag down a cab, but they all keep passing me by. I continue to walk down the street, trying to find my flat. I hear footsteps behind me. I can't be sure if it's one set or two, so I walk faster.

When I near the alley, two large hands reach out and grab me and pull me inside. A dirty hand that smells like motor oil clamps over my mouth. It's dark, and the man drags me kicking and fighting over to the trash bins. I lost my shoe somewhere, and my foot is cold.

He drops me to the ground, and I yell out, "Help me!" I'm slapped across the face. He's on top of me, and my hands are pinned above my head. This is it. I'm going to get raped in a dirty alley in Paris. "No! No! Stop, please!"

"Shh… Shh… Guilia, baby, wake up. It's okay. It's just a dream." That's Nico's voice. How did he get to Paris?

"Angel, open your eyes and look at me." That word, Angel. I heard it that night after I was jumped. I remember the way his voice sounds when he says it. I couldn't remember who said it, but I remember the word…Angel. My eyes flutter open, and I see Nico.

"There's my angel. It was just a dream. It's over now." His voice is calm and melodic while his thumb strokes my cheek. My brain is confused. I've heard his words before.

His body is warm, and his touches soothe as he rubs soft circles over the skin on my back. I know he'll keep me safe. I snuggle back down into his arms, and as I'm drifting off, I hear him say, "Sleep tight, Angel."

My eyes fly open, and I gasp. It wasn't a dream. I knew it! He was in Paris that night. I know he was. What the hell is happening to me?

‿

Nico

When we wake up the following morning, her body remains snuggled against mine. We both stir and stretch. I love the way this feels, waking up beside my angel in the morning. And I want more.

"Good morning, Angel. How did you sleep after your nightmare last night?"

"Like I was on a cloud. You always make me feel so safe." My heart is about to leap out of my chest. "But we broke the rules last night," she whispers.

"The rules?" We had an amazing night in each other's arms, and all she cares about is the damn rules.

"No feelings. No relationships. No clinging…"

"I remember the rules," I say, leaning on my elbow and looking down into her dusty-green eyes.

"I don't want to be your fuck buddy anymore," I say defiantly, and her eyes grow wide as if I just slapped her.

"What?" She tries to push me away from her, but I hold on tight.

"I want to be *more* than your fuck buddy." My voice is calm and sincere. "I know I said I wouldn't catch feelings for you, Guilia, but I lied. I can't do it. I tried, but I need more." Her head relaxes into the pillow, and I continue, "I hate it when I have to leave you to go home to sleep in my cold bed alone. I want to hold you after we come. I want you to ask me a million questions. I want to have morning sex with you, take a shower, then do it all over again. I want to listen to the way you breathe while you sleep and listen when you talk in your sleep."

"What do I say when I talk in my sleep?" she teases.

"Stay with me, Nico," I say in a high-pitched voice.

"I do not." She tries to shove me away.

"If you don't want more, I understand, but it's hard to act like I'm *just* your fuck buddy."

She kisses me tenderly. "I want more too, Nico. I didn't know if you did."

I sit up and scoot my back against the headboard. When she straddles my lap, I bury my face in her neck and growl possessively.

"You're silly." She giggles.

"And you're amazing." Those words cause a blush to spread across her face. I kiss her deep and long, and when I pull back from her, she says cautiously, "We need to go."

"What? Wait. Why? We just said…"

She puts a finger to my lips. "Rocky might be looking for me. What are we going to tell him if he asks where I was all night?" She moves off my lap and wraps the sheet around her body. As she walks away, she takes the sheet with her, leaving me naked. I fall over onto the bed, leaning on my elbows, and stare at her.

"God, you look sexy in my sheet."

Chapter 21
Gilly

After rising from the bed, Nico follows me to the bathroom and turns on the shower for me.

"I'll just tell him I brought you here because you didn't want to be alone in your apartment after the incident at the club."

"Do you think he'll buy it?" I ask.

"He doesn't have a reason not to. Besides, he said he trusts me with you. But if it makes you feel better, we can shoot some snide remarks at each other." He pulls out a new toothbrush and lays it on the counter.

"I don't think I want to tell him yet. Is that okay with you?"

"Yeah, I don't think I'm ready for him to beat the living shit out of me yet, either. You shower first. I'll make coffee." He kisses the top of my head and leaves.

"I thought you wanted to shower with me?" I give him a pouty face.

"We'll have plenty of time in the future for shower sex. We need to get moving."

"Fine."

In the future. Those words make my head spin. I step inside and shut the shower door. The scent of his body wash surrounds me, and I know if I use it, he'll be with me all day.

⤚

Stepping out of the shower, I wrap the white towel around my body and begin looking for my clothes.

"Hey, what did you do with my panties last night?" I yell. He walks into the bedroom, twirling them on his index finger. When I reach out to take them, he snatches them back.

"Nope. These are my property now."

"Oh, come on. You want me to go commando?"

"Sorry, it's my payment for last night."

"If you're going to keep my panties every time we have sex, I'll need to bring a few things over here."

"Whatever you need to do, baby, but I'm keeping these." He laughs as he holds them up to his nose and then stuffs them into his pocket. I finish pulling on my clothes and get ready for the walk of shame back to my apartment.

After Nico showers, we hop into his truck to go by my house to pick up a few things. When we're parked in the garage, he places one last kiss on my lips and croons, "I won't be able to kiss you goodbye in your apartment, so I wanted to do it now." I'm speechless.

As we approach the hallway, he says, "Look natural for the cameras, just in case Ethan has Daniel checking them." I unlock the door, and we step inside.

My brain can't process what I'm seeing. Blood pumps in my ears, and I can't catch my breath. My apartment is trashed. The drawers are tossed aside and their contents dumped on the floor. Nico closes the door, pushes me behind him, and takes out his gun. *Where the hell did that come from?*

"There's probably no one here, but stay behind me while I check." I cling to his back as he guides us around the apartment. Thank goodness we find no one.

They found me. They know I have the diamonds, and they're coming for me. The picture of my parents on the wall doesn't look touched, so at least they didn't find the wall safe. Idiots. Maybe it would be better if they had found the diamonds. They could take them and leave me the fuck alone.

"Who would do this?" Nico says out loud. I shrug, and he dials Daniel. I hear him tell him to look at the cameras from last night and see what happened.

"Come on, we need to go," he says, grabbing my hand. My legs won't work. He tugs on my hand again.

"I can't leave. I need to clean up this mess," I say in a haze.

"We need to get on top of this. I'll help you clean it up later. We need to talk to the boss." I can't believe this is happening. I hoped when I left Germany, they would stop looking for me, but I guess I was wrong.

We made our way to The Organization and headed straight for Rocky's office. "He knows we're coming," Nico says to Sasha as we walk past her desk.

As soon as Rocky sees us, he stands and comes around the desk.

"What the hell happened?" he asks, pulling me in for a hug. He takes me by the shoulders and pushes me back to look me over for injuries. "Are you hurt?"

"No, I wasn't there."

"Thank God," he says, looking between Nico and me. His eyebrows rise. "Where were you?"

"I was at Nico's house all night." His eyes home in on Nico.

"Why the hell was she at your house *all night*?"

"After I carried her out of the club, she was scared and didn't want to go home, so I took her to my house. We ate pizza and watched a movie. I don't want to think about what could've happened if she had been alone in her apartment last night."

Rocky nods in agreement. "Yeah, you're right. It was a good thing she wasn't there." Just like that, the conversation shifts back to the break-in.

"I have Daniel looking at the cameras. I gave the guys the night off because she was with me. He'll let us know when he finds anything," Nico says.

Rocky hugs me again. "I'm glad you're all right. I'll send some people over to clean up the place."

"Thank you."

"Who was the guy last night at Scarlett's?" Nico asks.

"His name is Fernando Ramirez." We all move to sit down by his desk.

"Do you think he's involved in the break-in?" Nico asks.

"How would he have found out where I lived so fast?" I ask.

Just then, Nico's phone rings.

"It's Daniel," he says. "Hey, Daniel. I'm going to put you on speaker." He clicks the button and places the cell on the desk.

"Daniel, what did you find?" Rocky asks.

"Three men dressed in black entered the apartment at 3:06 a.m.. Their faces were covered with balaclavas. One guy wore glasses, one was bald, and one wore a ball cap."

"How did they get inside?" Rocky demands.

"They picked the lock on the front door."

"How the fuck did they make it past the guard to get on her floor?"

"I don't know, Boss. I haven't figured that out yet."

"I want to know who was on watch and what the fuck happened."

"Yes, Boss."

"Go on."

"By the way they moved around the apartment, I believe they were professionals looking for something. They were in and out in about five minutes. They got into a black Tahoe that was parked across the street and headed for the highway."

"Thanks, Daniel." Nico disconnects the call.

"What are they looking for, Gilly?" Rocky directs his attention to me with a suspicious glare.

"What?"

"What did you do?"

"Why is this my fault?" I shriek and stand from my chair. "Fernando came after *me* at Scarlett's. I'd never seen him before last night."

"We don't know if this has anything to do with Fernando. What are *you* into, Gilly?" My brain can't think fast enough as he steps closer to me.

"Maybe it was his friends," Nico says. Rocky shrugs off Nico's comment and glares at me.

"Gilly?" Rocky prods.

"I don't know what you want from me, Rocky." It's my typical MO. I'm always the one getting into trouble. He's just assuming I've done something wrong, which I have, but why does he always figure me out so fast?

"They were looking for something, Gilly. What was it?" Rocky keeps coming closer, but I stand my ground.

"I. Don't. Know!" I yell a little louder and shrug.

"I can't help you if you don't tell me what's going on." We're standing toe to toe now.

I know he'll help me. But if I tell him, then everyone will know what I did while I was away. I was a jewel smuggler, for God's sake. I can't. I don't want to let my brother down. Let the family down. I can't tell him. Not yet.

"I. Don't. Know. Rocky." I square my shoulders, lift my chin, and stare right back at him.

"I can't make you tell me, but just know... I *will* help you." His voice is softer now.

"I know, little brother, but I can take care of myself."

Rocky turns to Nico. "You keep an eye on her. Don't let her out of your sight for one minute. I want a guard stationed inside the shop whenever she's there."

"Yes, Boss."

"Can she stay at your place while they get her apartment cleaned? Dominick has an ear infection and hasn't been sleeping at night, or else I'd have her stay with us. Just for a day or two, depending on what kind of damage there is?"

"Sure, Boss. Whatever she needs. You know I'll take care of it." Rocky slaps Nico on the shoulder and squeezes.

"I knew I could count on you for this job, Nico." Nico's eyes shift to mine, and he smiles that shit-eating grin of his. I know exactly what he's thinking. *If only he knew I was fucking his sister.* I turn back to Rocky.

"I want to talk to you about these cameras in my house," I say.

"What about them?" Rocky says.

"I want you to take them out." Confusion spreads over both of their faces.

"They saved you the other evening with Nathan Reed," Nico chimes in innocently.

"What the fuck happened with Nathan Reed?" Rocky barks. I give Nico the stink eye.

"He just got a little handsy on our date," I say.

"On your *date*? Nathan Reed is a—"

"I know what he is," I say, cutting him off. Rocky's head moves back and forth between Nico and me. "The security team saw it all go down on the cameras, and Nico saved me."

"Sounds like you're going to need a raise, Nico. Good work," Rocky says. Nico's eyes are wide with amusement, and I stick my tongue out at him. Rocky catches me out of the corner of his eye and shakes his head.

"As for the cameras, they did their job and saved you. If you'd been home last night, they would have saved you again. I think we need to keep them," Rocky says.

"But—" I start to argue, but he cuts me off and turns to Nico. "How many cameras are there?"

"Two in the parking garage, one in the hallway, elevator, living room, and... bedroom." With the word bedroom, Nico hangs his head.

"Bedroom!" Rocky and I yell in unison.

"I think it would be safe to get rid of the bedroom camera, don't you?" Rocky says through gritted teeth.

"Yes, Boss. Will do. Are you ready to go, Guilia?" Nico asks quickly. "I'll take you by the apartment to get some of your things."

All I can do is nod and think about him watching me on the camera in my bedroom. How long has he been watching me? What exactly did he see? Why would he do that to me? I trusted him.

I hug Rocky goodbye and thank him for his help. When Nico and I reach the truck, I let him have it.

"What the fuck, Nico! You have a camera in my bedroom! Why would you need that? Does everyone in security have access to my bedroom? To me naked! To me…oh my God!" The thought of the whole security team ogling me while I got off with my little pink vibrator flashes in my mind, and embarrassment washes over me.

"Have you been watching the videos after we had sex? How could you do this!" I scream at him, getting into the truck and slamming the door. I sit with my arms crossed over my chest and look straight ahead. My skin boils with rage. Nico climbs into the truck and shifts in his seat to face me. He takes a deep breath before answering my tirade.

"First of all, the whole security team doesn't have access to the bedroom camera, only I do. No one monitors your cameras but me. *If* I need backup, Daniel and Holden can access them at my request. Second, I would never allow anyone to see your naked body and live. Third, I told you when I was in the apartment, I turned off the cameras. Fourth…"

"That's enough." I hold up my hand. "I can't talk about this anymore."

He lets out a huff and starts the truck. There's only silence on the way to my apartment. His grip on the steering wheel is so tight his knuckles turn white.

After I wade through the rubble to get into the apartment, I change into more suitable work clothes and pack a bag to take with me. As we're leaving, the cleaning crew is coming in to assess the damage. I give them a key, and we leave them to it.

I don't know how to process this invasion of my privacy. He lied to me. I thought we had a mutual understanding. When we're safe in his truck, he calmly says, "I'm sorry. I didn't want you to find out about the surveillance this way. I was going to tell you."

"When?"

"I don't know."

"Why is there a camera in my bedroom, Nico?"

"So I could see if you needed help. I can't stand the thought of someone hurting you. You were so intent on finding a *fuck buddy*. I had to make sure you were safe. I'm not sorry I did it because if I hadn't seen what Nathan was doing to you that night, I never would've been able to help you."

"I want it removed."

"I will. I promise."

"And I want to see the views of all the cameras, so I know what can be seen. I should be able to run around my apartment in my underwear and not feel like I'm being watched."

"Is that what you think I do? Let everyone on the team see you naked! Do you think we sit around and drool at the screen all day? That's never gonna happen, Angel." He takes a calming breath and lowers his voice. "I would *never* do that to you, Guilia. I could never disrespect you in that way. I only want to protect you." By his desperate tone, I believe he wouldn't let that happen. He also knows Rocky would kill him.

He parks in a spot near the shop and comes around to open my door.

"I never want to hurt you, Guilia. I thought you knew me better than that by now." I take his hand and stand from the truck, smoothing out my skirt.

"Let's go to my office, and you can show me the cameras." I check in with the staff, and we head to my office. We sit behind my desk. I turn on my laptop and turn it toward him.

"Show me."

He logs into a website and types in an encrypted code. Within a minute, the screen is filled with views from several cameras. There are two views of the parking garage. One points at my car and the other view is a wider shot of the path I take to get to the elevator.

There's a view inside the elevator, and we can see the cleaning people carrying out bags of trash. The next view is of the hallway. It's pointed at my front door. So far, nothing bothers me. The next view is of my living room. I can see the couch, the hallway leading to my bedroom, and the front door.

"I would like to change this one, please," I say, pointing at the screen.

He shows me how to use the arrows to move the camera to the desired location. I move it until the view shows the front door and the couch only. I think I can walk down the hall and get to the kitchen without being seen in my underwear.

"Show me the bedroom camera view, please." He puts in another encrypted code, and the bedroom camera comes into view. His eyes never leave my face. The first thing I see is my bed, and my head drops.

"What's wrong?" Nico asks.

"You can see me in my bed."

"Yes."

"Did you watch me when we were watching our movie together?"

"Yes." Each use of the word comes out a little quieter than the last.

"Did you watch me use my vibrator the other night after we got off the phone?"

"Yes." I turn my chair to look at him in the face.

"Did you get off watching me?"

"Yes." He lowers his head.

"Oh Nico, why?"

Chapter 22
Nico

stare into her green eyes, trying to decide what to say. *I've been watching you on cameras for years. I'm obsessed with keeping you safe. I need to know everything you're doing every minute of the day. You're fucking mine.*

"It started because it was my job. To keep you safe."

"And now?" She sighs.

"Now, I can't get enough of you."

"Nico." A soft breath escapes her lips.

"I never meant to hurt you, Guilia."

"I know you didn't. But I need to feel comfortable in my home. I don't want to feel like I'm constantly being watched. Now that I know, I'll never be able to relax again."

"I'll remove the bedroom camera. I need to show you something else." I enter another code, and a real-time video of us sitting at her desk appears on the screen. It takes a second for her to realize what she's seeing. She looks around the room and spies the camera in the corner. She waves and laughs when she sees herself on the screen.

"You know what this means, right?"

"What?"

"We can never fuck on this desk."

"Was that ever a possibility?" I raise an eyebrow at her.

"Maybe. But now you've ruined it." A devious smile crosses her lips. "Are there any more?"

"Yes. There are three more." I show her the view of the front of the shop, the back door of the shop, and the inside of the shop.

"I'll need to tell my employees they're being watched for their security."

"That might be a good idea," I say. My phone chimes with a text. "It's Jackson. He's here to take his shift. I'm gonna go for now. What time do you want me to pick you up?"

"I think I'll stay until six today since we're getting here so late. And I told Lil I'd close the dress shop for her."

"Okay, I'll see you at six, and I'll help you close up."

I'm sitting at my desk when the boss steps inside.

"Boss?" *Shit, he looks pissed.*

I don't get to say another word before he leans over my desk and points his finger in my face.

"Why in the fucking hell are there cameras in Guilia's bedroom?" *He's going to kill me. He's going to kill me dead.*

"I was afraid she would bring some dickhead home, and he would try to hurt her. Once they leave the living space, there's no way to know what they're doing to her."

"You're sure there's no other reason?"

"Like what?"

"Like you're secretly a perv, or you're jonesing for my sister."

"Me? I'm not a perv. Besides, I told you I didn't want this assignment in the first place. But now that I have it, I'm going to do everything in my power to keep her safe." He pushes away from my desk with a huff.

"If I find out you did anything to hurt her, I'll kill you."

"I know you will."

Ethan leaves my office with a slam of the door, and I collapse into my chair. What the fuck am I doing? I've watched her from afar for years, and no one ever knew. Now, everything is suddenly falling apart.

Chapter 23
Gilly

Nico parks in front of the shop a little before six. Jackson stands and goes outside to meet him, and I can hear them talking from the doorway.

"Look, Boss, I can't sit inside the shop day after day. These women stare at me," he says, nervousness in his voice. His body is rigid, and he's pointing back toward the shop.

"You're ridiculous." Nico walks away from him, blowing him off.

"I didn't know women could be so nasty. I think they talk worse than men do." He leans in close. "They talk about us, ya know."

"Us. What do you mean, us?" Nico questions.

"Their men. Hell, all men."

"What are you talking about, Jackson? Have you lost your damn mind?"

"No. They talk about *everything*. Even the size of our dicks. Details, man."

"What the fuck?"

"Yeah. How big their men are. Not just length but… girth." He whispers the last word, and I try not to laugh out loud.

"Girth!"

"Yeah, man. I can't listen anymore. My self-esteem has been destroyed enough for today. Can someone else watch the shop tomorrow? Please. I'll do anything."

I've never seen Jackson come so unglued before. He's usually a stone-faced giant, but he's tugging on Nico's arm like a child who doesn't want to take a nap.

"Fine. I'll get Billy to sit here tomorrow." Nico shakes his head.

"Thanks, man. I owe you one." Jackson takes off to his motorcycle, and Nico heads for the shop. I take off running back to my office and try to make it look like I'm reading a magazine when he walks in.

"Are you ready to go?" he asks.

"Oh, you're here already. I didn't see you," I say, acting like I didn't just listen to their entire conversation.

He saunters over, his large frame towering above me. "You mean you didn't see me when you were listening to my conversation with Jackson through the door?"

"You saw that, huh?"

"Yep. Girth... really?"

"I can't help what my customers talk about." I giggle and pick up my bag. "All the girls are gone for the night," I say, throwing it over my shoulder and heading for the door to my office. Just as my hand hits the light switch, I'm pulled back into his hard body.

"What are you doing?" I gasp.

"I've waited all day to kiss these lips, and I can't wait a second longer." His kiss is hot and filled with lust. "Wanna be my fuck buddy tonight?" he whispers.

"Yes. Yes, I do. But I have to close the dress shop first."

"Okay, let's go." He follows me out the door.

All the shops are connected, allowing our customers easy access to all three shops. When my shop is locked up, we move into Lil's shop. Nico locks the door, and I go to double-check the dressing rooms.

Nico slides in behind me and pulls me into a dressing room. I'm so horny for him I can't see straight. We pull at each other's clothing, trying to free ourselves from them as quickly as possible. *Now this is what a fuck buddy is supposed to be like.*

His fingers travel between my thighs and find my clit. He's not wasting any time getting down to business. I can feel the wetness growing between my thighs as he slides two thick fingers inside me, and I begin to ride his hand.

"Sit down on the bench," I command, and he does as he's told without hesitation. He doesn't stop me when I take his hard length in my hand and stroke him. I bend down to lick the bead of precum from the tip, then take him deep in my throat. He groans but doesn't push me away this time. I can't believe he's finally letting me have my way with him, and all I want is to fuck his brains out. I swirl my tongue, and his head falls back. When his hands slide into my hair, I pull back.

"Not tonight, big guy. I'm going to ride until you come."

"Fuck yeah, cowgirl. Your saddle is waiting. Mount me, baby."

I straddle his lap and notch his tip at my entrance. Slowly, I slide down his length. I think I can feel him in my throat in this position.

"Oh fuck," I groan. Nico takes my ass in his hands and helps guide me up and down his cock. My hands are in his hair, while his lips are on my breasts. Our movements are wild and savage. The sound of our bodies slapping against one another fills the small space. My back arches, and I can feel the familiar tingle in my belly, signaling my orgasm is close.

"Nico, I can't hold on much longer. I'm gonna come."

"You take me so well, come for me." His voice is deep and sexy. He thrusts his hips up into me as I grind down on his dick, and we both moan as our release consumes us.

"Is this close enough to a coat closet for you, Angel?" We break into laughter, thinking about the movie we watched.

Nico carries my suitcase into his house and puts it on the bed in the spare room. Tonight feels more relaxed, like we've done this a hundred times. We stopped on the way back for Chinese food. I place the bags on the island, and we pull up stools to eat.

"Do women honestly talk like Jackson said?" he asks as he opens the food containers.

"Are we really going to talk about this again?" I sigh.

"Well, yeah. I didn't think women were like that." He sits on the stool beside me, and we fill our plates.

"What do you mean, *like that*?"

"You know, talk about men they're seeing and stuff they do with them," he says.

"Men talk about their sexual experiences, right?" I ask, with my mouth full.

"I don't, but yeah, some of them do." He takes a bite of his egg roll.

"Why can't women do the same thing?"

"I guess I never thought about it before."

"Because women are supposed to be all sweet and innocent," I say, batting my eyelashes at him.

"No, because what he said made it sound really dirty." He snickers.

"Haven't you read spicy books or watched porn?"

"Yeah."

"Don't you think women do that too?"

"I didn't think they would want to."

"I do. A hell of a lot of us do. Women like it just as raunchy and fucked up as men do."

"What do you read?"

"I like smut. The twistier and hotter the better."

"Who are your favorite authors?"

"Oh man. I like a lot of authors." I hold out my hand and start listing them off. "Shantel Tessier, Sadie Kincaid, Elodie Hart, Navessa Allen, Leigh Rivers, Kayla Grosse, Jescie Hall, Montana Fyre…"

"Okay, okay. I didn't realize there were so many."

"Honey, I could blow your mind with what these women write about."

"So if you had to pick your favorite book, what would it be?"

"Nah, I can't narrow it down to just one," I say, waving him off and taking my last bite.

"Okay, give me your top five. Who knows, maybe I'll read them." He begins clearing the containers and dishes off the island.

"Sure, you will." I laugh out loud. I don't even have to ponder this question. I just start spouting off my list. "*The Perfect Fit* by Sadie Kincaid, *Puck Shy* by Kayla Grosse, *Unfurl* by Elodie Hart, *Lights Out* by Navessa Allen, and *Dead of Wynter* by Montana Fyre. You can also listen to the first four on audiobooks. The narrators are amazing." I'm getting all tingly just thinking about the scenes in each one of these books I love.

"I might surprise you." He wipes the island clean.

"I hope you do."

"Will these books tell me what you like?"

"I know they'll give you lots of ideas," I say, with a wink.

"I have a lot of ideas of my own." I stand as he walks closer.

"You do? Tell me more," I purr, reaching up and wrapping my arms around his neck.

"I missed you today," he says, pulling me close to his warm body.

"You did?" I say playfully as he pins my back against the island.

"I missed this mouth." *Kiss.* "I missed this neck." *Kiss.* "I missed this little mole on your shoulder." *Kiss.* "I missed your smell." *Kiss.*

Dropping to his knees in front of me, he lifts my shirt and places a kiss on my belly. "I missed everything about you today."

My fingers run through his wavy hair, pushing it back away from his eyes and twisting my fingers through it. "I want you," I moan.

His hands lift my skirt and find my pink lace panties. He slides them down my legs, and I step out of them. I'm sure they went right into his pocket. He lifts me onto the island and returns to his knees. He removes my heels and places my bare feet onto his shoulders. The island is the perfect height for him to eat my pussy. I wonder if that detail was planned when he remodeled the kitchen. He runs his nose over my wet heat, sending chills across my skin.

"Lie back and relax." I do as he instructs, and the cold marble on my back causes my nipples to tighten. He feasts on my pussy until I see stars, and a wave of release rushes over me so strong I can't remember my name. When he lifts me from the island, I drop to my knees in front of him.

"I want you to come down my throat, and I won't take no for an answer."

"Yes, ma'am." That's all he gets out before I'm lowering his dress pants and boxer briefs to the kitchen floor. I don't even give him a chance to step out of them before my mouth is on his dick, licking and sucking. I have one hand on his ass cheek and the other at the base of his dick. It feels like velvet as I run my tongue in circles over its tip.

I look up to see him just standing there. One hand is gripping the island, and the other *hovers* over the top of my head. He looks like he's confused or in pain and not like he's enjoying getting a blow job. I pull him out of my mouth with a pop.

"Are you all right?"

He shakes the cobwebs away. "Yeah. I just can't believe you're here, in my kitchen, on your knees for me."

"Believe it, baby. Because I'm very real." I return my attention to the handsome man in my grasp and suck him into the back of my throat.

Chapter 24
Nico

My angel is on her knees for me, sucking my cock in the middle of my kitchen. She wraps her lips around my shaft and sucks me deep in her throat. I close my eyes and try to take in every sensation without moving.

"Nico!" she shouts, causing me to look down at her. "Baby, please. Tell me what I'm doing wrong?"

"Wrong?" *Oh my God, my girl thinks she's doing something wrong.* "Fuck no, Angel, you're doing everything right. I'm trying so hard not to come too fast because I want to enjoy that hot mouth of yours." A big smile stretches across her face as she takes my hand, placing it on the back of her head, and she motions for me to grab her hair and pull. I don't want to get so carried away that I hurt her, but God, I want to fuck her mouth so badly.

"Nico. Why are you being so gentle with me? I want you to fuck my mouth *hard*."

"I… I… I don't know if I can, Guilia. I don't want to hurt you."

She chuckles and flattens her tongue and massages the underside of my dick with it, and my cock twitches with need.

"You aren't going to hurt me. I'll slap your legs if you do. Otherwise, let me have it." Her gaze is dark and sultry, and my brain explodes as I watch her slide her lips back over my dick. I grab her head with both of my hands and push her mouth down onto my length until she gags. A moan escapes from her hot lips as I thrust my hips over and over.

I look down at my girl with my cock down her throat. Her eyes are leaking tears as she looks up at me with blown pupils. I use my thumb to wipe a tear away while slurping sounds fill the room. Closing my eyes, I do what my angel said and let myself go. I thrust deeper, harder, faster. I get lost in the way she makes me feel. Her tongue does a swirling thing to my shaft while she sucks, and I almost lose my mind.

"Oh fuck, Angel. Yes… that's it…" One more hard thrust and I fill her throat with my release. I pull her back a little and let her swallow. Every time her tongue swipes over my sensitive slit, my body spasms.

She sits back on her haunches, wipes her finger over her lips, and licks it clean. I pull her up by her shoulders. Her eyes are glassy, and her skin is flushed red. She's obviously very proud of herself.

"You are fucking amazing."

"I know." She winks at me and heads for the bedroom, swinging her peach of an ass the whole way.

Chapter 25
Nico

Before I take Guilia to work the next morning, we stop by her apartment. The cleaners are done, and you can hardly tell the place was a disaster yesterday.

"What are we doing here?" she asks. I take her by the hand and lead her to her bedroom. I pull the accent chair over and stand on it to remove the tiny camera from above the painting. When I step down, I hand it to her.

"I wanted you to see where it was." With a smile, she thanks me and puts it in her dresser drawer.

"I trust you, Nico." She places a kiss on my cheek. "Now let's get going."

At lunchtime, I stop by Miss Maria's bookstore and buy the five books Gilly told me about last night. I need to know what my girl likes, so I can help her bring her darkest fantasies to life.

Ethan gave the go-ahead for her to stay back at her apartment, so after work, I walk her to her door.

"Do you want to come in?" she asks.

"I think I'm going to head home tonight if you feel okay staying here alone. I have some things I need to catch up on before I leave tomorrow."

"No problem. Thank you for letting me stay with you."

"Anytime. Don't forget Billy and Jackson will be in charge for the next two weeks. The boss wants me to hunt down the leads from the break-in. You can always text me or call though."

"Maybe we can watch a movie on FaceTime."

"Sounds like a plan."

She unlocks the door and looks around the room. Feeling comfortable, she walks inside, says goodbye, and shuts the door. The click of the lock makes me smile.

That evening, I start reading the first book. Good Lord, I didn't know women read stuff like this. I pick out a few scenes I think I want to try with my girl.

Chapter 26
Nico

Two weeks later

Ethan has had me working with Daniel to find out who broke into the apartment. None of the leads have panned out. I don't know any more information today than I did when it happened. Whoever they were, they're not from around here. But the questions remain... what were they looking for, and why Guilia?

Billy, Jackson, and Joey have been training the newbie Tommy while they take shifts as Gilly's security detail. She told me on the phone the ladies like to mess with Tommy because he's so young. They talk raunchy, and it gets him all flustered.

I've made plans to take her to a special club tonight. I send her a text.

> I'll be there at six to pick you up.
> Wear something sexy.

GILLY
> Sexy, huh? What's the occasion?

> I haven't had my hands on you in two weeks. We're going someplace special.

> Can't wait.

When I stop at her office door promptly at six and look inside, she's leaning over her desk. She's wearing a short black leather skirt with the highest heels I've ever seen. Her legs look phenomenal. Her shirt is also made of black leather and has thin strips crisscrossing her back. Her hair is pulled into a messy bun on the top of her head, with little pieces hanging free. Her eyes are dark and sultry-looking. She looks sexy as hell. I lean against the doorjamb and whistle. She jumps and turns around with the biggest smile.

"You scared the shit out of me."

"You look fucking hot."

"Thank you. I'm ready to go."

"Maybe we should just go home so I can fuck you."

"You promised me a night out, Mr. Acosta, so we're going out."

"Fine."

We head for the car. Tonight, Benny is our driver. I don't want to drink and drive, and after she finds out where we're going, we're both gonna need a drink or ten.

Twenty minutes later, Benny stops in front of The Black Room Den. Guilia's body stiffens beside me, and I chuckle under my breath. She's nervous.

"The Black Room Den. Isn't it a sex club?" she whispers as if someone could hear her.

I open my door and step outside. Poking my head back inside, I say, "Yep." Her eyes grow wide, and I slam the door before she can speak. She's quiet when I come around to her side of the car. I hold out my hand and help her from the vehicle.

"Why are we here, Nico?"

"I've been reading *Unfurl*, and I thought you might want to check out a sex club." She opens her mouth to speak, but nothing comes out. "You went to places like this overseas, right?" She shakes her head quickly. "Really? I thought since you were into reading smut, you frequented places like this." I can tell my angel is scared out of her mind.

"Just because I read about it doesn't mean I've done it."

"But you fantasize about the things in the books, right?" Not giving her time to answer, I pull her toward the door.

We step up to pay our entrance fee, and the lady behind the glass asks, "Are you here to watch or play?" Her voice is void of any emotion, and she sounds bored out of her mind. I'm sure she has seen everything there is to see around this place. I look at Guilia and raise my brow. She looks like a deer caught in the headlights.

Turning back to the lady, I answer, "We're here to watch." A sigh of relief comes from Guilia's chest. We hold out our arms so she can place neon pink bands on our wrists, then we continue into the club. White means you want to participate, and pink means no touching.

The loud music rumbles in my chest. Gilly has a death grip on my hand, and her nails on her other hand dig into my bicep. There's a two-drink maximum, and I'm ready for mine. I snag us two seats at the bar and order.

"Are you nervous?" I ask.

"Maybe a little."

"It's okay. You don't have to do anything you don't want to."

"I don't want to do anything with anyone but you."

"Good, because neither do I. But we can watch." The bartender puts our shots of bourbon on the bar. Gilly shoots hers back before I even touch mine.

"Are you okay?" I laugh.

"Yeah, yeah, I'm fine," she says with a fake smile. Her eyes dart all around the room. At the end of the bar, two girls are kissing. In one corner, a woman straddles a man's lap, and she's riding him. Guilia's eyes stop on something behind me. I turn my head and find two guys making out.

"Stop staring, baby."

"I've never seen… two guys before, ya know… It's *so* hot." Her skin is glistening, and her pupils are blown. I signal to the bartender to bring our last drinks. He smiles when he looks at my girl. I'm sure he sees her reaction all the time. He sets the drinks down again, and she knocks hers back in a flash. I'm glad there's a two-drink maximum because she would be plastered if she could have more.

I throw my drink back and stand. "Come on. Let's take a look around."

She's walking in front of me, my hand on her lower back as I guide her through the space. The black walls are backlit with red lighting. People in various stages of undress are touching, rubbing, licking, and fucking each other. Her eyes are bulging from her head when we turn down a narrow hallway. The sign reads "You can look, but don't touch."

There are large windows on both sides of this hallway. If the curtains are open, you're free to watch. The curtains in the first room are closed, but we can hear moaning coming from inside. However, the curtains to the second room are wide open.

"Can they see us watching them?" she whispers.

"I'm not sure. Let's check it out and see if they notice us."

We stop in front of the window, and we see three people inside—two men and one woman. The first man sits on a black leather couch. His arms are splayed across the back of the couch, and his legs are open. The woman climbs onto his lap and positions herself above his dick. She eases down on him and begins moving up and down. She puts her hands on his shoulders and lowers her breast to his mouth. The second guy lubes up his dick to slide into her from behind. Gilly keeps leaning closer and closer to the glass. Her glare is so strong they have to feel it boring a hole through them. When her head bumps into the glass, I can't help but snicker. She snaps out of her trance and moves to the next window.

This room has one man and one woman. The man has her tied in an intricate rope system. She's strung up, weightless, suspended in the center of the room. Her body is totally on display.

"Oh my God," Gilly says under her breath. Her pupils are dark as coal, and I think she has stopped blinking. "Do you think that hurts?"

"She looks pretty happy to me. Look, she's dripping." Gilly's mouth falls open in disbelief.

When the man brings out a large black dildo, it looks like my girl's eyes are about to explode. The man begins slowly easing the dildo into the woman's pussy. She bucks and moans in satisfaction. Gilly moves closer to me and slowly rubs up against me.

"Does my girl need some relief?"

"Yes." I pull her in front of me.

"Put your hands on the glass." She does as she's told, and I slip my arm around her. I lift her skirt and I slide her panties to the side before my finger moves through her wet folds.

"You're dripping as much as she is, Angel." She doesn't speak, just nods. Never taking her eyes off the couple. I push one finger inside, and she gasps. Not wasting any time, I add another, and a little squeak comes from her throat. She watches as the woman writhes, and the contraption she's cinched up in swings slightly. The woman moans as he fucks her with the dildo, and Gilly moves her hips in circles as she rides my hand, quickly finding her release. I remove my fingers, smooth down her skirt, and suck my fingers clean.

"Are you ready to go?" I ask.

"No. One more window, please."

"Lead the way."

She takes my hand, and we stop in front of the last window. Behind the glass is one man and one woman again, but this time, the woman is in control. The man is tied to a Saint Andrew's Cross. He's blindfolded and has a black ball gag in his mouth. Saliva leaks from the corners of his mouth and slides down his chin. The woman is dressed in nothing but red straps crisscrossing her body, and she's holding a long, black whip in her hand. Her six-inch heels click on the concrete floor as she circles the man. Every few steps, she cracks the whip on the ground, making him jump. She hasn't hit him with it, but the anticipation has his dick standing at attention.

My cock is so hard in my pants I think I'm going to burst, but I need to stay in control for my girl. I need to give her this experience. Her face is stoic as she watches the woman drop the whip to the table and take a long flogger in her grip. She stands in front of the man and removes the blindfold. She rubs the flogger all over his body, letting him feel the soft leather before it hits his skin. She steps away and begins spinning her wrist. We watch as the flogger goes round and round like a propeller as she moves closer and closer to the man. When the tresses touch his skin, his body stiffens, his eyes shut, and he throws his head back.

"Do you think it hurts?"

"No, I think the leather is soft," I answer.

All at once, the spinning stops, and she flicks her wrist. A snap fills the room, and it touches his thigh. We both flinch as the man cries out, and his hips buck. His skin is pink, and she readies herself to strike again.

"That might have hurt a little," I say.

Gilly's eyes meet mine, and they're dark with desire.

"I want to taste you," she says.

"Here?"

"Yes. They can't see us, and there's no one else around." My eyes scan the hallway, and she's right. We're all alone. I nod, and she drops to her knees and unbuttons my pants. She only pushes them and my boxer briefs down to my thighs before her mouth wraps around my shaft.

"You look so pretty on your knees sucking my cock, Angel." I brush her hair away from her face so I can see her lips as they slip over my length. She looks up at me through hooded eyes, and I almost come down her throat right then.

Her tongue swirls over the bottom of my shaft as she plunges it deep into her mouth, hard and fast. I can't hear her moans over the music, but I can feel the vibrations on my cock. She grasps my balls in her hot little hand and squeezes. I brace my hand on the glass as she intensifies her strokes, and I'm close to coming. With one last suck, I explode into the back of her throat, and she swallows every last drop.

Looking up at me with those sated green eyes, she licks her lips and says, "I'm ready to go now."

We walk hand in hand as we weave our way out of the club and find Benny waiting for us at the curb. We climb into the back seat and sit in silence. Both of us are processing all the sights we just witnessed.

~

Gilly

"That was incredible," Nico says, letting out a ragged breath.

"You can read something in a book, but you don't get the full effect until you witness it with your own two eyes," I say. Silence fills the cabin again.

Benny clears his throat, causing our eyes to look up into the rearview mirror. "I know," he says.

"Know what?" Nico asks.

"Freddy told me. I swear, I won't tell anyone."

I turn to look at Nico.

"What did you tell Freddy, Nico?"

"He's not just my boss. He's my brother. I needed to talk to someone about the whole fuck buddy thing." He whispers the last three words. "And we need someone to run interference with your brother so he won't kill me."

"You can touch her now. I know you want to," Benny says with a grin before aiming the rearview mirror at the ceiling. Nico slides his arm around me and pulls me tightly into his body, and we make out like teenagers.

Benny pulls up in front of my building and opens my door. He takes my hand and helps me exit the vehicle.

"Thank you, Benny. I'm glad we have someone who knows about our arrangement we can trust."

"Of course, Miss Gilly," he says with a wink. Nico walks me to the apartment and takes a look around. When he's satisfied it's safe, he kisses me on top of the head and leaves.

Billy and Tommy were my babysitters the next day. I wanted to make Nico a nice dinner, so Tommy came with me into the grocery store. I send him to the end of the aisle to get some canned tomatoes, and I stay by the cart, checking my list.

Out of nowhere, I'm shoved forward, and I lose my balance as a deep accent says, "Entschuldigung." I know that word. It's German for excuse me. It happened so fast. All I could see was his bald head.

"Are you okay, Miss Gilly?" Tommy asks as he puts the can of tomatoes into the cart.

"Yeah. We need to go."

We park in Nico's driveway, and a text comes through to Billy. He's acting weird. He opens my door, hands me the two bags of groceries, and points me at the front door.

"Nico said we need to get back to the office. You're to go inside and lock the door." Confused, I nod and head for the front door. I unlock it and step inside, but the house is dark. When I reach for the light switch, nothing happens. I flick it a few times to be sure and let out a huff. I open the door to call out for Billy to come back, but they're already pulling away.

"Dammit!"

I make my way to the island, bumping into a stool. As soon as the bags hit the island, the lights turn on. I get a weird feeling in the pit of my stomach as something catches my eye in the living room. Or more like someone. I see a man sitting in a chair in the corner. I gasp, panic surging through my body. My eyes focus, and I see the man is dressed in head-to-toe black and is wearing... a mask. Just like the one on the cover of *Lights Out*. It's a blue skull, but it looks like a child painted it. *Did he make it himself?*

"I see you recognize my mask," he says. My insides do a backflip when the voice comes out distorted. Deep and menacing, just like in the audiobook I love so much.

The day I listened to that part of the book; I was at the gym on the leg extension machine. When the narrator spoke, it was the hottest thing I'd ever heard. I could've come right there on the machine. I'm sure I looked crazy with my mouth hanging open in disbelief. Probably the way it looks right now. I close my gaping piehole.

"Oh my God," I say under my breath.

"By the look on your face, Angel, you're a little surprised to see me here."

"Yes. Yes, I am."

"I read the book *Lights Out* and thought I would try the *masked man* thing and see how you like it."

"Nico, what the hell are you trying to do to me?"

"Bring your fantasies to life, *fuck buddy*." With every word out of his mouth with the voice modulator, my pussy clenches. I gulp as he stands and strides toward me.

"I'm not fucking your knife," I declare.

"We can skip that part," he says with a laugh. When he's standing in front of me in that mask, even though I know it's him, my heart races with excitement. He runs his hands down my arms and grabs my wrists. In one swift movement, he tosses me over his shoulder and takes me to his room.

The lights are off, except for a small amount of light coming in through a crack in the curtains. He throws me on the bed and climbs on top of me, and I can see his silhouette above me. His hands roam over my body, rubbing, pinching, and teasing. My body is needy for what he's about to do to me. He knows what I want, and he needs to give it to me now.

"Please," I beg.

"Please what?" His voice is still distorted. I feel the wetness flood my panties.

"Please fuck me…masked man." Without another word, he yanks down my pants, taking my panties with them, and flips me onto my stomach.

"Head down. Ass in the air. Now!" I scurry to my knees and do what he says. The loudness of the word *Now* causes my core to jump with a thrill. I know he would never hurt me, but man, this is so fuckin' hot. His hand lands on my ass with a loud crack, and I yelp. He does it again on the other cheek, and I push my ass up higher.

"My girl likes that."

"Yes. I liked that."

A hand comes down again, and I moan. He rubs my ass cheeks, and his hand glides to my drenched pussy. He wastes no time in plunging two fingers inside me but immediately removes them. He places his fingers in front of my mouth.

"Look how wet you are, Angel. Suck."

My tongue darts out, and I suck his fingers clean. The next thing I know, his hard cock is at my entrance, and I gasp.

"When did you…?" I start to ask when he removed his clothes, but his fullness stifles my words. He thrusts inside me hard and deep as I cry out his name. He smacks my ass between thrusts. The sensations are overwhelming. I've never felt like this before.

"I want to feel you come all over my cock." That voice pushes me over the edge into the abyss. I cry out with pleasure as his cum fills my core.

He drops to the bed beside me, still wearing the mask. My hand reaches out and pulls it from his face.

"Did you know her uncle's name is Nico?" he asks. *What a strange thing to say right after we just had the hottest sex of my life.*

"Yeah. Why?" I chuckle.

"'Cause my name is Nico." He waggles his brows at me.

I can't stop laughing. "But you're not a grouchy old mobster."

"No, but I do work for the mob. I thought it was a cool coincidence."

"If you say so, baby." I pat him on the shoulder and cuddle up to him. "That was so fuckin' hot. I like it when you read my books."

A loud rumbling laugh comes from Nico. "Yeah, me too. Who knew reading smut would be so educational?"

Chapter 27
Gilly

A month has passed since the bald man ran into me at the grocery store. There's been no sign of him. I think it was just a coincidence. There are lots of tall, bald German men in the world. I'm sure it was just an accident.

Nico's been away a lot lately, and I've been busy working on inventories and shipments at the shops. The bell dings. It should be Billy here to pass me off to Jackson, so I grab my bag, turn off the lights, and walk to the lobby. There stands my friend Kara.

"Oh my God! What are you doing here?" I scream as I pull her into a big hug.

"I wanted to surprise my girl!" Kara squeals.

"Oh my God. You did! How are you?"

"I'm good, but, girl, you look amazing," she says.

"You're so tan. Where have you been?" I ask, turning her around so I can get a good look at her.

"Greece. On Sebastian's yacht. It was amazing, G. You have to come with us sometime." Sebastian is a douchebag she hangs out with when she wants to be spoiled and fucked with no strings attached.

"I would love that—"

"Miss Gilly, Jackson is here." Billy interrupts.

"Yes. Thank you, Billy." I turn back to Kara and ask, "Are you staying a few days?"

"Of course."

"Then you're staying with me." We loop our arms and walk toward the SUV. Billy drags her bags to the car and piles them in the back.

"To my apartment, please, Jackson."

"Damn, girl, you have your very own security force. Do you live in a mansion too?" she asks.

"Nope, just an apartment uptown." We talk nonstop on the ten-minute drive. Jackson brings all the bags in and puts them into my spare room.

"Do you know if you will be leaving the apartment tonight, Miss Gilly?" he asks. I look at Kara and back at Jackson.

"As far as I know, we'll be staying in tonight. If something changes, I'll let you know. Thank you, have a good night." I close and lock the door. Kara walks around and checks out the place.

"I thought you were kidding when you said you didn't live in a mansion. This apartment is so…quaint, G. Don't you miss our life in Paris, Milan, Dubai…?"

"I do, but I don't." I walk over to the kitchen and take down some wineglasses, pouring us each a glass. "I don't miss all the stress of taking pictures and making videos every day and having to post, post, post. I don't miss everybody knowing who I was and wanting a piece of me." I hand her the glass. "I do miss the beautiful sights we got to see, and the nice people we met. And of course, my best friend." I give her a little squeeze.

"I've missed you so much. We always had so much fun," she says.

"I've missed you too." I take a sip of wine and turn toward her on the couch, tucking my leg underneath me. "Tell me what you've been up to."

Kara started as my assistant after my online presence took off. She kept all my affairs in order, and as we spent more and more time together, we became very close friends. She doesn't know about my life here or what my family does for a living, and I hope she never finds out.

"I'm sorry I left so abruptly," I say.

"Are you ever going to tell me his name and what the hell happened?"

"Whose name?"

"The name of the asshole who broke your heart and caused you to run away from your life."

"It wasn't a guy, K," I say.

"What the hell was it, then?" she snaps.

"I got into some trouble and had to get the fuck out of there."

"What did you do, rob a bank?" She laughs.

"No. But let's just say, I came into the possession of something that didn't belong to me, and I didn't know how to return it."

"G. What did you do?"

"I can't tell you."

"But we always used to tell each other everything," she says, putting her hand on mine.

"I don't want to talk about it. Are you hungry? Let's get something to eat."

We order Mexican food, and when we're both well-fed, she says, "Let's go out. There has to be a club or something in this town."

"There are a few good clubs around. I'll let Jackson know we want to go out," I say, reaching for my phone.

"Do you have a new man who's keeping you prisoner?"

"What?" I say, chuckling awkwardly. "Why would you say that?"

"Do these men escort you everywhere you go?"

"Yeah. So? My brother is overprotective."

"Your brother is doing this to you? Can't you go anywhere without them?"

"I can do whatever I want, K. I'm not a prisoner. It's for our safety."

"Safety from what?" *Mobsters who will kill me if they find out I took their diamonds.* Yeah, I can't say that.

"Safe from all the crazies in the world."

"Your brother must be a nervous wreck."

"No, he's not. He just likes to take care of me. Aren't you tired from your trip? Let's wait until tomorrow to go out," I suggest.

"Oh, come on, it will be like old times. Let's go, please," she begs like a two-year-old.

"It's still early, so why the hell not?" I concede.

It takes us about two hours to get ready. Kara wears an off-the-shoulder black mini dress with Jimmy Choos, and I have on a shimmering red cocktail dress and my favorite Louis Vuittons. I thought about leaving the team a note, but Kara rushed me out the door so fast, I didn't have a chance. We climb into my pearl BMW i8, and I start her up. It's been so long since I've driven, I hope I remember how. I pull out of the parking garage and head for the Jade Club.

Kara turns on the radio, and "Woman" by Kesha comes on. She reaches over and turns it up full blast, and we sing at the top of our lungs. When I pull into a parking space, we're laughing, and my throat is already hoarse.

The Jade Club is a dance club, and it's more upscale than Scarlett's. It's decorated just like the name sounds, with jade-green walls, gold trim, and accents. It's only about eleven, so the party is just getting started.

"This place will do," Kara says, nodding her head in approval as we take a seat in a booth in the back against the wall. *Why don't I remember Kara being this stuck-up before?* I head to the bar and order a bottle of champagne, and they follow me to the table with it.

"Woo-hoo!" she yells. "You splurged on the good stuff."

"Only the best for my girl," I say. We down a few glasses, and I remember ordering a second bottle when "Power" by

Little Mix comes thumping through the speakers, and we head for the dance floor. The lights are flashing, and the dance floor is crowded. Everyone is bouncing off everyone else.

It's not long before two guys come in behind us and join in. I don't turn around and look to see who it is quite yet. I have my buzz on, and I want to enjoy it. Kara's guy is cute. He has dark hair and deep brown eyes. She has her arms around his neck while she grinds on his thigh. The guy behind me places his large hands on my hips, and I circle against him and run my hands through my hair and across my chest. Time to get a look at my guy.

I turn to check him out and stop dead in my tracks.

Chapter 28
Nico

Jackson and Billy have been in charge of watching Guilia for the past month. Ethan has had me on assignments for The Organization, but I still keep track of my angel with the cameras and phone calls. My plane landed about an hour ago, and I'm finally making it home. I've been trying to call her, but she's not picking up.

My patience is growing thin, so I drop my shit by the door and head to my office. I log into my laptop and start checking the cameras. All the shops are dark, and when I look back on the video I see her leave with Jackson and another woman hours ago. Jackson escorts the same woman, along with a shit ton of luggage, into the apartment. When I see Guilia's car is gone from her parking space, I call Jackson.

"Where's Guilia?"

"In the apartment, Boss."

"Where's her car, then?"

"Boss?" I can hear the confusion in his voice, and a bad feeling rolls through my gut.

"Her car is gone," I snap.

"It can't be."

"Jackson, I'm looking at the fucking camera right now, and there's no car in her spot."

"Her friend came in from out of town. I took them home myself. She said if they decided to go anywhere, she would let me know. I didn't get any calls. Maybe they snuck out."

"Why would she sneak out? We take her anywhere she wants to go."

"Maybe she wanted to go somewhere alone with her friend." Her friend is the one she talks about from Europe. The one who worked her to death and loved money. Maybe she talked her into taking off somewhere.

"Go to the apartment and check it out. I'll coordinate with Daniel."

"On it, Boss." I hang up with Jackson and call Daniel. I told him to track her car and her phone. I put trackers on both of them when I took over her security detail. The next call I have to make will be a bad one, to the boss. I have to tell him I lost his sister. Pacing around my living room, I decide to wait for the two updates before I make the call.

The first to call me back is Jackson.

"Boss, you were right. They're gone."

"No shit. Did she leave a note?"

"I didn't find one."

"Go to the parking garage and see if there's anything out of the ordinary there."

"On it."

Daniel rings in next.

"I have her car, Boss."

"Where the fuck is she?"

"The Jade Club."

"How long has she been there?"

"About an hour."

"Thanks, Daniel." I grab my keys and head for the Jade Club. I call the team to meet me there.

Twenty minutes later, I pull into the parking lot and locate her BMW i8. If she's drinking, she's not driving it home, so I have Billy and Tommy take it back to her apartment. Jackson comes inside with me. I send Marco around the building to the left and Pete to the right, leaving Sean in the parking lot to await further instructions.

The place is packed. The music is blaring, and the lights will give you an epileptic seizure if you stare at them for too long. I signal for Jackson to go around the other side of the dance floor, and I circle the room, but I don't see her.

There's a bottle of Dom Perignon sitting on a table in the back of the room, and what looks to be the girl from the video sits nursing her glass. I walk over, and she looks up at me. Her face is sweaty, and her skin is flushed.

"Are you Guilia's friend?"

"Yeah, what's it to ya?" She's had way too much to drink and can barely keep her head up.

"Where is she?"

"I don't know. She was dancing behind me one minute, and the next minute, she was gone."

"Gone? What the fuck do you mean, gone?" She points at Guilia's phone lying on the table.

"She. Is. Gone. She left her phone and her purse." I pick up the phone and see all my unanswered calls on the screen. Jackson works his way around the room and meets me at the table.

"Did you see her?" I ask.

"No, Boss."

"Fuck!" I slam my hand down on the table, and the woman jumps.

"I'm Nico, her head of security. This is Jackson, my associate."

"I'm her friend Kara McClain. I just got in from Greece."

"Where was the last place you saw her?"

"We were dancing over there." She points at the center of the dance floor. "These two big guys came up and started dancing with us. I turned my back for a minute, and she was gone."

"What did the guy dancing with her look like?"

"He was tall and bald." Fucking hell. My eyes lock with Jackson's.

"Why, what's wrong?" she asks.

"How long has it been?" Not sure she has any concept of time in her drunken state, but maybe we'll get lucky.

"Maybe ten minutes." I grab Guilia's phone, and we take off to search.

"Hey!" she yells. I turn and raise an eyebrow at her. "You can't just leave me here," she whines.

"I'll come back. Stay here." She huffs out a breath, but she stays put. I'm not certain she can even walk. I send Jackson to check out the offices on the third floor, and I check the bathrooms and head for the basement.

When I get to the basement, the lights are dim, and the music is muffled, just some bass thumping through the walls. The first room is empty. When I head for the next, I hear someone struggling, but I don't understand what they're saying. Drawing my gun, I approach the door. I hear a woman whimpering. I push the door open and see Guilia tied to a chair with a bag over her head. I clear the room and rush to her side, but when I touch her, she lets out a muffled scream.

"Angel, Angel. It's me, Nico," I say, tentatively touching her on the shoulder. She must be gagged under the bag because I can't understand anything she's saying.

"It's okay. I'll get you out of this." I use my knife to cut the strings off the bag and remove it from her head. Her blond hair falls over her shoulders, and I can see not only did she have a bag over her head, but they also blindfolded and gagged her. I remove the mask covering her emerald-green eyes, and she squints from the light.

The bit gag in her mouth is so tight it's making marks on her skin from the rings on either cheek. The gag fits over her head and has a long silicone bar to bite down on across the front. It's connected by a round metal ring on each side. I loosen the buckle on the side of her head and pull it off.

"Nico! Oh my God!" she squeals. I cut the ropes binding her wrists and ankles, and she leaps into my arms. I press my lips to hers for a moment.

"We need to get the fuck out of here," I say.

"It was him. Nico. It was the bald man again." Her words come out breathless and broken.

"Kara said a bald man came up and danced behind you, and then you were gone. Can you walk?" I ask her. She nods and I look over her body quickly for injuries. I pray I don't see anything other than marks from her restraints.

"You saw Kara?"

"Yes, upstairs. We need to get you the hell out of here." I slide her sweet body behind mine as we move into the hall. It's all clear, so I take her hand and pull her toward the elevator.

"Marco, Pete, I got her," I say into the earpiece. "Meet me in the parking lot. Jackson, grab her friend and get the hell out of there."

Everyone confirms.

As soon as the elevator doors open, we move to the exit at the front of the club. The strobe light bounces off the sparkles on her dress, and she looks like a flame dancing across the floor. She clings to my arm, and we make it outside.

"My car's here somewhere," she says as the night air causes her to shiver. I remove my jacket, place it over her shoulders, and pull her to my side.

"I had Billy and Tommy drive it home. You and your friend can ride with me." She sees Kara across the parking lot and dashes for her.

"Oh my God, are you all right!" Kara says as they hug each other tightly. "Where did you find her?"

"In the basement," I say, pulling them both to my truck. "Get in. Let's go!" We all climb inside, and the other guys hold down the perimeter while we barrel out of the parking lot, and then they fall in behind.

"Tell me what happened, Angel. And don't leave out any details."

"We had some champagne, and we were dancing. My head was swimming from the bubbles. I felt someone come up behind me and start dancing with me." My blood pressure rises at the thought of my angel dancing with another man. "Kara was across from me dancing, so I turned to look at my guy, and it was him, the bald guy. I couldn't move. All I could do was stand there. I should've run, but my feet were stuck to the floor.

He threw me over his shoulder and carried me to the elevator. I kicked and squirmed, but he was too strong for me. He tied me to the chair, and when I wouldn't stop screaming, he slapped me and put that thing on my head."

"Did he say anything?" I ask.

"Other than stupid bitch?" That means she was fighting her ass off. "He said something like you're going to pay for this and wait until he finds out. That was all I caught."

"Who was that guy?" Kara asks.

"Hell if I know," I say.

Kara has a death grip on Gilly's arm and her face is turning a light shade of green.

"Kara, are you okay over there?" I ask.

"Yes, but this is a little too much excitement for my jet-lagged ass." She leans her head against the window.

"We'll be back at the apartment in fifteen minutes."

Guilia lays her head on my shoulder, and before I know it, she's sound asleep. I listen to the soft sound of her breathing and hold her head, so it doesn't slide off my shoulder. I whisper into the earpiece again.

"Billy, can you hear me?"

"Yes, Boss."

"Go to the apartment and make sure it's clear."

"On it."

"Jackson."

"Here, Boss."

"Call Ruck and tell him to meet us there. I want him to check the girls over." Ruck is our doctor. He was a Navy SEAL in another life and has seen every kind of injury imaginable. He's patched us all up a time or two.

Billy leaves Tommy in the apartment and comes to the

garage to help me with the girls. He lifts Kara like she weighs nothing, carries her to the spare room, and lays her on the bed. I follow with Guilia.

"I got you, Angel. You're home now," I say as I lay her on the bed. Her eyes flutter open, and a crooked smile crosses her soft face. "I called Ruck to come check you and Kara over. He'll be here in a few minutes. Can you stay awake for me, baby?"

"I'll try," she says weakly as I press a kiss to the back of her hand and hold it to my cheek.

Ruck comes in a short time later and checks her for injuries while Gilly goes in and out of consciousness. There are no signs of a head injury or broken bones. She consumed a lot of champagne, and the adrenaline from the evening has long since worn off.

"She has a few scratches and bruises. She's going to be sore tomorrow, but overall, she'll be fine. I left her some pain relievers, but keep an eye on her. If anything changes, call me," Ruck instructs once he's finished checking her over.

"Thanks, Ruck."

"Can you come with me to check on the other girl? I don't want her to wake up to a strange man touching her," he says.

"Sure, give me a sec." He leaves the room. I cover Guilia with the duvet and kiss her forehead. "Sleep tight, Angel."

I go to the other room and wake up Kara. She lets Ruck check her over and goes right back to sleep. She's just drunk and jet-lagged, like she said. She'll be hungover in the morning but will be just fine. I usher everyone out of the apartment and take a seat in the barrel chair in the corner of Guilia's bedroom, where I watch her sleep for the rest of the night.

Chapter 29
Gilly

The sun rising behind the blinds tells me it's way too early to get up.

"Fuck," I groan as I pull the covers over my head and roll over.

"Good morning," a deep voice says. I lower the duvet down just below my eyes so I can see the man who made that sexy sound.

"Nico?"

"Yes, Angel. How are you feeling?" His voice is deep and menacing.

"Like my head is going to explode." Visions of last night seep back into my brain; the alcohol, the bald man, and the hood over my head. I spring to a seated position.

"Where's Kara?"

"She's asleep in the spare room." I let out a sigh of relief and fall back on the pillows and moan. I look across the room and see Nico sitting in my chair in the corner. His left ankle is propped on his right knee, his arms are splayed across the top of the round accent chair, and he's tapping his fingers. Oh my God. Father used to do that when I was in trouble.

I'm eight years old and sitting across from my father in his office.

"What did you do this time, Guilia?" he growls.

"I didn't do nothin'," I snap.

"Then why were you sent to the principal's office again?"

"Because that little brat Caroline made me punch her."

"She made you punch her?" A combination of confusion and a chuckle comes from his lips as he tries to keep a stern look on his face.

"Yeah, she took my lunch money, and I told her to give it back or I'd punch her. She wouldn't give it back, so I did."

"You did what?"

"I punched her. Right in the mouth. Took my lunch money back and got in the lunch line. Then Mrs. Jasper pulled me out and sent me to the principal's office."

"Why are you always in trouble, Guilia?"

"I didn't start it. Caroline did."

"I heard what you said, Guilia. But you are a Martinelli. You can't let people like her get to you. You must stay in control at all times. You must be a good girl."

"But—" My father raises his hand, and my lips snap closed. He sits in his chair, tapping his fingers, contemplating my punishment.

I have the same sinking feeling in my gut as Nico taps his fingers. He stands and moves across the room and sits on the side of the bed.

"Guilia," he says, holding my hand in his. "Are you okay?"

"Yes. I was just thinking about my father." He leans down and presses his forehead to mine, giving me Eskimo kisses with his nose, and I giggle.

"Did you find the bald man?" I ask.

"Daniel is working on it. Are you hungry?"

"Yeah. I could eat."

"You go shower, and I'll make pancakes, and then we need to talk," he says. I have a sinking feeling I'm about to be in a lot of trouble again.

Chapter 30
Nico

make pancakes and set them on the island. Guilia glides down the hall, wearing her fluffy pink bathrobe. Her wet hair hangs down her back.

"I checked on Kara. She'll probably sleep for a week," she says as she sits on a stool at the island.

"I need you to tell me what the hell is happening here, Guilia. You can't tell me some bald guy who danced with you for two minutes at Scarlett's weeks ago is doing all of this to you."

Her brows scrunch up, and she stuffs a big bite of pancakes into her mouth and says, "I don't know what you're talking about."

"Who's the bald man, Guilia?" She shrugs and stuffs more pancakes into her mouth. She's hiding something from me, and I'm going to find out what it is.

"Angel," I say, pulling her plate away from her, "I can't help you if I don't know what I'm up against." She lets out a huff and swallows.

Looking around to make sure no one is listening, she says, "I got into some trouble in Europe."

"What kind of trouble?"

"I have something that doesn't belong to me," she says

under her breath, side-eyeing me. My mouth flies open, but she cuts me off. "Before you say anything, I didn't steal it. I just kinda… ended up with it," she says with a shrug.

"What is it?" I ask. She mouths a word to me, but I can't make it out.

"What?" I whisper back. She does it again, but this time, I swear she's trying to say diamonds.

"Did you say—" Her hand claps over my mouth, and she shakes her head from side to side.

"Let's go take a walk, and I'll tell you everything."

"A walk?"

"Yes, where no one can hear us." I slide the pancakes back to her hesitantly so she can finish eating.

Before Kara wakes up, we leave the apartment. I station Tommy in the hall outside the door with strict instructions she's not to leave and to let her know we'll be back shortly.

We dress like we're going for a jog and start walking in the direction of the city park. We sit on a bench away from all the people.

"When I tell you this, you can't hate me."

"Guilia, I could never hate you." I take her hand in mine.

"When I was gone, I started out doing the whole social media thing."

"So far you aren't telling me anything I don't know." *Because I was in the shadows watching you during most of it.*

"It all started as a way for me to express myself. It was supposed to be fun and exciting, but over time, it became work. Kara kept me so busy with appearances, I didn't know where I was half the time. I had to be responsible to the sponsors and to my followers and to show up every day, whether I felt like it or not. 'Slap a smile on your face and keep going,' she would say. I wasn't enjoying it anymore."

"I know all of this."

"I had no control over my life anymore. I needed something that was just mine again. Something I could control. Do you understand what I'm trying to say?"

"I understand."

"When I was in Dubai, a man named Lorenzo approached me."

"Approached you to do what?"

"To run jewels for the international mob."

"Do what!" I yell. Her eyes grow wide, and she scoots away from me.

"I'm sorry. I'm sorry. I didn't mean to scare you. Go on. Go on," I say, scooting closer to her.

"He would give me the packages, and it was my job to get them through security and carry them on the plane, train, or whatever. He would tell me where to hand them off and who to give them to. Sometimes I didn't even have to travel. I would meet up with them at a designated location, make the drop, and leave."

"How long did you do this?"

"About two years."

"Two years!" She stiffens again. "I'm sorry, Gilly, but this is a lot of information for me to digest." Some of this time must've been when Antonio had me handling the security for his wife when she got sick.

"I know." She looks down at the ground and kicks at some rocks with her foot.

"What happened next?"

"I was in Germany, and Lorenzo sent me to Charlottenburg Palace to hand off a bag of diamonds."

"And?"

"And nothing. No one ever showed up. I sat there for two hours and nothing. The whole time, I was texting Lorenzo for instructions, but he never answered me again."

"What did you do?"

"I ran. I went back to the hotel, grabbed my shit, and left. I lay low for a couple of weeks, but I was scared. I got tired of running and hiding and decided I needed help."

"That's why you moved home?"

"Yes. Mother and Father were gone, and I knew Rocky would help me, but I just... I can't tell him, Nico."

"Why not?"

"He'll be disappointed in me. Everyone is always disappointed in me. I do stupid shit and get myself into trouble," she says. I pull her in close and wrap my arm around her. She rests her head on my chest.

"Don't talk like that. You're not a disappointment."

"My whole life, I've always been the troublemaker, the wild child."

"You stand up for yourself and speak your mind. There's nothing wrong with that."

"How am I going to tell him I screwed up again? I'm supposed to be a responsible business owner now."

"You didn't screw up, Angel. And you won't be alone. I'll go with you. Come on, let's walk." We wander around the park and talk, making our way back to her apartment. When we get there, Kara is awake and sitting on the couch. A plate of pancake residue sits on the coffee table in front of her. I relieve Tommy as Gilly plops down beside her friend on the couch and huddles under her blanket with her.

"Where have you been?" she asks.

"We went for a walk and ended up in the park. How do you feel?"

"I'm so tired. How much did we drink last night? I don't remember getting back here."

"We had *a lot* of champagne."

"Do you remember what happened to the bald man?" I ask her.

"Yeah, he took G. You found her, and we left," she says.

"You got the gist of the story, I guess. Can you tell me anything else about the bald man?" Nico asks.

"No. One minute, they were dancing, and the next minute, she was gone." That's basically what she said last night.

Gilly stands and heads for the bedroom.

"Where are you going?" Kara asks.

"I need to go see my brother. You rest. We won't be gone long."

⌒

Gilly and I are in the car on the way to The Organization.

"Have you read any more books I recommended?" she asks, trying to lighten the mood.

"Yeah. I read *The Perfect Fit*."

"Did you like it?"

"I see why *you* liked it." I chuckle.

"What's that supposed to mean?"

"Three guys and one girl. You could have all the cock you ever wanted, whenever you want it."

"I know, right!" She sounds a little too excited. "What else did you get from it?"

"That you need a nickname."

"I have a nickname. You already call me Angel."

"But each of the men has a different name for Lilly."

"So?"

"I think you need another name. One a little more… sassy."

"Sassy. Hmm. Like hot lips?" She puckers her lips at me playfully.

"I was thinking… Peaches."

"Peaches? Why Peaches?"

"Because when you walk away, your tight ass looks like a peach." She gasps and giggles.

"You think so, do you?"

"Sure do. I like to hold that ass tight while I fuck your sweet pussy."

"Nico. You need to stop, or I'm going to make you pull this truck over and fuck me before we get there."

"I could arrange that."

"No. My brother would know we just had sex. Eww"

"You're right."

We make our way to see the boss. Sasha isn't at her desk to make a face at us like she does when we walk by without getting her approval. After knocking first, we let ourselves in.

Chapter 31
Gilly

I walk over to Rocky, hug him, and sit in one of the dark leather chairs in front of his desk. He speaks first, as usual. "So what did you need to tell me?"

I wring my hands until Nico coughs, and my eyes land on him. He nods, telling me to go on.

"When I was in Europe..."

"Yeah."

Just blurt it out. Maybe it won't hurt as much.

"I used to smuggle jewels for the mob."

"You what?!" I wince as those words hurl across the desk at me.

"I used to..."

"I heard you the first time. You don't need to say it again. Why would you do something like that?"

"I was tired of doing the whole influencer thing and wanted to do something more... exciting."

"I'm sure being a jewelry smuggler was exciting." He shakes his head and leans back in his seat. "Tell me."

I tell Rocky everything. How I met Lorenzo. How I was supposed to meet the man at the fountain, but no one ever showed. How I ran and how I still have the diamonds. He sits there, expressionless.

"Did you ever hear what happened to Lorenzo?" he asks calmly.

"No. I ran and didn't look back."

"Did anyone ever approach you before the bald man showed up in Johnsonville?"

"No."

"I'll have Daniel see if his contacts have heard anything about missing diamonds. Where are the diamonds now?"

I reach into my purse, pull out the black velvet bag, and place it daintily on his desk by the strings. He raises an eyebrow at me.

"You've been carrying millions of dollars' worth of diamonds around in your purse this whole time?" He's flabbergasted.

"No. They were locked in the wall safe in my apartment until I took them out today." I nod for him to take the bag, and he does. Slowly, he pours the contents into his large hand.

Nico leans over to take a look and whistles. "That's a lot of fucking bling."

Talking quickly, I say, "Rocky, I didn't know what to do with them. I couldn't dump them somewhere because I knew they would still hunt me down looking for them. There was no one I could give them to because Lorenzo handled everything. I don't know who they belong to. I didn't know what to do, so I ..." My head falls into my hands.

"You came home... Like you're supposed to when you need help." He pours the diamonds back into the bag and comes to my side of the desk. "Guilia, you're my sister, and I love you. I wish you would've trusted me with this sooner, but now that you finally have, we'll fix this."

"How? I don't know who..."

"We'll get our hands on the bald man and beat the answers out of him. I'll fix it." He pulls me into his chest, and I cry the tears I've been holding in for weeks.

"I'm so sorry. I'm sorry I'm such a fuckup."

"You're not a fuckup, Gilly," he says, holding me tight. "You just have a knack for getting yourself into situations that are a little *different*." He pulls me back to look in my eyes. "It's going to be okay. I'll put the diamonds in the safe in the basement. No one will ever get to them there." He points at Nico. "Take her home and make sure she stays there until Daniel can do some digging."

"Will do, Boss."

He kisses me on top of my head. "Stay out of trouble for a couple of days, okay, sis?"

I give him a nod, and we leave his office. As we're walking past Sasha's desk, Nico tells her thanks.

"I didn't do anything. You all seem to come and go as you please around here. It doesn't matter what I say about it, even though *I am* his assistant." Nico stops and turns back to her.

"I didn't know it bothered you so much. Why didn't you say anything?"

"It's none of my business what the boss does. I figure if he doesn't kill you, it must be okay. But a little respect once in a while would be nice."

"You're right. I'm sorry we haven't been checking in with you first. I'll do better in the future."

"Thank you. I would appreciate it," Sasha says.

Nico drives us back home, and Kara is waiting when we get there. As soon as we come into the room, she bombards me with questions.

"What did your brother say? Did he know who the bald man was? Are you safe?"

"Slow down, K. My brother says I need to lie low for a few days. Are you good with that?"

"I have to leave tomorrow anyway, but I want to make sure you're safe," she says, concern showing on her face.

"I'll be here to watch her. She'll be just fine," Nico says. "I'm going to go pick up some food. Tommy will be in the hall, and Jackson is downstairs. You both are perfectly safe here." I follow him to the door.

"Thank you."

He leans in close. "You know I would do anything for you, Peaches," he whispers the last word so Kara can't hear and smiles a dirty grin at me.

"So you're in love with the bodyguard?" she asks as I close the door and lock it.

"He's the head of security for my brother."

"Oh, so that makes a difference. He's still just a glorified bodyguard."

"He's so much more than that, K."

"Tell me."

"There's not that much to tell." I head to the kitchen and pour us some wine. "When Rocky said he wanted me to have security, I was pissed at first. I didn't want these people following me around everywhere. But who wouldn't want to be driven everywhere and protected by an army of good-looking guys? Nico's been very good to me."

"Very good to you. In the bedroom?" She smirks.

"K. He's turned out to be a nice guy." *I can feel the blush on my skin, but I'm not going into my sex life with her.*

"It doesn't hurt that he's easy on the eyes either, with all that olive skin and the dark, dreamy locks."

"He *is* good-looking, isn't he?" I beam.

"Good-looking? Hell, he's fucking gorgeous. Not to mention the part where he swooped in on his white horse and saved the day. Good God, G, are you blind?"

"I'm not blind. I know what he is." I chug my wine down and stand. "Are you ready for a refill?"

"How about something a little stronger?"

"You got it." I bring down the Macallan 18 from the cabinet and two glasses. Walking back over, I place it on the coffee table and give each of us a healthy pour.

"Now, that's what I'm talking about." We toss back a few drinks, and I'm starting to feel a nice buzz settling in.

꙳

We have the music turned up, and we're dancing around the living room. Nico clears his throat loudly, and we both jump, causing us to burst into a fit of laughter.

"Looks like you two started the party without me," he says, raising an eyebrow at us.

"Sorry," we both singsong at the same time.

We put our glasses down and head for the island to eat. Nico stays for dinner, but I think it was just to make sure he saw me put food in my mouth. When we're done and all cleaned up, he leaves Kara and me to continue our evening alone.

"Remember the night we were in Rome at that billionaire's house?" I ask.

"Yeah, it was a fun night."

"When you went off with him, did you have sex?" I ask.

"Nah, he took me to the wine cellar to show me his collection. He rambled on and on about how the grapes were stomped by the feet of orphan children or some shit. It was so boring."

"What about when you went out with the Russian guy?" she asks.

"No, we only had one date. I never seemed to have repeat callers for some reason. But you did," I coo. "Jose. Remember him?

"How could I forget?"

"He was so suave and debonaire. I thought for sure he would steal your heart," I say.

"Not my heart, just my pussy." We had so much fun together back then. "God, he was so good in bed."

"Whatever happened to him?"

"He married some supermodel," she says before tossing back the rest of her drink.

"Oh, what about Darian?"

"I haven't thought about him in years," she says.

"Did you fuck him?"

"Yes, but why are you asking me about all the guys I fucked, G? You were around for most of them, don't you remember?"

"I remember, but my sex life back then wasn't as exciting as yours." *Because you fucked every guy you saw.*

"It's not as good as it's all cracked up to be." She lowers her head.

"Sex every night with a different guy. How can that be bad?"

"Yeah, some guys aren't so nice. Others aren't so good at it. Once in a while, you get a guy who knocks it out of the park. But not every time."

"I'm sorry, K. You always made it look like you were having the best time."

"I was, for the most part."

"Don't you want to fall in love and settle down someday and have a gaggle of kids?"

"A gaggle of kids?" She laughs. "I don't think so."

"Why not?"

"I'm just not the settling down kind or the mothering kind, for that matter, G. I want to see the world and live every day to the fullest. I remember when you thought like that too."

"I did. But I'm older now, and I think I want something different."

"Now that you met Mr. Security Man. Hmm?" she purrs. Maybe."

"Don't worry about me. I'll be just fine." She smiles.

"I just want you to be happy."

"I am happy! And I can do whatever I want. With whoever I want. Wherever I want."

"Aren't you lonely?"

"Sometimes, but I try not to think about it and move on."

"Always on to the next big thing," I say, and we clink glasses. "Speaking of the next big thing, what are you doing for money these days?"

"Oh, you know, a little bit of this and a little bit of that. Mostly social media still. My clients aren't as big as you were, but they will be when I'm done with them."

"I'm sure you'll build them into social media sensations before you know it."

We spent the rest of the night reminiscing about our adventures in Europe. We got ourselves into a lot of trouble. It's only been a couple of years, but I feel like it was a lifetime ago. I feel like a different person. I'm not the same rebellious girl who ran from her family to make a new life for herself anymore.

I have my own business now. I'm close to my siblings again, and I have a nice man in my life. Kara, on the other hand, is still the same shallow person she was back then. She's only out for herself and anything she can do to make a buck. She's still my friend, but I'm kind of glad she's leaving tomorrow.

"Where are you headed next?" I ask.

"Los Angeles. My parents live there. I haven't seen them in…" She pauses to count on her fingers how long it's been. "Six years. Wow! Time flies, doesn't it?"

"It sure does."

⌒〜

Kara leaves early the following morning and takes an Uber to the airport.

Rocky calls.

"What'd you find out?" I ask.

"Daniel has a lead on the diamonds. Word is, they belonged to the Bratva. Your friend Lorenzo was having you pass them off to the Germans," he says.

"Did Daniel find out anything about Lorenzo?"

"Yeah. They found his body in Berlin around the time you said you ran."

"Damn it. I was afraid of that. Any more information about the bald man?"

"His name is Alexander Schültz. His father is the head of the German Mafia."

"So he's not the man from Scarlett's?"

"Nope. Two totally different bald guys. What are the odds?"

"Did he come here alone?"

"We don't know yet. We haven't gotten any leads on where he's hiding out. We need to find a way to draw him out."

"What can I do?" I ask.

"Are you up for being bait?"

"Umm. Depends on what I need to do."

"We need him to follow you, so we can grab him. Maybe walk around Main Street and shop or take a jog. I don't care what you decide, but you need to be visible."

"Yeah, I can do that."

"Nico can coordinate everything with Daniel. Gilly, we'll get him."

"Thanks, Rocky."

Chapter 32
Gilly

'm dressed in my workout clothes the next day and ready to go for a jog by nine. I put the earpiece Daniel gave me into my ear and give it a test. "Can you hear me?"

"Yes, but you don't have to talk so loud. We'll be able to hear you, even if you whisper," Daniel instructs.

"Oh. Sorry," I whisper.

"You've got this," Nico says. "Now go take your run like you always do. Stay on the route we mapped out, and Marco will meet you at the coffee shop on your way back."

"I'm nervous."

"You've got this. Nothing is going to happen to you. We got you, Gilly."

I put my phone in my armband and exit my apartment building. As I run, I see members of the team sitting on benches and leaning against buildings and trees. There's no sign of Alexander. I run two miles, turn around, and start back. I stop at the coffee shop like I always do to cool down.

When I enter the coffee shop, Marco is seated in the corner, looking at a magazine. I pick up my iced Americano and take a seat by the window. I remove my phone from my armband and start scrolling. I'm looking out the window when I see him, and my breath hitches.

"What's wrong, Gilly?" Nico asks in my ear.

"He's standing on the street corner, waiting to cross," I whisper.

Marco stands and throws his trash in the waste receptacle directly behind me. His eyes shoot up and zero in his stare at Alexander Schültz. He nods to me and exits the building and turns right on the sidewalk.

"Everybody, close in on their location," Nico says to the team.

"Gilly, get your stuff and start walking home like you always do." I do as I'm told. I pick up my phone, I smooth down my shirt, and head out of the coffee shop to the right. I walk with my head up like I have no idea he's there. I'm confident the team will get him. I walk past a few stores and Nico says, "Take a right into the alley."

"What?" Panic shoots through my body.

"Marco is in the alley ahead of you. Walk in and Marco will grab him."

"I can't go in the alley."

⌁

Nico

I know she doesn't want to go down the alley because of what happened in Paris, but I need her to get him into the alley.

"I know you don't want to, but I need you to lure him in, Guilia." Her breathing becomes ragged, and she fumbles with her phone and drops it.

"Guilia, are you all right?"

"No, I don't feel so good. I... I can't breathe," she says quietly. *She's having a panic attack. Shit!*

"Take some deep breaths. You can do this. As soon as you turn into the alley, you'll see *Marco*. It's going to be okay. I'm coming up behind you as fast as I can." If I run, it will draw attention to myself, so I'm walking as fast as I can.

I hear her take a deep breath, trying to get herself under control, and she starts moving forward again.

"Boss, something's wrong with her. She's walking so slow, and her head is down," Billy says into my ear. *Where did my self-confident woman go?*

I tune back into Guilia, and I can barely hear her speaking. "I can't. I can't do it."

"Snap out of it, baby."

"I can't do it." She sniffles like she's crying and she's muttering to herself.

"Marco, you're going to have to grab him as he walks by the alley instead. She can't bring him to you."

"On it, Boss."

"Gilly, just keep walking. You don't have to go down the alley. Just walk on home."

She's not answering me at all now. I don't think she's even listening to us anymore. *Fuck it.* I take off running. I can see her on the block ahead of me, but I don't see Alexander. I don't care about him at this point. I need to get to my girl.

"Does anyone have eyes on Alexander?" I call out.

"No," calls out over the earpiece six times. We lost him while Gilly was having her meltdown.

"Dammit!" I bark. I take large strides and finally reach Gilly.

"Guilia... Gilly... Angel," I say, approaching her cautiously. I don't want to spook her, but she's not answering me, so I touch her on the shoulder. She startles and jumps back away from me. When her eyes meet mine, she throws herself into my arms.

"Benny. Bring the car!" I shout. He pulls up alongside us a few seconds later. I lower her into the back seat, climb in beside her, and pull her onto my lap. "Take us to my house. Everybody else, go home," I say, defeated. I take our earpieces out and toss them to Benny.

"I got you, baby," I say, brushing the hair back out of her face and place kisses in her hair.

"I'm sorry," she mumbles.

"Don't be sorry. I had no idea you wouldn't be able to handle the alley. This is all my fault."

Benny drives us to my house in silence. I carry her inside and settle her on the couch.

"Are you okay? Do I need to call Ruck for you?" I take the throw off the back of the couch and wrap it around her shoulders.

"No, but I need…" She can't get out what she wants to say.

"What is it, sweetheart? I'll get you whatever you need."

"I need to tell you what happened to me in Paris."

I know what happened to her in Paris. I was there, but she doesn't know that. I saw what that monster did to her with my own eyes, but maybe if she talks about it, she can move past it.

"Tell me."

Quietly, she begins to speak. "I went out partying with my friends one night. I had too much to drink. I only lived a few blocks from the club, so I started walking home."

"Where were your friends?"

"They took a cab to another club. I just wanted to go home. When I walked near the alley, a man grabbed me." Her body is tense, and tears fill her eyes. I take her hand in mine and stroke it. "I was so scared. I tried to fight him, but he was too strong. He dragged me to the back of the alley and threw me down on the concrete. He kept calling me a bitch. When I yelled for help, he hit me across the face. He pulled on my clothes and put his hand down my pants. I must've passed out because I don't remember anything else. I woke up the next day in my bed, still clothed."

"This is why you couldn't walk down the alley today?"

"I couldn't do it. Just the thought of the alley took me back to that night."

"It was a panic attack," I say, pulling her to my body and holding her tightly.

"Do you want to know what's really strange?" she asks.

"What."

"I swear I remember hearing your voice that night."

"My voice?" *Oh shit. She heard me. What the fuck do I say?*

"You called me Angel, and you told me to sleep tight." *Now I'm going to have a panic attack.* I stand from the couch and go to the kitchen. I stare into the refrigerator, trying to decide what to do, what to say. I don't want to lie to her anymore, but she'll hate me if she finds out about all the times I watched her for Antonio. I feel her hand on my shoulder. Turning to look into her eyes, I know what I have to do.

Chapter 33
Gilly

He's been staring into the refrigerator for a long while. I walk over and place my hand on his shoulder.

"Nico, what's the matter?" He reaches in and pulls out a bottle of water and turns to look at me.

"Nothing. I'm fine," he says nervously.

"It took you all that time to decide you wanted a bottle of water?" I know I disappointed him today by not walking into the alley, but is he that mad at me? "I'm sorry I messed up everything," I say.

"You didn't mess up anything, Angel." His head drops, and he looks ashamed. "We need to talk."

We make our way back over to the couch and face each other. I'm afraid whatever this is between us will be over before it even gets started. He takes my hands in his, and his eyes bore into my soul.

"I've been lying to you."

"What?" My heart sinks in my chest.

"I'm sorry, Angel."

"Who is she?" I ask quietly.

"What?"

"What's her name?"

"No. There's no one else for me, Angel. It's only ever been you."

"Then what's going on?"

"Has anyone ever told you what it was like here after you left for Europe?"

"No. I just assumed everyone went on with their lives like normal. The only one who missed me was my mother."

"Do you really believe that?"

"Well. Yeah."

"That's so far from the truth, Guilia. We all missed you, but your father went crazy."

"I told Mother he would be angry if I left without a word, but she said he would never let me leave if I told him."

"He wasn't angry. He was furious with you, with your mother. Hell, he was mad at the whole damn whole world."

"She never told me that."

"I think she kept a lot from you because she wanted you to be happy and live your life the way you wanted. If you knew how he was acting, you might've given up on your dreams and come home. She didn't want you to do that."

"What happened?"

"After you left, The Organization went on high alert. He searched everywhere for you. He had teams out following every lead they could find. It took him nine months, but when he found out you actually left the country, he went ballistic. He killed five men that week."

"He did what! No, Nico, he wouldn't do that." *I never knew about any of this.*

"He sent Freddy and me to collect deadbeats who owed him money. He tortured them within an inch of their life, then he killed them with his bare hands."

"Oh my God. I can't believe my father would do something like that. I knew he was vengeful, but I never saw that side of him."

"Trust me, we never saw him behave like that either. He was out of control."

"I can't believe this."

"It was different when your mom died. He just disappeared into his room. Carmine took over the day-to-day operations, and we didn't see Antonio for months. When he did finally come back to work, he looked like he'd aged twenty years."

"I knew he was devastated by my mother's passing, but no one ever told me what was going on."

I didn't come home when Mother died. I was afraid if I came back to the States, my father would keep me from ever leaving again. I knew it wasn't beneath him to put me in a cell and throw away the key, so I stayed away. It was the hardest decision I ever had to make. I felt like I let my siblings down, and I never truly mourned her death.

"When he found you, you were already on your way to becoming a big shot influencer. He wanted to drag you back home, but he knew he couldn't because the world was watching. So instead, he sent a team to watch you."

"Watch me?"

"Yes. He sent a team of two men to track your every move. To keep you safe."

"I *knew* it felt like someone was watching me."

"He rotated the teams every six months. When he asked for volunteers...I always volunteered."

"You?"

"Yes. I volunteered as many times as he would let me."

"You volunteered?" *He volunteered to stalk me all over the world.*

"Yes, six months on and six months off. I was usually paired with Beckett."

"So you *were* there in the alley that night. I did hear your voice."

"Yes. Beckett and I were watching you in the club that night. We saw your friends get in the cab and leave you standing on the sidewalk. You were wobbly on your feet, but started up the street toward your flat. When you came to the entrance of the alley, poof, you were gone. We took off running, but by the time we got in the alley, he already had you pinned to the ground."

"What happened to him?"

"Beckett took care of him."

"He killed him," I say matter-of-factly.

"He was on top of you with your pants down to your knees, his hand between your legs, and his mouth was on your breast."

"He hit me in the face. That was the last thing I remember. Who was it? I never saw their face," I ask.

"It was the guy from the bistro who got handsy with you. The one you punched in the nose."

"He was an ass."

"Beckett pulled him off you and took care of him." I let out a sigh and lean back into the couch. "You were unconscious when I got to you. I fixed your clothes, picked you up, and took you to your apartment. I put you in your bed. I didn't know you heard what I said to you until tonight."

"How many other times?" I ask briskly.

"Angel?"

"How many other times did you rescue me that I didn't know about?" I snap.

"Why does that matter now?"

"Because I thought I was on my own. Taking care of myself. I thought…"

"Guilia, you did take care of yourself."

"Obviously, I didn't because you had to rescue me."

"That's what we were there for. To stay in the shadows and protect you only when you needed it," he says. "I was so fuckin' proud of you when you punched that idiot in the face. But I wanted to be the one to beat his ass for you."

"You saw everything I did. Everywhere I went?"

"There wasn't much the teams didn't see, Angel."

"You missed the part where I was smuggling diamonds though, didn't you?" Nico doesn't move a muscle. "You didn't answer my question. How many? How many other times did you have to save me, Nico?"

"Just once."

"When?"

⤿

Nico

"Do you remember when you were in Florence at the fashion show?" I ask.

"Yes."

"You had a stalker."

"No. I had an overzealous fan," she says dismissively.

"He was a fucking stalker, Guilia."

"Ryan was his name, I think." She scrunches up her nose, trying to remember.

"His name was Ryan Marino," I say without hesitation.

"Yeah, that's it. He sent me white roses every day."

"With threatening notes inside about how he was going to fuck you and then kill you."

"What? No. I never got any notes like that." Her voice sounds panicked. She stands from the couch and begins to pace.

"Yes, you did. We just removed them before the flowers were delivered. He wanted you all for himself."

"What happened to him?" There's a long silence. "Nico… what happened to him? He just stopped coming around."

"He stopped coming around because he was dead."

"You killed him too?"

"It was either kill him or he would kill you, and I wasn't going to let that happen."

Florence Fashion Show. My angel is sitting in the front row with Kara. She received another message in the flowers this morning from Ryan. It read, "I'm coming for you. Today's the day, my love."

"We have to find him before he finds her," Beckett says. We searched the entire downstairs of the venue but came up empty.

"He has to be up there." I point to the catwalk and the rafters. "Let's go check it out," I say.

We climbed the tiny ladder to the catwalk and stayed out of sight while we searched. We didn't want to panic the people below, but we had to find him. We were halfway across the platform, which hovered above the runway, when we caught sight of him. He was crouched down with a sniper rifle pointed at Guilia.

"Split up." I motioned to Beckett. Slowly, I walk toward Ryan. He was so zoned in on you he didn't see me come at him from the side and knock the rifle from his hand. I put him into a chokehold and tightened until he lost the battle.

"We sat up in those rafters for three hours, waiting for the rest of the fashion show to be over and for everyone to leave. When the coast was clear, we strung him up over the stage and made it look like he hung himself." She drops back down on the couch beside me.

"Why didn't I ever hear any of this on the news?"

"Because the venue didn't want to be associated with the death, so they kept it on the down-low. Besides, you and Kara flew out the next day for Dubai." I put my arm around her shoulders. "Angel, don't you see? It was my job—hell, it was all our jobs—to make sure you were safe. Your father had enemies all around the world. He was afraid someone would try to hurt you to get to him. We let you live your life the way you wanted, but we were there if you needed us."

"All the time I spent away was a lie." Her voice cracks. She shrugs my arm off.

"No, it wasn't. We didn't make you an internet sensation. We didn't make you a fashion icon. You accomplished all of those things on your own. You should be so proud of yourself. You fought so many battles and won them all on your own. I watched you do it, Angel."

"I guess."

I take her face in my hands and force her to look at me. "You are Guilia Arianna fucking Martinelli, and don't you ever forget it."

"I won't."

"I hated lying to you. Do you hate me?" I ask.

"No. I don't hate you." The silence taking over the room is deafening. "I think I need to be alone," she says softly.

"Oh. Sure. Okay. I'll just go, then," I stammer. I stand and grab my jacket. "What time do you want me to pick you up tomorrow?"

"I don't think I'm going anywhere tomorrow."

"Angel?"

"I need to process everything you said. I need to think about my life and what I want. I'll be fine. I won't leave the apartment. I swear."

"Okay, Angel. But if you need me, I can be here in ten."

"Thanks."

I kiss her on the top of the head and leave.

Chapter 34
Nico

watch her the next day on the living room camera, wishing to God I still had the bedroom camera hooked up. She looks so sad, roaming around the apartment. She stares out the window for a long time, takes a nap on the couch, then goes to her room. She spends hours in there. It's killing me not knowing what she's doing. Is she in distress? Does she need me? At seven in the evening, I text her.

> Are you awake?
>
> Are you hungry?
>
> Are you okay?

Just when I decide I'm done watching and I'm going over there, she shows up on the living room camera. Her fluffy pink robe is pulled tight around her waist, and she has a pint of ice cream in her hand. Whew, she's okay. It looks like she's going to watch a movie. I zoom the camera in on her face and see her eyes are red and puffy. She uses her hand to wipe a tear away. I can't do this anymore. I'm worried about her. I call Freddy.

"What's up?" Freddy asks.

"I need your help. It's Guilia."

"What happened?"

"She had a meltdown."

"What do you mean, a meltdown? You were supposed to be trying to catch Schültz."

"We had him in our sights, but when I wanted Guilia to lead him down the alley to Marco, she panicked."

"Because of Paris."

"Yeah. We lost Schültz, and now she's a mess because she remembered me putting her in bed that night."

"You confessed, didn't you?" His voice is dismissive.

"I had to, dude. I couldn't lie to her anymore. She figured it out. I had to come clean. I came clean about a lot of stuff."

"Like what?"

"I told her about Antonio having her followed until his death, how I signed up to watch her, the stalker Becket and I killed. You know… *stuff*."

"What do you need me to do?"

"I need you to call Lillianna and see if she'll come talk to her. I think she's depressed, and she won't answer my text messages."

"You're watching her, aren't you?"

"Yeah," I say on a sigh. "I don't want her to be alone."

"Maybe she needs to be alone, Nico."

"She can be alone in her bedroom. I'm only watching her on the living room camera."

"I'll call Lil."

"Thanks, Bro."

About an hour later, Lil is sitting on the couch. Guilia's head lies in her lap while she cries. It's killing me to see her like this, and once again, I can only watch.

Chapter 35
Gilly

"You know Father was just trying to keep you safe, right?" Lil says as she brushes the hair away from my face.

"I know he thought he was doing the right thing, but I left so he couldn't control me. As it turns out, he was controlling me the whole fucking time," I say through more tears.

"He wasn't controlling you, Gilly. You did whatever the hell you wanted. You traveled the world and built a social media empire. He had nothing to do with any of that. He let you live your life. He just sent the guys there to *watch* you. To be sure if you ever needed help, you would have it. Did you ever need help?"

"I guess I did, but I didn't realize it."

"What the hell does that mean?"

"Nico said he and Beckett killed a man who was stalking me." Her hand flies to her mouth, and she gasps. "He had a rifle and was going to shoot me at the Florence Fashion Show."

"Guilia. I'm glad they were there, then."

"They also saved me in the alley in Paris."

"You wondered how you made it home."

"It was them. Becket killed the man, and Nico carried me home."

"Sounds like I need to thank Beckett."

"But Lil—"

She cuts me off and lifts me off her lap to make me look at her. "You can be mad at Father all you want, but not at the men who were sent there on orders to protect you. Be grateful they were there."

"I thought I could trust Nico."

"Guilia, if you can't tell by now this man cares for you, you're fucking blind. You know that? He volunteered over and over to be there for you. He chased your wild ass all over the world, and he's *still* protecting you today."

"What do you mean?"

"Who the fuck do you think called Freddy and asked me to come over here tonight? Nico."

"Oh."

"Come on, let's finish watching your movie, and then I need to get home to the kids." We snuggle down in each other's arms on the couch, cover up with a blanket, and watch the movie. She's holding me tight, just like when we were kids, and I would get into trouble. Lil could always make me feel better.

"Lil."

"Yeah?"

"Do you hate me?"

"Oh my God! Gilly." She laughs. "Are you fucking crazy? I love you. You're my baby sister!"

"I know, but I let everyone down when I stayed away so long. When I didn't come home for the funeral."

"Gilly, if you don't stop this shit, I might have to get physical with you."

"Why?" I chuckle.

"Because we all knew Father would chain you up in the cellar if you came home."

"My thoughts exactly. I wanted to be there so much, Lil. I miss her so much."

"I know you do, honey. We all do. She was the glue that held us all together. She ran interference between us and Father."

"She couldn't stop him though."

"She did sometimes."

"She couldn't stop him from forcing you and MeMe into arranged marriages."

"No, but she saved you."

"She did, didn't she?" I snuggle into Lil closer, and I think of Mother while the movie rolls in the background.

Nico

When the movie is over, Lil leaves. I watch as Gilly locks the door, turns out the lights, and heads down the hallway toward her bedroom. I guess I won't see her again until morning.

Just when I'm ready to close my computer, I get a message telling me a camera came online. It's the camera from her bedroom.

It's positioned in a different spot, but I can still see her. She lies down on her bed and wraps up in the blankets. She waves at the camera and then shuts off the light. My angel will be okay.

Early the next morning, I get a text.

GILLY

Morning.

Morning.

Did you decide what we're going to do next to lure in Alexander Schültz?

Yeah. I thought we would go to a hockey game.

A hockey game?

I thought I would take my girl on a date.

Your girl?

You're still my girl, aren't you, Gilly?

Yes.

Pick you up at six.

Tonight, I drive her BMW i8, and the team falls in line behind us.

"There will be lots of people around, and it's a long walk from the parking lot to the arena. He'd have plenty of time to approach us. Plus, we might even get to see a good game and some fights on the ice."

"Sounds like fun."

"Look behind your seat. I got you something," I say, gesturing to the back.

"What is it?" she says with a smile.

She unbuckles her seat belt and almost climbs over the seat to reach the bag. Flopping back down, she reattaches her seat belt to make the incessant dinging noise stop. She opens the bag and pulls out a jersey with Acosta written on the back and the number seventeen.

"I don't understand. You don't play hockey." Confusion etches across her face.

"No, but in *Puck Shy*, Cherry wears Lucas's jersey."

"So you had a jersey made with your name and a fake number on it?"

"Yeah. Tonight, you can pretend I'm playing for you."

"But you're not playing hockey." My girl looks so confused.

"I know I don't play, but can't you pretend?"

"You're getting into this book thing a little too deep, don't you think?" She giggles.

"It's been fun so far, hasn't it?"

"Yes."

"Then think about it this way. Tonight, after the game, I'm going to take you back to my place and fuck you wearing *my* jersey."

"There *it is*. I'm in."

Chapter 36
Gilly

I couldn't stop thinking about wearing his jersey while he fucks me tonight. We're supposed to be drawing in the bald man, but it feels more like a date. We stroll to his truck after the game. People whiz by us, trying to get out of the parking lot before a line forms, but we take our time. Nico's head is on a swivel the whole time, but no one follows us. It takes thirty minutes of sitting in line to emerge from the stadium parking lot and head for Johnsonville.

"Do you see anyone tailing us?" I ask.

"Nope, not a soul. Maybe he won't show up tonight?"

"Do you think he bugged my apartment and heard the plan?"

"I had your apartment swept for bugs, but I can do it again if it'll make you feel better."

"If he did hear us talking, then he'll know we're going to your house," I say.

"We're going to find out because we're almost there."

He pulls into the garage, and we walk inside. Nico walks through the house, gun drawn, but doesn't find anyone waiting to jump out at us. When he comes back into the living room, I'm standing in just his jersey.

"Holy shit."

"You approve?" I ask, turning from side to side.

"Fuck yes." In three strides, he's standing in front of me. "Do you like wearing my jersey, Peaches?"

"Yes."

Dusting his lips over my ear, he says, "Do you want me to fuck you while you wear it?"

"Yes."

Nico picks me up bridal style and takes me to his *office*.

"What are we doing in here?"

"Remember when West fucks Lilly on his desk?"

"Yeah."

"I'm going to fuck you on my desk."

"Am I being punished?"

"No, why do you ask?"

"Because he was punishing Lilly and Xander, remember?"

"Have you been a naughty girl?" he says in a teasing voice.

"No. I'm an angel, remember," I purr, batting my eyelashes at him cheekily.

"Then I'm just going to fuck you hard over my desk for the hell of it, Peaches." He turns me to face the desk and eases my body down. The cold hardwood of his desk causes my nipples to pebble.

"Spread your legs wide for me, Angel."

"I thought I was Peaches," I say, looking back at him over my shoulder.

"Spread your legs wide for me, Peaches," he corrects.

I giggle when he says it. He's so sweet. My big Mafia man, acting out scenes in a book for me.

He runs his hands up my thighs, pulling up the jersey as he goes.

"I'm going to fuck this pussy so hard," he growls.

"Yes, please."

I can feel him kneeling behind me. He slips a finger inside my pussy. "You're always so wet and ready for me, Peaches," he groans just before his tongue sweeps through my folds.

"I've been thinking about this all evening," I coo. I widen my stance and push my hips back as far as I can, searching for more. "Nico, please, I need your cock inside me. I can't wait any longer," I moan.

He rises to his feet, and I hear the sound of his zipper sliding down. His pants hit the floor, and then I feel his tip at my entrance. I push my ass back, and he groans.

"You're my needy little slut tonight, aren't you, Peaches?"

"Yes," I whine. "Nico, please," I beg as he pushes his cock deep inside me with one stroke. "Oh. Nico."

"That's it, baby, take my cock." A loud moan pours from both of us while he holds himself deep in my pussy.

He begins to move, drilling into me hard and fast. I grip the edge of the desk and try to stay where he put me. The sound of our bodies slapping against each other is music to my ears. My orgasm breaches the surface after just a few strokes.

"I-I-I..." I can't get the words out as my pussy clenches around his cock. He continues to thrust into me, not giving me a chance to come down as he fucks me through my first orgasm of the night.

He lifts my hips and pulls me back toward him. With a loud crack, he slaps me on the ass.

"Oh!" I squeal.

"You like it when I spank you, don't you, Peaches?"

"Yes," I pant. His slaps make my pussy clench around his hard length, and before I know it, I'm barreling toward my second orgasm. He leans forward and gathers my hair in his fist, and my head rises from the desk. More slaps ring through the air.

"Nico. Oh Shit."

Slap.

"Nico, I'm going to..." The tightness of his grip on my hair and the smacks across my ass cause my pussy to flutter around his cock once again. Am I about to come for the third time, or has this been one really long orgasm? They're coming so fast, it's hard to tell. I like it when he takes charge, and I don't have to think about anything except the way he makes me feel.

"I'm coming, baby. Come with me."

"I can't. Not again."

"Yes, you can. Give me one more," he growls into my ear as he thrusts into me hard. Four? I've never had four orgasms in one night in my life. I can feel my juices sliding down the inside of my legs.

He lowers my head to the desk. I hear some shuffling around and then the low hum of a vibrator. I try to turn my head to see what he has in store for me now, but I can't. He holds me down with a hand between my shoulders.

"Is my girl curious?"

"Yes."

"You don't have to see it to know what's coming." Visions of the giant black vibrator the man used on the lady at the sex club spring to mind. When the vibration lands on my clit, it's too much for me to take. My body and mind are on overload.

"I love the sounds you make when you come on my cock," he grits out as my pussy flutters in ecstasy around him. My body is exhausted. I feel like I'm floating. His body becomes rigid, and he comes deep inside me, and I swear I can feel his cum shooting off inside me.

He runs his hands down my back and moves to caress and soothe my achy neck. I'm totally spent. I have nothing else to give. I don't think I could make a complete sentence if I had to. When he pulls out of me, my legs collapse beneath me. He picks me up and carries me to the bathroom, then deposits me on the counter.

"We need to get you cleaned up. Don't move." He turns the tap on in the bathtub, and hot water begins to flow. The room fills with a cloud of steam. He lifts the jersey over my head and kisses me sweetly on the forehead.

"I got you, baby." He lifts me in his arms once again and stands me in the tub before climbing in beside me. He sits down in the massive soaker tub and pulls me down onto him. I settle in between his legs and melt into his chest.

"I love this tub," I coo. I feel him chuckle lightly through his chest as steam wafts around us and the water fills the space around our bodies. It feels like heaven.

"Nico," I hum out his name in my sated state.

"Yes, Angel."

"Thank you for saving me in Paris and Florence."

"Angel, you don't have—"

"Please let me finish."

"Okay, sweetheart, go ahead."

"Lil helped me see why Father kept a team watching me all the time. How he needed to feel like he was keeping me safe because I was so far away from him. I understand why you and the others were there. You were just doing your job." He releases a long exhale. "But I thought of something last night."

"What, Angel?" he asks as he pulls me in tighter to his chest, resting his nose in the crook of my neck.

"I was the assignment that went bad, wasn't I?"

"Angel." His voice pleads with me to stop, but I can't.

"I was the person you were talking about. I'm the person you almost lost while on assignment for my father. I'm the reason you're so strict about security."

"Yes. I failed you that night. You got hurt, and it was all my fault."

"You *saved* me. You did what you were supposed to do. Take care of me. You picked me up, put me to bed, and watched me on the cameras *all night* to make sure I was okay…didn't you?" He nods. The silence between us seems to last forever.

Chapter 37
Nico

"Do you know why I put the number seventeen on the jersey?" I ask.

"No, why?"

"Because I've been in love with you for seventeen years."

"Nico?"

"It was the night Freddy and I showed up at the mansion. I saw your big green eyes peeking out from behind a door, and I couldn't breathe. I was only fourteen, but I knew in that moment, I had to have you for my own."

Freddy and I arrive at the mansion around nine o'clock. We're soaked to the bone from the pouring rain. We just left our father lying on the living room floor, dead.

"We need to see Mr. Martinelli," Freddy says. His voice is trembling and impatient.

"You'll have to come back tomorrow," Wade, the butler, says in his stuck-up voice.

"That'll be too late. We need to see him tonight," Freddy insists. My eyes scan the room and connect with a girl. She's peeking through the crack of a door. Her big green eyes are wide, and her dark blond hair falls into her face. She's

beautiful, and my heart skips a beat.

"Young man, do you know what time it is? Mr. Martinelli does not accept visitors at this hour," he says, motioning for us to use the door.

"What's all that blasted noise, Wade?" Antonio Martinelli himself stands at the top of the stairs.

"Sir, the Acosta brothers would like a word with you. I told them to make an appointment." Mr. Martinelli descends the staircase and looks us up and down. We're chilled to the bone, and there's blood on Freddy's clothes. He seems to take pity on us, or maybe he's just curious why two teenaged boys would have the balls to show up unannounced at his home in the dark of night covered in blood. He holds his hand out to stop the butler from talking.

"It's okay, Wade. I'll speak to them now. Boys, come with me." We follow him past the staircase and the beautiful young girl hiding in the shadows to his office. I'm drawn to her like a magnet. I need to know more about her.

"There's never been anyone else. Only you, Angel. If I couldn't be with you, at least I could be nearby, keeping you safe."

Chapter 38
Gilly

*D*id he say... love?

I lean up and turn around in the tub, taking his face in my hands and forcing him to look up at me.

"You what?"

"I love you." The words escape his lips like a warm breeze crossing the ocean.

"That's what I thought you said." My lips crash down on his, and tears leak from my eyes. One of his hands is in my hair, and the other is on my face, wiping away the tears.

"Why are you crying, Angel?" he croons.

"Because I love you too. I've loved you since we were in high school. I used to watch you from the sidelines while you played football. I never had the nerve to talk to you or ask you to dance."

"Oh God, I don't want to talk about dancing."

"Why not?" I pull back and look at his flushed face.

"You remember the night we won the championship?"

"How could I forget? That night was incredible."

"I had decided I was going to ask you to dance. When I got up the nerve and started walking toward you, fucking Ronnie beat me to it."

"Oh, I remember that. I wish I had known. Ronnie was a dick." Our laughter echoes off the tile walls.

༼

Nico

I wake up early with my angel in my arms. Her back snuggled to my front. Her soft body molded into mine.

"Mmm. Good morning." She reaches up and runs her fingers through my hair. Her fingernails rake over my scalp, sending chills up my spine.

"Morning, sleepyhead." I roll her over and cuddle her into my chest. Twirling a lock of her hair around my finger with one hand, while the other gently strokes her arm draped across my torso.

"I wouldn't have slept so late if *someone* hadn't fucked me into oblivion last night," she says with a giggle. "I like being fuck buddies with you."

"Me too, baby. Me too," I say, curling my foot around hers, not able to get her close enough to me. "What are we going to do today, my little reader of smut?"

"Well, first, I'm going to lie in bed with my boyfriend."

"Okay, I'm down with that. And then what?"

"Maybe make him some eggs and toast."

"With strawberry jam?"

"Yes. You know me so well."

"And then?"

"I need to go to the mansion for a little while. Lola found a box of stuff with my name on it when she was cleaning out for the renovation."

"That sounds intriguing."

"It's probably just stuff from my old room or something. But I want to go check it out. What are you going to do?" I ask.

"I need to go into the office for a little while, but I'll be back early."

"Okay. I'll meet you back here for dinner."

"Sounds like a plan. Will you be my dessert?"

"Mm-hmm."

Chapter 39
Gilly

make it to the mansion around two in the afternoon. Lola sits me down at the dining room table and places a cardboard box in front of me.

"Which closet did you say you found this in again?" I ask.

"The one in your mother's room."

Since Lola and Rocky moved into the mansion, they've been renovating a little at a time, trying to make the house feel more like their own. No one has touched my mother's room since she passed away. Father would sleep in there sometimes, but overall, he kept it as a shrine to her. I guess it's time we all need to move on.

"What's inside?" I ask.

"I don't know. I didn't open it. I didn't want to pry." Lola walks to the doorway. "I'll leave you alone to go through it."

"Lola…" My voice pleads for her to stay.

"It's okay, Gilly. If you need me, I'll be in the other room." She motions for me to open the box and leaves.

I look over the brown box. My name is written in Mother's handwriting across the top, and I smooth my hand across it. I pull the tape away and lift the flaps. Lying on top is a plain white envelope with my name on it, and underneath it is mementos from my childhood. I set the letter to the side and lift the objects out one at a time.

The first thing I see is my teddy bear. I carefully lift him out and hug him to my chest.

"Oh my gosh. Tiger. I haven't seen you in years." My emotions swing from elated to sad in a matter of seconds. He feels as soft as he did when I used to cuddle him close in my bed at night. He helped me through the many times my father sent me to my room when I got into trouble. My tears soaked his fur when I rode out storms too afraid to run to Lil's or MeMe's room. I set him safely on my lap, and we continue going through the box together.

Inside are hair bows and ribbons—little toys and knick-knacks. The tiny white christening dress I wore as a baby, and in the very bottom, I find a picture. It's of Mother and me. I'm sitting on her lap. I must be three or four years old, and we're laughing. I flip the photograph over, and there's a note. It reads: ***This is my favorite picture of us.***

I clutch the picture to my chest, and tears fill my eyes. I loved my mother so much, and I wasn't there when she needed me. I was halfway across the world when she lay in her bed dying. I could've dropped everything and flown home to be with her, but I didn't. I was scared. Scared my father wouldn't let me leave. Scared of what he would do to me when he saw me again. Maybe even a little scared he could've hurt me. I let my fear keep me away when she needed me the most.

"I'm so sorry, Mother," I cry out loud. New tears fall onto Tiger's fur, and he's there to catch them for me once more.

Lola taps on the doorframe.

"How are you doing in here?" she asks. I turn to look at her through my tears, and her face drops. "Oh, Gilly. Are you okay?" She scoots a chair up beside me and takes my hand. I squeeze my eyes shut, wishing away the tears, but they keep flowing. She brushes the pieces of tear-soaked hair out of my eyes and tucks them behind my ears.

"What can I do to help you, honey?" she asks.

"I wasn't here for her, Lola."

"Shh. It's all right."

"No. It's not. I let him keep me from her when she needed me the most. I loved her so much," I cry.

"She knew you loved her, Gilly. She knew all of her children loved her."

"But I…"

"You can't beat yourself up like this. You did what you thought was best at the time. You can't go back and second-guess yourself now. It wasn't safe for you to come back here."

"But I should've been here for her. I was so selfish. I was more worried about myself than my mother. I even missed the funeral. I let her down. I let my siblings down. And I let myself down."

"Ethan and your sisters know why you didn't come home. They love you and wanted you to be happy. I wish I had gotten to meet your mother. Ethan said she was a great woman."

"She was the glue that held this family together." I try to wipe my tears away.

"What's this?" Lola asks, picking up the envelope. I wipe the tears on my pants.

"I don't know. I didn't open it. I don't know if I can."

"Sure you can. It's from her. Maybe it's a letter or a picture or something." I shrug. "Come on. Open it," she urges me.

"Will you open it for me? I can't."

"Are you sure? I'm sure it's private." I nod. "All right. If you're sure."

Lola carefully opens the envelope and pulls out several sheets of paper. She opens them and presses them out flat on the table. "It's a letter."

I shake my head, and more tears fill my eyes. I can't put any words together. I just point at it and Lola knows what to do.

"My Dearest Guilia..."

As she reads, I close my eyes and hear my mother's melodic Italian voice.

> *If you are reading this letter, I have lost my battle with this horrible disease, and I have gone to be with my God.*
>
> *You and I share a special bond, my darling daughter. Possibly more than you know. Out of all my children, you are the one most like me. You may not realize this about your boring mother, but I too was once a free spirit like you. Anxious to see the world and all it had to offer.*
>
> *Your father was a different man when I fell in love with him. He was gentle and kind. Protective and sweet. Very quickly after I met your father, we decided we did not want to be goat farmers for the rest of our days. We would lie in the grass, in our secret spot by the pond, and daydream about what our lives could be like.*
>
> *My dream was to move to France and work at the Jeu de Pauma. To be surrounded by the perfection of Monet, Degas, and Renoir. Eat gourmet food and drink the best wine. Evening strolls along the Seine with Antonio, watching as the lights on the Eiffel Tower illuminated the night sky.*
>
> *Your father's dream was to create a world where he was in control. Where he no longer had to take orders from others. Where he gave the orders, and his soldiers obeyed without question. He wanted to eat the finest food, live in the largest house, and have amazing children to continue his legacy.*
>
> *We ran from the life his father arranged, just as you have had to run from the plans your father made for you.*

Building The Organization took a toll on him. More than I think he ever thought possible. He was no longer allowed to show the world his softer side. He had to be strong and brash all the time. He built a wall around his heart and sometimes forgot to open the door and let his family back in. But I believe in my heart he thought he was doing what was best for the family. He loved you, Guilia. If he didn't, he would not have fought so hard to find you and bring you home.

I know you're mad at him and that's why you've stayed away from your family, from me, for so long. I understand the reasons you had to leave. Don't you ever feel guilty for leaving to follow your dreams. Know you have been in my heart every minute of every day since you left. I am so proud of you, my darling daughter. I am proud of the strong, independent woman you have become. I am proud of you for following your own path and building your own empire.

I love you with all of my heart. I'm sorry I will not be able to meet the man you find who makes you happy. I hope he is good to you. That you can laugh and cry together. That he allows you to be strong and holds you up in times of need. I regret I will not be there to watch your babies grow. To love and spoil them like all grandmamas do.

My wish for you, my dear, is that you never stop fighting for what you want out of this life. We only get one, and there is no way to know what day will be your last. Live each day to the fullest and continue to live your life on your terms. Be the woman you have always strived to be and most of all, be happy.

I love you,
Mother

Lola and I sit and embrace one another and cry for a long moment.

"She loved you so much," Lola says.

"This means so much to me, Lola. It means she wasn't disappointed in me at the end. How did she know I would need to hear this from her?"

"Well, she said you two were alike. She must've known you would be hard on yourself and wanted to ease your pain."

"Did you find a box for Ethan and the girls?"

"No. There was only this box for you and a book. A diary, I think. Ethan has it." I begin to put the items back into the box.

"Thank you so much for this, Lola."

"Of course, honey."

"I need to get going."

We load the box into my trunk, and I drive straight home. I'm eager to share the letter with Nico.

Chapter 40
Gilly

The fourth shop in our little empire went up for sale an hour ago, and the girls and I want it. We're meeting with Mason Real Estate to put in a bid first thing this morning.

"Thank you for meeting with us, Mr. Mason. We know you're a very busy man," Lil says.

"Anything for you ladies. Thank you for contacting me. Please have a seat," he says as he motions for us to sit. "Now, what can I do for you today?"

"You listed a property this morning and we would like to make an offer on it."

He opens his laptop and picks up his pen. "Which one are you interested in?"

"The one at 129 Market Street. It's the fourth section in the row of shops we already own," MeMe says.

Setting down his pen, he says, "I'm so sorry, ladies. The property is already under contract."

"So fast! The listing just went live a few hours ago," I say.

"It's a hot piece of property. Great location," he says with a smile.

"We know," we all say in unison.

"Is there another property you ladies are interested in?" he asks.

We all look at each other in disappointment and shake our heads. We've been waiting a year for this place to go up for sale, and it's gone already.

"Mr. Mason, I'm sure you understand our interest in this property. We own the other three units. Can you please see if the owners would take a bid from us? I'm positive we can beat the other offer," I say.

"I would love to entertain other offers, ladies, but the deal is cash, and it's basically complete."

MeMe stands. "Well, thank you for your time." Lil and I just look up at her. *Is she crazy? We can't leave yet. We have to fight.* She stares us down so Lil and I concede, follow suit, and stand. We exchange pleasantries and leave the building. We load into the SUV and Benny begins the drive to The Organization.

"I can't believe it's gone," MeMe says.

"He wouldn't even give us a chance," Lil says.

"There has to be something we can do."

We're all defeated and sit in stunned silence for the rest of the drive.

Walking into Rocky's office, he looks up from his desk as we file inside.

"What the hell is wrong with all of you?"

We each plop down in a chair and hang our heads.

"You know how we wanted to buy the other shop?" Lil says.

"Yeah."

"Somebody bought it out from under us."

"What do you mean, *bought it out from under you*? Did you have a contract?"

"Well, no," I say. "It just went on the market a few hours ago. We went in person to put an offer in."

"And…"

"And he said it was basically sold. He wouldn't even entertain another bid. Said it's a *done deal*."

"I'm sorry, girls. You each have your own shop. What did you want another one for, anyway?" Rocky asks.

"We hadn't decided what we were going to do with it yet. We needed to buy it first," MeMe explains.

"I know you're disappointed, but maybe the new owner will put something good in there."

"Sure."

"Right."

"Whatever." We all chime in succession.

There's a knock on his door, and Nico walks in. His laser gaze seeks me out.

"Oh, there you are," he chides. "Benny said you were visiting the boss."

I nod and think this is a chance to make everyone think we hate each other.

"I went out with my sisters today. Is that a crime?" My bratty tone comes out loud and clear.

"No. It's just harder to keep track of you when you're running all around town, that's all," Nico clips back.

"Whatever," I say like a spoiled teen.

"I'm going to be your babysitter tomorrow," he snarks. "What time do you want me to pick you up?"

"Ten is fine," I say, waving him off.

"Okay, then. Don't get into any trouble today." He shakes his finger at me and leaves.

Like the little snot I'm trying to be, I say under my breath, "Don't get into any trouble today. I'll show him trouble." After I dig my lipstick out of the bottom of my purse, I look up, and the three of them are staring at me.

"What?"

"Why do you hate him so much?" MeMe asks. "He seems nice to me."

"I don't hate him. We just don't get along."

"Well, ladies, if there is nothing else you need, I have work to do," Ethan says, dismissing us. We all stand, hug him good-bye, and start down the hall.

"Hey, I need to use the restroom," I say. "I'll meet you in the car." I go to the restroom and apply my cherry-red lipstick, just like I imagine Cherry wears in *Puck Shy*. Nico is standing at the end of the hall when I exit the bathroom. His eyes grow wide, and his mouth flies open. I stop beside him, waiting for the elevator.

We both face forward, and under his breath, he says, "Are you trying to kill me, Peaches?"

"I don't know what you're talking about, Mr. Acosta," I tease.

"The lipstick. That's not your normal shade."

"Sue a girl for trying something new. Do you like it?" I coo and pucker my lips.

"You know I fucking like it, and you know I want you to wear it tonight when you wrap those luscious lips around my cock."

My insides get all jiggly, and I can't help but chuckle as I step into the elevator. Giving him a little wave, I say, "See you tonight, Mr. Acosta."

Chapter 41
Nico

Guilia is trying to fucking kill me with those cherry-red lips. They're what wet dreams are made of, and I haven't been able to stop thinking about her all day.

I pull my Camaro into her parking garage and check the cameras. I rotate the camera view and find her standing at the stove cooking. Her hips sway back and forth to music piping out of her phone on the counter. I turn off all the cameras and make a beeline for the apartment.

When she opens the door, my name is all I allow her to get out of her mouth before I step into her and press my body to hers. Pushing the door closed with my foot, I greedily attack those beautiful, fucking cherry-red lips.

"Did you turn off the cameras?" she pants.

"In the parking garage before I came in." My hands roam over her body, pulling and tugging on her clothes. She's still dressed in the red wrap dress from earlier. She makes a sniffing sound and jumps away from me.

"Oh no! Dinner!" she yells as she runs to the stove. "Dammit!" She pulls the pan off the burner and sets it on a towel on the counter. I come around behind her and rest my chin on her shoulder, looking down at the pan of whatever it was supposed to be that's now burnt to a crisp. I place my hand over hers on the spoon, and we push the piece of meat around the pan.

"We could eat the parts that aren't burnt," I suggest. She tosses her spoon into the pan and lets out a frustrated breath.

"I was trying to make a nice dinner for you."

"There's plenty here I can eat."

"It's burned. Are you crazy?"

"That's not what I'm talking about eating," I say as my hand slides down and cups her pussy.

"Oh." Her demeanor changes back into my temptress.

"Gemme those lips back," I coo as I kiss her senseless.

She's so pliable in my arms. I think I can do anything to her tonight. It's time to play out my scene from the last book I read. I lead her to the bedroom and shut the door behind us.

"I've brought a few things to play with tonight. Is that okay?"

"What do you have in mind?" she coos.

"Will you let me edge you?"

"I… uh…I guess?" she stammers. I'm not sure she knows what she's just agreed too.

"You know I'll never hurt you, right?"

"Yes, I know that, but I don't…"

"Have you ever had someone keep your pleasure from you?"

"No."

"Since you were a brat in Ethan's office today, I should punish you, don't you agree?"

"Yes… Sir." There's that goddamn word again, sir.

"I like the word Sir on those cherry-red lips. You can address me that way tonight."

"Yes, Sir."

My dick swells with anticipation. Down, boy, or we'll never make it through tonight.

"Strip," I say. My voice low and menacing. She doesn't hesitate for one second. Her ruby red dress pools around her feet in a flash, and it's followed by her bra, panties, and shoes. She takes one step toward me.

"Stop right there," I instruct, setting my bag on the bed. I reach inside and pull out a pair of fur-lined handcuffs and sit down on the end of the bed.

"Crawl to me," I demand. Her eyes grow wide, and she seems to fight with her inner self for a moment about giving up control. She takes a deep breath, then slowly lowers herself to the floor and begins to crawl across the carpet to me.

"That's my good girl," I praise. A sheepish smile slides across her lips. She stops when she reaches my legs. She sits back and rests her hands on her thighs, palms up, and lowers her gaze from me.

"My girl learned a few things on our sex club visit," I praise, and she nods.

"Look at me." She raises her hooded eyes to mine. "You're so fucking beautiful on your knees for me." I take her chin between my fingers and kiss her deeply. When I release her, I show her the handcuffs.

"Climb up on the bed. Head down, ass up. I'm going to cuff your hands behind your back."

"Yes, Sir." Her words are soft but obedient.

"Have you done anything like this before?"

She shakes her head.

"I'm going to need you to use your words tonight, Angel."

"No, Sir. I've only had the spanking you gave me."

I secure her wrists in the cuffs and pull them behind her back, attaching them together with the clip, making sure they're not too tight. I rub my hand down her back to let her know I've got her.

"Are you all right?"

She nods her head and catches herself before she says, "Yes, Sir. I'm fine."

"Good girl. You take directions well, Angel."

"Thank you, Sir."

I climb off the bed and go back to my bag, pulling out a

black vibrator. It's definitely not as big as the one we watched the woman at The Black Room Den take, but it's bigger than the little pink one she plays with.

I lean down and show it to her. Her eyes grow wide, and a blush falls over her face. I think my girl is embarrassed.

"What is it, Angel? You can speak freely with me. Tonight doesn't have to be all yes and no responses." Her eyes are wide. "Talk to me, baby."

"I've never used one this big before."

"It's okay," I say, stroking her cheek. "I won't give you more than you can handle. That's what your safe words are for."

I see a little tear escaping the corner of her eye. *Is she afraid of me?*

"Angel, are you afraid. We'll stop right now."

"No, Sir."

"I'm not going to hurt you."

"I know, Sir."

"I only want to bring you pleasure. You can stop the scene anytime you feel uncomfortable by saying your safe word. This is all new to me too. We're going to learn together."

"Yes, sir." She rubs her tears on the mattress and tries to relax.

"Are you're arms uncomfortable?"

"No, Sir." She gives her ass a little shake, telling me she's ready for what I'm about to give her... or not give her.

"Tell me your safe word?"

"Red."

"And what word do you use if you need to pause and talk?"

"Yellow."

"And if you want to keep going?"

"Green."

"Good girl. Are you ready?"

The little tentative word comes from her mouth once again. "Yes."

"Yes, what?"

"Yes, Sir."

"That's better."

I move in behind her, rubbing her ass cheeks in my hands. I'm a little nervous too, but I won't ever let her see that. I've never taken control of a woman before quite like I want to take control of my angel tonight. But I've done my research and not just smutty book research. I engaged the almighty Google, YouTube, and a little porn, and I think I have a grasp of the concept. I want to make her feel good while allowing her to let go of some of the control she grips so tightly.

"I'm going to give you a few slaps to each side to warm you up." I relax my arm and slap her ass twice on the left and then twice on the right. Massaging her flesh after. She wiggles her ass and my dick twitches.

"What's your color, Peaches?"

"Green," she coos.

"I'm going to give you a few more, a little harder this time.

"Yes, Sir."

This time I alternate spanks to each side. Her body flinches, but she doesn't use her safe word.

The next time, I slap a little harder still, and a louder moan seeps from her lips. Her eyes are closed, but her brows are scrunched. Her ass is turning pink right before my eyes.

"How are you doing, baby girl?"

"I... I... Green," she declares.

I try a few of the smack-and-grab motions I learned, and her ass clenches. With each slap, I knead her cheeks to sooth the sting before I make the next ones a little harder, waiting on her to use her safe word, but it never comes.

I'm starting to wonder if it's me. If I'm doing it correctly. I place a few smacks to the backs of her thighs and she winces, but again she says the color green.

She's not making it easy for me to learn her boundaries. I rub her now red hot flesh in a circular motion, soothing her. I think we've had enough of spanking for tonight. I brush her hair from her face and kiss her tear-stained cheek.

"You've been a very good girl. We're going to move on to edging now."

"Yes, Sir."

Tomorrow we're going to have a little conversation about safe words. I pushed her body hard, and she didn't use any of them.

I turn the vibrator to the first setting, and her body stiffens. I run it down the length of her spine, allowing the sensations to flood through her whole body. Slowly, I bring the toy up to her pussy and slide it between her folds. Her hips begin to rock, and it doesn't take long to hear the wetness escaping her core. Her panting fills the room, and I can tell my girl is needy and ready to come, but I can't let that happen, not yet, so I pull the vibrator away.

"Um. What just happened?"

"That's edging, sweetheart. I get you to the point of climax and take it away."

"But why would you want to do that?"

"That's your punishment."

"Punishment? Why am I being punished, Sir?"

"Because you were a brat in front of everyone at the office. That behavior earned you a punishment."

"Oh."

"You're not allowed to come until I give you permission."

"What?"

"That's what edging is, baby. Didn't you know what it meant when you agreed to it?"

"Well, no."

"Don't ever agree to something when you don't know what it is, Angel."

"Well, I don't think I like edging after all, so just let me come." I can't contain my laughter at her bratty little attitude.

"Oh no. We started it. Now we have to finish it. Unless…" Maybe this will give her the reason to use her safe word. "Unless you're going to use your safe word?" Guilia thinks for a long moment.

"No, Sir. Please continue."

"Are you sure?" Why is she refusing to use her safe words. She's earning more punishments all the time.

"Yes," she says softly. "You'll let me come now?"

"Not. Yet." I slap her ass.

"Ah!"

I return the vibrator to my girl's pussy. This time, I sink it inside her wetness, and she starts to ride it. Circling her hips as I slide it in and out. When I angle it up into her G-spot, she gasps, and her knees buckle.

"Ooh, I found something you like?" Watching her ride the vibrator does things to my dick I can't explain.

"Yes, Sir," she purrs. Her legs quake, and her back bows, and I pull it away once more.

"Oh my God!" she yells. My girl gets *mad* when her orgasm is denied. I make a mental note of that. A dark chuckle comes from my chest. The look of frustration on her face sends a thrill to my balls.

"Nico, please," she begs.

"Oh, Angel, what did you just call me?" I growl and swat her tender ass.

"I'm sorry. Sir, please, I need to come."

"Soon, Angel, soon. I haven't had my taste yet."

I run my hands over her body, stroking and massaging her soft skin. I lull her into a relaxing state of mind. When she pushes her ass back into my swollen cock, I groan. Unclipping the cuffs, I instruct her to lie down on her back.

"I need to taste this sweet pussy," I growl. She doesn't argue as she climbs into the center of the bed, and her long blond locks unfurl across the pillow. I climb above her, kiss her soft lips, and snatch the pillow from beneath her head. Her head bounces on the mattress and she gives me a quizzical stare before I raise her cuffed arms above her head and clip them to the hook on the headboard.

I run the back of my fingers down her cheeks and place a soft kiss to her lips. "Are you okay, sweetheart? Do you want to stop?"

"No, Sir."

"Color?"

"Green."

I settle between her soaked thighs and run my index finger through her folds, playing and teasing her greedy little pussy.

"You're drenched. My angel likes being spanked." Her cheeks redden and she smiles shyly.

I bury my face between her legs and suck her engorged clit into my mouth. She rocks and groans as I feast on her sweet cunt.

"Oh! Sir... I...Please." Her cries of frustration building.

"I think my angel is trying to tell me she wants me to let her come," I say pressing two fingers into her slick center while I suck on her clit.

"Yes. Yes, please," she moans. I massage her G-spot and her legs begin to shake, but once again, I pull away.

"Nico!"

My eyes snap to hers and she looks really pissed off now. I tighten my stare and her mouth drops open when she realizes what she said.

"I mean... sir," she says coyly and bats her eyelashes at me.

I think my angel has reached her point of no return. Time to put her out of her misery.

"That's better."

"Have you learned your lesson, Peaches?"

"Yes, Sir."

"Will you stop being a brat to me in public?"

"I thought we had to be snarky, so everyone thought we hated each other?"

"I don't want to hate you anymore. I want the world to know how much you mean to me."

"Yes, Sir." I climb up her body and kiss her sweet lips.

"But right now," I notch my cock at her hot entrance, and she gasps for a breath. "I want to fuck this desperate cunt of yours, long and hard. And make you come harder than you ever have before."

"Yes, please."

Chapter 42
Gilly

When we wake the following morning. I'm cuddled into Nico's side. I wince at the slight discomfort on my backside when I stretch.

"Does your ass hurt, Angel?" Nico asks, pulling me back into him. "Did the arnica cream help last night?"

"A little. I'll definitely remember what you did to me all day today."

"I told you the edging was worth it."

"The orgasms were incredible. Was that what you got from reading *Dead of Wynter*?" I ask.

"Yes. When Everett spanks her and paddles her over the arm of the couch and when he edges her. We're both still learning. Next time we try edging, you'll know what to expect and you can trust me."

"I do trust you, Nico."

"I'll need your complete trust for you to allow your body and mind to submit to me entirely. I want you to be able to relinquish all control to me. To let yourself let go and get out of that pretty head of yours. It'll take time. If you want that, I mean. If you didn't like it, we don't ever have to do it again."

"I liked the orgasm part the most." She giggles. "I would like to try it all again sometime. But can we let my ass heal first?"

"Of course. But we need to talk about something that's been bothering me," he says.

"What is it? Did I do something wrong?"

"Fuck no, Angel, you were perfect. I'd like to know why you didn't use a safe word last night." My body stiffens at his words. "I spanked you really hard, but you never changed your color."

"No, Sir."

"You don't have to call me Sir when we're not in a scene, sweetheart."

"Oh."

"You're supposed to use the safe words to communicate what you're feeling, but you didn't, did you?"

"No."

"Why not?"

"I didn't want you to think I was…"

"Was what, Guilia?"

"Weak."

"Weak? You're the strongest woman I know, Angel. Fuck. The safe words are there to keep you from getting hurt. They're not a sign of weakness."

"I wanted to be strong for you. I didn't want to give up."

"Give up? Angel, I could've hurt you very badly last night if I'd kept going. Were you ever going to use your safe word?"

"No," I admit quietly.

"Angel, you have to promise me the next time we play, you'll use the safe words to tell me when you've reached your limit. I need to be able to trust you too."

"I will. I promise. I'm sorry." He places little kisses to the top of my head, while he holds me close. The silence is awkward as I try to think of something to lighten his mood.

"What book are you going to read next? This has been a lot of fun."

"You'll have to give me some new titles to pick up."

"I'll make you a list." I get out of bed, head to the bathroom, and Nico follows.

"I need to go to work for a meeting. Are you going into work today?" he asks.

"I thought I would play hooky today. Can I stay here?"

"Of course, you can," he says, placing a gentle kiss on the tip of my nose. I love how he gives me little kisses everywhere.

"My big bad mobster boyfriend is really a big softy," I say.

"Don't let it get out. I have an image to protect." His smile is warm and his eyes are soft. He looks content.

"Can I go for a jog?"

"Sure, I'll call Joey. I think he can keep up with you."

"Great, I'll make you something to eat before you go to work." He enters the shower, and I throw on my robe and make us lunch.

He walks down the hallway in his black dress slacks and gray button-down. He slides in behind me and puts his arms around my waist.

"Look at you being all *domestic*," he says into my neck. I turn and face him, placing a light kiss on his lips and fix his collar.

"And look at you all *hot as fuck*." I pull him by the hand. "Let's go back to bed."

"Nah, nah, I have to be in your brother's office in an hour."

Looking down at the watch that isn't there, I say, "We have fifteen minutes. Let's go." He tugs me to him tightly and kisses me sweetly.

"We need to figure out how to tell your family we're a thing."

"A thing?"

"A couple, together, you know what I'm trying to say," he says, throwing his hands all around.

"That I love you," I purr.

"Yes, and I love you back."

I suck his bottom lip into my mouth, and he hums. "We need to eat so I can leave."

"Fine," I say with a pout. Both of us sit down at the island and eat the salads I prepared.

"Why don't we take the whole family out to dinner at Lowell's and tell them. Rocky won't be able to kill you in public," I say with a teasing grin.

"Gee, that makes me feel so much better, thanks," he grumbles.

"But seriously, we need to think about what we're going to say."

"I'm going to say, I've been stalking your sister for years. I love her, and I want her to bear my children."

"Bear your children! Hold on now," I say, as he bursts out into a belly laugh.

"I'm just kidding. You're making it too hard. We'll figure it out. Can we talk about it more tonight when I get home?"

"Yeah." He kisses me on the cheek and heads out the door. I clean up the kitchen and get ready for my run.

Joey rings the bell around two, and we head out. When we return around three, Joey leaves me at the door, and I go straight to the bathroom for a long, hot shower.

It's four o'clock when I emerge from the bathroom, dressed in one of Nico's black T-shirts and a pair of his gray boxer briefs. *Why are men's clothes so comfy?*

I chuckle when I see his large form sitting in a chair in the back of the living room. He's in a black ski mask like bank robbers wear this time, and he's dressed in all black. He must've changed his shirt.

"Are we doing *Lights Out* again?" I ask. He shakes his head, and I walk a step closer.

"Oh, I know this is from *Carnage*." He shakes his head again. I'm about six feet from him when he stands, and I realize this is not Nico. I turn and try to run, but he grabs my arm and spins me into his chest. His grip is tight, and my wrist aches.

"Who are you? How did you get in here?" I struggle in his grip. He drags the mask off his head, and I see the face of the bald man, Alexander Schültz.

I scream, but he backhands me across the face. My eye burns, and I feel wetness sliding down my cheek.

"What do you want from me?" I yell before I feel a prick in my neck, and everything goes black.

Chapter 43
Nico

I walk into my house around five o'clock.

"Honey, I'm home," I singsong like they do on those shows from the fifties. I check the bathroom. "Gilly?" The bedroom. "Peaches?" There's no sign of her. I call Joey.

"Joey."

"Yeah, Boss?"

"When did you get back from your jog with Gilly?"

"About three o'clock, why?"

"Did she tell you she was going somewhere else?"

"No, Boss. She said she was taking a shower and going to make you dinner."

I hang up the phone and head for the kitchen. I check the island and the refrigerator for a note, but I don't find one. Nothing seems out of place. *What the fuck.* I dial her cell, but she doesn't pick up. Pissed off, I call it again. That's when I hear it. The faint sound of a ringtone in the distance. I run to the bedroom and find her purse sitting in the chair where it always lands but no phone. I dial her number again and hear the ringing sound, louder now. I find her phone lying by the bathroom sink.

I dial Ethan.

"Boss. We have a problem."

Chapter 44
Gilly

I wake up with a groan as I try to lift my head. My neck is killing me, and I feel like I ate a cotton ball.

"What the fuck is going on?" I slur as I try to open my eyes.

"Ah, the princess awakes," a deep voice says. The light burns my eyes when I squint, trying to focus. I see a man sitting in a chair across the room. It's not the bald man this time. He's an older man. Maybe the mid-to-late fifties, if I had to guess. He has jet-black hair, which looks like it's either a toupee or he colors it black, and bushy black eyebrows to match. His fat gut hangs over his pants onto his lap.

"Who are you?" I ask.

"Why. I'm going to be your new husband," he says. I hear his thick German accent now.

"Like hell you are," I snap.

I thought for sure he would say something about the diamonds, not that I was going to be his wife. His belly jiggles as he laughs loudly.

"What the fuck are you talking about? I don't even know you."

"Oh, forgive me, princess." He stands and walks over to me. I can see he's on the shorter side.

"My name is Alfred Schültz. I believe you met my son, Alexander."

"The bald man?"

"Yes, that's him." Alexander steps into the room, and my heart begins to race. I pull on the ropes restraining me, but I can't budge them.

"Alexander, meet your new momma."

"Momma! What the fuck!" I yell. *This guy has lost his mind.*

"Okay, it is a little far-fetched to think you could be his momma, but you get the idea." Alfred chuckles.

"Why in the hell do you think I'm going to marry you?"

"Because your father and I made a deal."

"My father's been dead for two years."

"Oh, I know, my dear, but you were supposed to have been mine the day after your high school graduation." *I knew it! I fucking knew it!* Father arranged a marriage for me too, just like he did for Lillianna and Maria. Of course, they get good-looking, tall, dark, and handsome and just as I predicted, I get short, fat, and old.

"I'm not marrying you," I say, shaking my head wildly.

"Your father and I had a deal. It was signed, sealed, and delivered. I gave him five million dollars in return for your hand in marriage. The only problem was you…"

"Ran away the day after graduation," I complete his sentence.

"Yes."

"My father is dead now, so that makes the contract null and void."

"No, it doesn't. I already paid my money for you."

"My brother will give you the money back with interest. Just let me go."

"You're coming back with me to Germany to be my bride, to produce more sons for me." *Produce* more sons. Like hell I will. He comes over to me and takes a piece of my hair between his fingers. "You are as beautiful today as you were back then." My skin crawls at the thought of this disgusting man touching me. He runs the backs of his fingers across my eye, and I wince. There must be a mark there from when Alexander hit me.

He crosses the room and slaps Alexander. "I told you not to hurt her!" he yells up at him. Alexander says nothing. He just takes the hit.

"I'll never marry you," I say.

"My, you are a feisty one. You are going to keep me young. I like it. But you don't have a choice in the matter, Guilia."

Nico has to know I'm gone by now. He'll find me. He has to.

Chapter 45
Nico

'm on the phone with Daniel, trying to figure out where in the hell Guilia went. We found Billy lying in the bushes, with a bump on his head the size of a golf ball.

"Did you find Guilia on the surrounding cameras yet?

"Almost there," Daniel says. I can hear the sounds of typing in the background. Daniel found the bald man on the camera carrying her over his shoulder, out the front door, and putting her into a black van. He's been tracking them using the cameras set up throughout the city.

"Gotcha!"

"Where is she?" I snap.

"She's in a hangar at the airport."

"The airport? Drop me a pin and get a team headed there now!"

"On it. Do you want me to tell the boss?"

"No. I told him I would be the one to call him with the location," I say.

I hang up with Daniel and call Ethan.

"Daniel thinks he's found her."

"Where the fuck is she?"

"She's in a hangar at the airport. I'm headed there now. He's sending a team."

"You better get to her before they get her on a plane. If they move her out of the country, we may never find her."

"On it."

I drive like a bat out of hell to the airport. Daniel pinned her to hangar twelve and alerted security to let us pass. Two of our black SUVs full of armed soldiers follow me to the hangar. It's after midnight when we park out of sight and surround the building.

I don't want my angel to be in the middle of a gunfight. Maybe if we can take the perimeter guards quietly, we can surprise her captors. They probably just want their diamonds back. Ethan is on the way with them. If we can have a peaceful trade, this can all be over, and I'll have my angel back.

"Boss," Jackson says through my earpiece.

"Copy."

"They have her tied up in a back room. There's an old guy and the bald man in there with her. There are six guards in the surrounding area."

I turn to my right and see our black Escalade pulling in. It holds Ethan and the bag of diamonds.

"Get my sister the fuck out of there, Nico," the boss demands.

"You heard him, take them out. But let's try to do it quietly, so we don't spook him. We don't want him to run with her."

The team moves on the six men. It only takes two minutes, and they're dragging them to the center of the hangar by the jet. They shot three of them, and the other three are tied together, back-to-back-to-back. Beckett and I move down the hall toward the room where he's holding my Guilia.

We burst through the door, and we're halted by the scene in front of us. The old guy is behind my angel and is holding a gun to her head. The bald man stands at his side, pointing his gun at us.

"Don't take another step," the older guy barks in his thick German accent. My gun is pointed at him, and Beckett's is aimed at the bald man. We're at a standoff and I'm not leaving here without my girl.

Guilia has dried blood on one side of her face, but I can't tell if she has any other injuries. She's tied with ropes to a wooden chair by her wrists and ankles.

"Nico!" she yells. The old man tightens his grip on her shoulders, and she winces.

"It's gonna be okay, Guilia," I say calmly.

"And who might you be?" the older man asks.

"I'm the head of security for The Organization, and you are?"

"I'm Alfred Schültz, capo di tutti capi, of the Schültz family, Germany. And this is my oldest son and my second, Alexander. I believe you've met." *Germany. What the fuck are they doing here?*

"I'm going to need you to let her go," I say.

"Ah, young man, that won't be happening. I'm going to need *you* to drop your weapons."

"That's not happening either, old man," I say.

"She's returning to Germany with me tonight. She's going to be my wife."

"Wife!" I laugh. Guilia is shaking her head and mumbling to herself.

"Yes, my wife. Tell him, my dear." He gives her shoulder a little shove, and she begins to speak.

"My father set up an arranged marriage for me to Mr. Schültz. I was supposed to marry him the day after graduation. He paid my father five million dollars for me."

"Holy fuck, Antonio, what did you do?" Ethan says in my ear.

"We'll give you the money back, and you can give back Guilia."

"Oh, I don't think so. I have waited too many years to find her. She's mine," he says.

"That's not going to work for us."

Ethan comes through my ear again. "Tell him I want to meet with him, Nico."

"Rocco Martinelli would like a moment of your time before this gets out of hand."

"I don't see him," he says, trying to look beyond me.

"He's outside."

"Well, send him in. I want to get this over with so I can take my bride home." He runs his hand over her shoulder, and she cringes at his touch. I might have to cut that hand of his off if he doesn't keep it to himself.

In two minutes, the boss stands behind me. He touches my shoulder, and I take one step to the left. Never taking my aim off of Schültz. He walks into the room, and I move one step back.

"Ah, Rocco. How are you, my boy?" Schültz asks.

"Better than you're going to be if you don't let my sister go, Alfred," he says in a deep menacing tone.

"Your father and I made a deal."

"My father is dead." The boss's voice is cold.

"A deal is a deal, my boy."

"Don't call me that. I'm not a boy anymore, old man."

Alfred makes a tsking sound. "I see you *are* just like your father."

The skin on Ethan's neck turns red and I know his blood is boiling. He doesn't like being compared to his father.

"It's come to my attention I may have something you covet more than you do my sister."

"Never."

Ethan holds up the velvet bag of diamonds. Alfred's eyes widen at the sight of the little black bag dangling from Ethan's finger.

"Where in the hell did you get those?" he barks.

"Let's just say they recently came into my possession," Ethan whispers, like it's a secret. "I heard you stole them from the Russians."

"I didn't *steal* them. I made a deal for them, but they were never delivered to me."

"I think what's in this bag is worth a lot more than the five million dollars you paid for my sister. Why don't we trade?"

Alfred's body is thrumming with excitement. I think those diamonds just gave him a hard-on.

"I need to see them first."

Ethan points at the table across the room, and Alfred uses his gun to direct him to go ahead. He walks over and carefully pours them onto the table. Alfred points the gun again for him to back away. Ethan raises his hands and takes a few steps back.

Alfred moves away from Guilia, and Alexander takes his place. He aims his pistol at her head and takes a handful of her hair and yanks her head back. She cries out in pain, and I'm going to have to kill Alexander for touching my woman as well.

Alfred walks over to the table. His eyes gleam, as if he's in a trance, as he looks at the pile of sparkling diamonds.

"Wunderschone Juwelen," (beautiful jewels) he says under his breath. Alfred thinks long and hard. Finally, he waves his gun to Alexander. "Untie her." Alexander doesn't say a word. He's such a good little son doing everything his daddy says without complaint. He holsters his weapon, so Beckett and I follow suit.

Alexander goes to work releasing the ropes holding my girl. Her eyes dart around the room as she takes in the situation. She rubs her wrists but doesn't make any sudden movements as she waits for instructions from Ethan.

Alfred points at Ethan to put the diamonds back in the bag. His jaw grinds, hating taking an order from another Don, but he would do anything to get Guilia out of here. He fills the bag, holds it up, and drops it into Alfred's outstretched hand.

"It was nice doing business with you," Schültz says with a devious grin on his face.

"I want to be clear. Your arrangement with my father is null and void now. You'll leave my sister alone and go back to Germany."

Schültz holds out his hand to Ethan, and they shake. "Yes, of course, my boy."

Ethan steps back and they move to the doorway. The boss nods in our direction. Beckett and I each take one step back and allow them to leave the room.

The boss holds out his hand for us to stay put. Guilia stands and files in behind me. Her hands grab my shirt, and she buries her face in my back. Suddenly, we hear shouting in what sounds like... Russian? Then there's gunfire and silence.

"It's all clear, Boss," someone says through the earpiece. Ethan strides from the room, and we follow.

As we approach the hangar, eight dead bodies are now scattered across the concrete. Blood seeps from beneath them all.

I reach my arm around to hold Guilia in place. "Stay behind me and close your eyes," I say as we walk out to meet the Russians.

Pakhan Ivan Vilkolov of the Bratva, stands beside a black BMW x7. He's tucking the black velvet bag into his suit pocket. With one gesture of his hand, Ethan tells us to stay put, and he walks forward to meet Ivan. As he gets closer, he holds out his hand to Ivan.

"Comrade, I cannot thank you enough for recovering my lost treasures. If you need anything in Russia, you come to me," Ivan speaks in his thick Russian accent. Their handshake is long and hard with lots of shoulder slapping.

"I will. Thank you for helping me save my sister."

"Of course."

"Safe journey home, my friend," Ethan replies, as the group of Russians load into their vehicles and leave the hangar.

"Beckett, get the cleaning crew in here to clean this mess up before the sun comes up and someone finds out what happened here tonight," Ethan orders. Then he motions for us to move forward toward the vehicles.

I hear Guilia take a deep breath and watch as she moves out from behind me, headed for Ethan. The need to keep touching her is all-consuming, but I have to wait until we get in the car.

My girl has her eyes set on her brother.

"How was the Bratva just here?" she asks.

"I told you I thought the diamonds belonged to the Russians. When I called and talked to Ivan, he flew here right away. He was on his way to the mansion when I got the call from Nico. He agreed to turn around and meet us here instead and to let us use the diamonds as bait to save you from Schültz. His only stipulation was he wanted to be the one to take him out."

"I should've thanked him," she says.

"He knows you're grateful." Ethan chuckles.

Ethan walks around to the trunk, and Guilia starts to move closer to the car. I want to take her in my arms and smother her with kisses, but Ethan is here. He still has no idea how we feel about each other, and this is not the time or the place to have that conversation. She looks a little shaky.

"Are you all right?" I ask. She nods and reaches her hand out for the car, but she's not even close to it. As she begins to go down, I scoop her into my arms.

"I've got you, Angel," I say so only she can hear. I carry her to the car and set her on the seat and scoot in beside her. I pull her onto my lap and brush her hair out of her face.

"You're okay. I've got you," I say, kissing the side of her head.

"Nico?"

"Shh. It's over. You're safe now. I've got you, Angel."

I look up and see Ethan standing in the doorway. His eyes connect to mine, and he closes the door without a word.

Chapter 46
Gilly

'm sitting on Nico's lap in the back of a car. The darkness surrounds us as his hand pets my head, and he's covering me with gentle kisses.

"You're okay. I've got you," he keeps repeating.

"Nico?" My voice is groggy.

"Shh, we're going home, Angel."

"I'm sorry," I whisper.

"Why are *you* sorry? He kidnapped you. I'm the one who should be sorry."

"What?"

"I wasn't there when you needed me, *again*."

"You saved me, *again*."

"But he took you from *my* home. A place I thought you were safe."

"Nico, stop. I was safe there. What happened to Billy? Is he okay?"

"Alexander hit him pretty hard on the head. He has a concussion, but he'll be fine." Benny hands him his jacket over the seat, and Nico covers me with it. He pulls me in closer to his warm body. "I thought I lost you." His forehead connects to mine, and he runs his nose over mine.

"You didn't lose me. You found me." He peppers me with kisses. I don't have any energy, and my limbs are weak, so I cuddle into his chest and try not to pass out again.

"When was the last time you ate?"

"The salad I made us for lunch."

"I'm sure you're dehydrated and the adrenaline is wearing off."

"They drugged me with something," I say.

"You might be having some side effects from whatever they gave you too. We're almost home. I'll have Ruck come and look you over. Then you're going straight to bed. I'll wait on you hand and foot until you're ready for me to fuck you senseless."

"You don't have to do the waiting-on-me-hand-and-foot part. But you can do the fuck-me-senseless part."

"Not until Ruck says it's okay." I'm too exhausted to argue.

"Fine," I say with a pout. "I'm going to close my eyes for a minute, okay?"

"Okay, baby. I won't let you go."

"Benny, call Ruck and have him meet us at Guilia's apartment."

"Yes, Boss."

When we pull into the parking garage, Nico won't let me out of his arms.

"My legs work just fine, ya know," I scoff.

"I don't care. I'm not letting you out of my arms."

He carries me through the apartment and deposits me on the counter in the bathroom, and runs me a hot bath. After he removes my clothes, he gathers me into his arms again and stands me in the center of the tub and motions for me to sit.

"Aren't you getting in with me?" I ask.

"Not this time, baby girl. You relax and soak. I'm going to make you something to eat." Reluctantly, I sit in the tub and lie back. The water feels amazing, but it's not the same without his chest to snuggle into.

When Ruck arrives, Nico helps me out of the tub, dries me

off, and helps me into my panties and one of his T-shirts. I sit on the side of the bed while Ruck checks me over.

"You were very lucky. It could've been so much worse," he says, placing a bandage on the cut by my eye.

"Why do I feel so faint?"

"Nico said you went for a run and haven't eaten all day." I nod. "On top of that, you were sedated. I'm sure you're feeling lethargic from whatever they gave you. Get some food and water into your system. I'm going to leave you a sleeping pill to take when you're ready to go to bed. It will help your body relax and heal."

"Thank you."

Ruck helps walk me to the couch. He goes into the kitchen to talk to Nico, and I cuddle up in a blanket. My body feels so heavy, and I just want to sleep. The front door closes, and the lock clicks.

"Don't go to sleep, baby, you need to eat," Nico says, setting a tray on the coffee table in front of me with some pasta and a big glass of water. "Eat and then sleep." I sit up and give him a dirty look, but I start to eat.

"Thank you for taking care of me," I say. He pulls the blanket around my shoulders.

"Are you really going to watch me eat? Where's yours?"

"I'll eat when I know you're taken care of," he says.

I finish my plate of food and can barely keep my eyes open. He picks me up off the couch.

"Okay, you're going to bed, sleepyhead." I whimper, but I know I need to sleep.

"Can you hold me until I go to sleep?" I ask.

"Of course."

He gives me the sleeping pill, and I wash it down with some water. I lie down, and he covers me with the duvet, then goes around the other side and climbs in behind me. His warm body surrounds me, and I snuggle back into him.

"I think Ethan knows," he says, winding my hair around his finger.

"Knows what?"

"About us?"

"Why do you think that?"

"Because he saw you sitting on my lap in the car. When I kissed you on the head, he was staring right at me."

"What did he say?"

"Nothing. He just shut the door."

I can't think anymore as the pill takes hold of me. I drift off into the first good night's sleep I've had in two years.

The diamonds are gone, the bald man is gone, and I'm back in Nico's arms.

Chapter 47
Gilly

A week later, I go for a run, trying to get back to some sense of normalcy. I stop by the coffee shop for my iced Americano, and I'm standing off to the side waiting for my name to be called when someone taps me on the shoulder.

"Guilia?" he asks in a heavy Russian accent. I turn to see Boris standing behind me. Boris from Russia, Boris. The same Boris who took me out on one date and never called me again, Boris.

"Boris, it's good to see you. What are you doing in America?"

"I'm here on business," he says.

"It's been what, four years?"

"About that, yes. How are you?"

"I'm good. How about you?"

"Better now since I ran into you. Would you like to sit?" he asks.

"Sure, let me send a text, and we can chat."

I send a message to Marco to tell him I came across an old friend from Russia, and I'm going to stay at the coffee shop and talk for a while.

We take a seat in the back. This is going to be an odd conversation since we only went out on one date, but we'll see where this goes.

"So what kind of business are you here for?" I ask.

"I work for Pavlov Oil."

"Oh, wow. What do you do for them?"

"I'm an engineer."

"Do you go out on those big rigs in the ocean?"

"No, I usually work in the office." He chuckles awkwardly.

"Oh."

"What are you doing in Johnsonville?" he asks. "Traveling the world get too boring for you?"

"Something like that."

"Where do you work?" he asks.

"My sisters and I started some small businesses downtown."

"Small businesses. That sounds nice." If I didn't know better, I would say he was being condescending.

"Let me save us both a lot of time making small talk. Why didn't you call me after our date?" I ask.

"I was persuaded not to."

"What the hell is that supposed to mean? *Persuaded.*"

"A man in black cornered me in the alley next to your apartment and told me—in no uncertain terms—to stay the fuck away from you or he would kill me."

"Oh, he did, did he?"

"Yes, and no offense, but we had just met, and you weren't worth dying over. But now that fate has brought us together again, maybe we could..."

"Stop right there. It was really nice to see you again, Boris, but I think I'll pass."

"But, Guilia, why?"

"One, you weren't willing to fight for me."

"We only had one date," he pleads his case.

"And two, I'm looking for a man who will respect me and treat me right, and you, Boris, are not that man," I say as I look him up and down. His words seem to get stuck in his throat because none seem to come out as his mouth hangs open.

"It was great to see you again, Boris. Have a nice life."

Chapter 48
Gilly

Rocky beats us to the dinner invitation and invites the whole family to Lowell's for dinner on Friday night. Nico and I are in the car as Benny drives.

"Marco said you met up with an old friend at the coffee shop after your run. Do I know them?"

"Oh, I think you might remember him."

"Him?" *Do I see a spark of jealousy in his eyes?*

"Yes. His name is Boris. I went out with him once in Russia."

"Oh." I raise an eyebrow and stare at him. "I can explain," he says.

"You can explain what, Nico?" I ask innocently.

"I'm the reason you didn't have a lot of second dates back then."

"You are? Why?"

"Because I was a jealous fuck, all right?"

"What would you do to keep them from coming back?"

"I would put the fear of God into them."

"You would threaten them with death, according to Boris."

"Well, maybe a little of that too."

"Nico!"

"I'm sorry, Angel. I couldn't bear the thought of you getting close to someone, and then I'd *have* to kill them."

"You didn't kill any of my dates, did you?"

The thought of him killing someone just for dating me is ridiculous, but Nico doesn't answer my question.

"Nico! Did you kill someone because they went on a date with me?"

"Just once."

"Oh my God! Who?"

"That little twerp Landry."

"Ah, he was nice." I think about it for a split second and add, "But he was a little weird."

"He was a *little* weird, all right."

"What happened?" I ask.

"When I cornered him to tell him to stay away from you, like I did all the rest. The little bitch freaked out and pulled a knife on me. I had to get rid of him after that."

"My protector." I giggle.

"You're not mad?"

"Nah. He was an idiot."

"Thank fuck," he says, pulling me in close.

"Are you nervous about telling everyone tonight?" I ask.

"Hell yes, I'm nervous. Ethan's going to kill me in the middle of the restaurant. Old mobster style, with a gun aimed at me under the table."

"Nah, he wouldn't kill you in the middle of the restaurant for all the witnesses to see. He would take you out back to the alley to do it," I tease.

"Gee, thanks." A little shine of sweat is forming on his brow. I take his hand in mine and squeeze it.

"It's going to be okay."

"Do you know what you're going to say yet?" he asks.

"Me? You were supposed to come up with something to say."

"I know, but I'm too nervous. You do the talking."

"You're the man, you do the talking," I squeal.

"Where in the rule book does it say the man has to do all the talking?"

"Rule book?"

"Yeah. Don't all women have a list of rules their men are supposed to follow?" His smile is naughty,

"You're in the damn mob. You negotiate all the time."

"This isn't a negotiation, Angel. We're going to tell him we've been dating for months, and I've been his sister's secret fuck buddy. He's going to kill me."

"We'll do it together," I concede. "He'll respect that."

"Okay, but you talk first," Nico says.

"Nico!"

Benny pulls up to the curb, and Nico helps me out. The first thing we see when we enter the vestibule is the coat check closet, and we burst out laughing. Maybe this won't be so bad after all.

Rocky reserved a small banquet room upstairs. It's big enough for the whole family. The space allows the kids a place to play while the grown-ups talk. Once everyone has arrived, Rocky taps his knife on his water glass, and the children running wild around the room come to an abrupt halt. They take their seats beside their respective parents, and the room gets quiet, waiting in anticipation for Rocky to speak.

"I brought you all here tonight to make an announcement." He holds his hand out to Lola and she goes to stand by his side. "I bought the fourth shop for Lola. She's turning it into a coffee shop."

Oh my God and congratulations erupt from the family. MeMe, Lil, and I all jump from our seats and surround Lola, showering her with hugs and kisses.

"Why didn't you tell us the day we came to your office?" Lil asks Rocky.

"Lola wanted to be there when we told you. I didn't want to ruin it for her."

"This is amazing! We all have a shop now," MeMe says, hugging Lola.

"Have you come up with a name yet?" Lil asks.

"No, not yet. I thought maybe you all could help me come up with a fun name," Lola says.

"What about the shelter?" I ask.

"Amelia does a great job overseeing the day-to-day operations. Marissa has been an excellent addition and has assembled a great team to keep everything moving smoothly. I'll continue to work there until we renovate the shop, and then I'll split my time between the two for as long as they need me."

"Okay, ladies, you can all go to lunch tomorrow and work out the details. Let's eat," Rocky says.

We chitchat through dinner. Lola seems so happy, and I'm happy for her. All four sisters are working together now. We can support each other with the shops and the family. The kids can ride the bus there after school and do their homework in the back. It will be incredible.

Nico squeezes my leg, and I look at him. He mouths to me, "Tell him."

"You tell him," I mouth back.

"What are you two whispering about down there?" Rocky asks.

I almost choke on the spit in my mouth when I try to speak.

"I, um. We, um, have something we'd like to say." Nico nudges me with his elbow to stand. I push him on the arm, but I stand anyway.

"Um, yeah, uh." My mouth is as dry as the Sahara. "Nico and I are kind of a thing," I blurt out quickly and plop back down in my seat and brace for the explosion.

"You're what?!" Rocky bellows. Both Nico and I hunker down into each other. Nico closes his eyes and scrunches up his face as if my brother is going to kill him right here in front of all the kids. Rocky stands, walks over, and stops behind Nico's chair. He claps his hand on his shoulder, and Nico winces, squinting even tighter now. He braces himself for a beating.

"It took you long enough," Rocky says as he slaps him on the shoulder hard enough to hurt. Nico opens one eye and looks at me. I shrug because I don't know what the hell is happening either. We turn our heads and look up at him.

"You said what now?" Nico says. Rocky laughs and holds out his hand to shake. Nico turns his seat and stands. He takes Rocky's stretched-out hand.

"Why do you think I forced you to *babysit* my sister?" We both look at one another, our mouths hanging open. "Because I knew you two were perfect for each other." I smile at Nico, and he puts his hand in mine. "The little show you put on in the office the other day was pretty good, but we all knew better."

I look at my sisters, who are all smiling like Cheshire cats.

"You all knew?"

"Don't look at me. I didn't tell anyone," Lil says, holding up her hands.

"I knew something was going on when he came to the bookstore and bought some of your favorite books," MeMe says in her dreamy-eyed romantic way.

"I guess we aren't the good actors we thought we were." Nico chuckles.

"I guess not." He gives me a quick peck on the lips, and all the kids say eww.

"We'll be right back," Nico says as he pulls me from the table.

"Where are you taking me?" My high heels click on the tile floor as he leads me down the stairs and across the restaurant. "Nico."

"You'll see." He stops us in front of the maître d' stand and shoots the man a wink. The man uses his key to unlock the door to the coat check closet. We walk inside, and the man closes us in with a click.

"You didn't?" I say, shaking my head at him with the broadest grin on my face.

"I did." His dirty smile is wide as he pulls me into his arms and spins me so my front is against the wall.

"You're crazy. You know that?" I purr.

"Mm-hmm," he coos as his hand slips up under my dress and into my panties as I press my ass back into him.

We emerge from the tiny room, and Nico tips the man a hefty sum. We walk back to the table hand in hand with sated smiles on our faces. Thanks, Lucy Hale, for my coat closet sex.

Chapter 49
Nico

Guilia and I are lying in bed after our evening with her family. She's cuddled into my side with her right arm and leg tossed over me, holding me tightly in place. The room is dark except for the soft glow from the television, where *Friends* is still playing. I can't sleep because the woman I've loved from afar all these years sleeps peacefully across my chest. I no longer have to watch her from a distance or on cameras in secret. I can touch her and kiss her, make love to her, and fuck her relentlessly the way she likes it. It's not a secret anymore and I'm never going to let her go.

Graduation day.

I sit in the stands and watch Guilia cross the stage to receive her diploma. Of course, she's summa cum laude. I wouldn't have expected anything less from this intelligent, strong woman.

I've been working for Antonio and The Organization for the past two years. I started as a bouncer at Scarlett's, just like Freddy did. Paying back our debt for making our old man disappear.

My angel beams from ear to ear. Her blond hair, with bright pink tips, shines in the sunlight. Tomorrow, I'm going by her

*house and asking her out on a date. I've waited long enough.
We're both adults now. The worst thing she can do is say no.*

Guilia stirs in my arms and rolls onto her other side. I wrap
my body around hers from behind and listen to her soft breaths.

*The next day, I pace the floor in the apartment until I gather
enough courage to make the trek to Guilia's house. Antonio
will kill me if he finds out, but I have to see her. I have to talk
to her. I need to know if we can be anything to one another.*

*I drive up to the mansion on my motorcycle. I remove my
helmet and hang it off the handlebar and stride, with the last
bit of confidence I have, to her front door. Ringing the bell, I
bounce on my heels, impatiently waiting.*

*A teary-eyed Lucia answers the door. I've been on Mrs.
Martinelli's security detail once or twice this year. She's a kind
lady who treats all the soldiers with respect.*

"Mrs. Martinelli, are you all right?" I ask.

*She wipes her eyes with a tissue and motions for me to come
inside. She takes a deep breath to compose herself.*

"Yes, I'm fine. How can I help you, Nico?"

"I came to speak to Guilia."

"She's gone." *She bursts into tears again, and her cries fill
the porch.*

"What?"

"She left right after Antonio did this morning. She's gone."
Tears stream down her face.

"I'll get the guys. We'll go after her and bring her back."

She puts her hand on my forearm. "You can't do that, my
dear."

"Why not?"

"Because I helped her leave."

"You what?" *Why in the hell would she help her leave? I
don't understand any of this. She can't be gone.*

"I haven't told anyone, but I need to talk to someone."
*She waves me into the living room, and we sit side by side on
the couch.* "Guilia came to me a few weeks ago and said she
wanted to leave."

"Leave?"

"She was afraid her father would force her into an arranged marriage like he did her sisters." She wipes her eyes and blows her nose, trying to compose herself.

"Why would you let her go?" I ask.

"I had to, Nico. She doesn't want to live this life. She wants to be free."

"Does Mr. Martinelli know?"

"No, not yet, and you mustn't tell him." She waggles her finger at me. "We need to let her get as far away as she can before he begins looking for her."

"He's going to be mad."

"He'll be beyond mad. He would burn the world to the ground to find his baby girl."

"I still don't understand why you would let her go."

"Guilia has always been independent and strong-willed, you know that. We can't force her to stay here. She would be miserable. She has to be free like a butterfly."

"But you're miserable without her." Not to mention I'll be miserable without her.

"I'll be fine. When Antonio and I ran from our parents and came to America, we were in love. We built an empire out of nothing, our way. I think my Guilia is like us. She will build her own empire and conquer the world."

"Is she in love with someone, and they left together like you did?" I hold my breath as I wait for her response.

"No. No. Nothing like that."

"So she's just... gone."

"Yes, and I don't know where."

I take a deep inhale of my angel's scent while I snuggle my face into her neck and think about the day Antonio found Guilia in Europe. He had been looking for her all over the States. When he found out she left the country, he lost his damn mind.

Freddy and I were sent to find Nolan James and bring him to the warehouse. We grip him between us as we drag him. All the while, he pleads his case.

"You've got the wrong guy. Let me go. I won't tell him you let me go. Please," he begs.

We've learned not to engage with the people we bring to Antonio. They all have sad stories and try to coax you into letting them go. We bring him in the door, kicking and screaming, and strap him to the chair in the center of the room. This is the protocol for taking care of business in The Organization. Freddy and I stand at attention by the wall, awaiting further instructions.

Antonio was waiting for us in the shadows. He walks silently into the space and addresses Nolan.

"You thought you could run out on paying me, didn't you, Nolan?" His voice is dark and evil.

"N... N... No, I was going to pay you. I swear it. I just need more time." Antonio punches him in the face. His head snaps to the side, and blood seeps from his right eye.

"I'm tired of waiting." He punches him with his other fist. Now, both eyes are swelling and bleeding.

"Please. Please. I'll do anything!" the man pleads.

"String him up!" Antonio yells. Without hesitation, Freddy and I go straight to work, releasing him from the chair and reattaching his handcuffed wrists to the chains hanging from the ceiling. We pull on the chains, and his squirming body rises and hangs in front of us. His toes barely touch the floor.

"You can't do this. I-I-I have a family."

"They'll be better off without you," Antonio says with clenched teeth as he walks over to the table where the various torture devices are displayed. He chooses a cattle prod to begin with. The next time Nolan speaks, Antonio shocks him in the side with it. His entire body jerks while he lets out a horrendous scream.

Freddy and I stare straight ahead. We know we can't show any emotions, or Antonio will turn on us. I saw it when Buck lowered his eyes while Antonio tortured someone. He showed weakness, and Antonio could smell it a mile away. He flew across the room and beat the shit out of Buck, right beside me.

We watch as Antonio takes all his frustrations about Guilia

*out on Nolan. He cut off fingers and toes, sliced skin from his
body, and so many more things I would like to forget.*

*When Nolan's naked body hangs lifeless from the ceiling, An-
tonio calls for Freddy and me to go find another man on his list.*

*Day and night, the man never slept. He tortured and killed
five men in all. When he had nothing left to give, he collapsed
from exhaustion. We took him home to Lucia.*

*While he was recuperating, he came up with the plan to
have Guilia followed 24/7 while she was gone. I decided that
if I couldn't be with her the way I wanted, I could be there for
her this way. Watching her. Protecting her. So I signed up as
many times as Antonio would allow.*

The clock on the nightstand shines 2:30. I pull away from
Guilia to find the remote and turn off the television. I go to the
kitchen for a drink of water and climb back into bed beside
her, but I still can't sleep.

Moscow.

*Guilia is out on a date with Boris. She met him during a photo
shoot at the Kremlin. He took her to dinner, and he walked her
back to her hotel room. I hack into the hotel camera feed and
watch as his hands are on my angel, and my blood begins to boil.*

*She doesn't let him inside, thank fuck for that, but they stand
in the hallway, and he kisses her good night. She goes inside
and closes her door, leaving him standing in the hall. He takes
the stairs to ground level, and I'm there to greet him at the
entrance to the alley.*

*Wearing all black with a mask over my face, I throw him against
the wall. Holding my switchblade to his throat, he begs like a little
pussy, "Take my money, whatever you want, just don't hurt me."*

"I don't want your money."

"Please don't kill me," he begs.

"Shut up! I have a message for you."

"A message?"

*"You will never contact Ms. Martinelli again. Do you
understand?"*

"Whatever you want. Just don't hurt me." What a sniveling

little coward. I push him to the ground and leave the alley. I'm the reason she never had second dates while I was on her security detail.

I run my hand through my hair. I feel bad for doing those things to her. I know it messed with her self-esteem, but I couldn't let anyone get close to her. I was selfish and afraid I would lose her forever, and she was mine.

She spent six years traveling the world and dominating the internet. Antonio let me have six tours on her secret security team. I would have done more, but he put me on Mrs. Martinelli's security detail when she got sick. I helped take her to and from the doctors' visits until she could no longer make the trips. Then I would go pick up the doctors and bring them to her.

"You're a nice young man, Nico," she says, putting her hand on mine.

"Thank you, Mrs. Martinelli."

"I wish my Guilia was here."

"Me too, ma'am."

"I think she would like you. Maybe you could sign up for her protection team."

"I would like that, ma'am."

"Take good care of her for me, Nico."

"I will, Mrs. Martinelli, I promise."

She passed away a few weeks later, while I was in Paris keeping watch over Guilia. When she got the call from Ethan, I wanted to go to her and console her. Watching her in pain was the hardest thing I've ever had to do. She refused to fly home to attend the funeral. She was so sad. I had to do something to cheer her up.

There's a knock on her door. I watch her on the camera as she looks through the peephole and shouts, "Who is it?"

"Delivery." She opens the door to find the flowers I sent her. The card reads, **I'm sorry for your loss.**

There's a look of confusion on her face, but she brings the flowers inside and sets them on the coffee table. They were irises. The flower of France.

Chapter 50
Nico

I wake up the following morning beside my angel.

"I love you," I say softly before she even opens her eyes.

"I love you more," she coos.

"Are you head over heels yet?" I ask.

"What?"

"Remember during our first dinner together when you said you left town because you didn't want an arranged marriage like your sisters. You wanted to fall head over heels in love with someone."

"Yeah, I remember."

"Well, are you?"

"Yes, Nico Acosta. I am head over heels in love with you." Her kisses are warm and gentle before I pull back and whisper, "Are you happy?"

"Nico, what is wrong with you. What is with all of these questions. Of course, I'm happy."

"Remember the letter your mother wrote you."

"Yeah."

"She said she was sorry she would never get to meet the man that makes you happy. Well, she did meet him. I mean me. She actually told me to take care of you."

"Oh Nico. You never, told me that."

"Maybe she knew somehow how much I loved you already."

"I feel warm all over. Thank you for telling me that.

"Let's go away together."

"What?"

"Let's go away together."

"Are you sure?" She raises her eyes to mine.

"I'm sure."

"Where do you want to go?" she asks, pulling my arms tighter around her.

"I told you that night at Anthony's, when you threw all those questions at me, I'd like to spend some time in a cabin in the woods. Let's go do that."

"That's a great idea," she says, scooching up in the bed. Goose bumps run across her skin, and I pull the duvet up around her.

"Do you think Rocky will let you off for a few days?" she asks.

"Well, I'm supposed to get a week's vacation. Maybe he'll let me take it now."

"A whole week of just the two of us in the woods. That sounds amazing and so relaxing. We can take walks, and naps, maybe swim in the lake—"

I cut her enthusiasm short with a kiss to those pouty little pink lips of hers. "I wasn't thinking about doing all of those things."

"What do you want to do?"

"Have sex with my beautiful girlfriend, uninterrupted for an entire week."

"We'll have to eat, ya know," she says with a smirk.

"Okay. We'll stop now and then to eat." We both break out into laughter. "Let's go take a shower and go talk to the boss."

"I think you can call him Ethan now," she says.

"Uh, no thank you," I quip.

It took us longer to get out of the house than I'd planned. We spent a half hour in the shower having morning sex until all the hot water ran out. But here we are now, standing in front of Sasha's desk.

"I know the boss is not expecting us, but do you think we could have a moment of his time?" I ask her politely.

"I'll check. Have a seat." Sasha calls the boss.

She replaces the receiver and says, "He can see you now."

As she pulls the door closed behind us, she mouths the words, "Thank you."

Chapter 51
Gilly

"Thank you for seeing us," I say, giving Rocky a big hug.

"Of course. What can I do for my favorite sister today?"

"Your favorite sister, huh? What do you want, little brother?"

"Nothing. I'm just happy for you and Nico." He gestures for us to sit. "So what's up?"

"Remember how you told us we could have a week's vacation when you took over The Organization?" Nico asks.

"Yes. And I know you haven't taken yours yet, but I let you off the hook because you were watching out for my sister."

"Well, I was wondering if I could take it now."

"Now?" He raises his eyebrows.

"I thought maybe we could go to the cabin in Big Bear for the week," I say.

"You have a cabin in Big Bear? You didn't tell me that," Nico says.

"We hadn't gotten that far yet, honey." I pat him on the hand and give him the stink eye.

"I don't think it'll be a problem since Gilly's stalker has been eliminated and she'll be with you the whole time."

"Great! See you in a week." Nico jumps to his feet and pulls me by the hand to the door. "Thanks, Boss."

"Hey, on your way out, will you tell Sasha I need to see her for a second?"

"I love you, Rocky. Thank you."

"I love you too, sis. You look happy."

"I am."

Chapter 52
Rocco, Rocky, Ethan, Boss...

S asha comes into my office.

"You wanted to see me, Boss?"

"Yeah, have a seat." She sits across from me, ready to take notes. "You don't need to take any notes. I just wanted to talk to you."

"What about?"

"Remember when I took over The Organization and said everyone would get a week's paid vacation?"

"Yeah."

"Well, you've never taken yours."

"Well, I, um..." she stammers.

"I want you to take it now."

"Now?"

"Yes, now."

"But I don't want to take a vacation," she says a little too loudly. She knows better than to raise her voice to her Don, and she lowers her head to me.

I let it slide this once, and I say, "Look, everyone needs time to get away and decompress, and that includes you. So get the hell out of here."

"But what the fuck am I supposed to do for an entire week? I've never been on a vacation before."

"Go to the mountains, hike, and camp, or go to the beach, lie in the sun, and read a good book. I. Don't. Care. I don't want to see your face in this office for a whole week." Her mouth springs open to argue, but I put up my hand to stop her.

"Got it?" I say firmly.

"Got it," she says dejectedly.

When Sasha leaves the room, I call Lola.

"Hey, I figured out a way to get Sasha out of here, but it's up to you to get her on the plane."

"Thanks for the heads-up. I'm almost there," Lola says.

〜

THE END

If you liked this book...

Please leave a review on Amazon or Goodreads.

Follow me on...

Tik Tok: @authormkmanson
Instagram: authormkmanson1
Facebook: authormkmanson

Coming Soon in 2025...

Forced Vacation
Come Back

Acknowledgments

Thank you to my husband, Rodney and kids, Frank, Austin and Kaitlynn for all of your support and patience throughout this whole publishing process. You always kept me moving forward. You believed in me, when I didn't believe in myself. You all mean everything to me.

Thank you to Christy Jones at Ellen Christy Intimate Portraits for taking the photo for this amazing cover. For all of our lunches where we talked so long, we were the only ones left in the place. For everything you've helped me with, from banners to bookmarks. Thank you for seeing my vision and bringing it to life.

Thank you to Frank Manson for all the time you've spent on logos, cover designs, and 3D printing. Thank you for climbing the mountain with me.

Thank you to Edits4Indies, Barren Acres Editing, and Bravia Books for making my books better with your mad skills.

Thank you to Gabriela for your marketing expertise. You have been such a wonderful teacher, and I hope we continue to work together for years to come.

Thank you to Shae, Beth and Christy for being my beta readers. Your comments and suggestions have helped me so much. Your enthusiasm for the characters made me feel like I was on the right track.

Thank you to Deanna, Taylor and Kathy, for always being there for me to bounce ideas off of. For being the first to read everything I write. I couldn't have done it without you.

Thank you to the Mexican Dinner Group. Your support means the world to mean. Love you all!

Thank you to all the readers for choosing this series. I hope I brought Nico and Gilly alive for you the way they live rent free in my head. Buckle up for the ride, because Book Three is coming up next—you guessed it—it's all about Sasha, your favorite badass assassin.

If you liked this book, please help a girl out and leave a review on Amazon or Goodreads. Thank you for your support

About the Author

M.K. Manson began a journey of self-discovery on her 58th birthday. It started her on a path to become a dark romance author. She has been a lover of smut for years. Whether listening to audio books or poring over paperbacks, she reads all genres and loves a dark and twisty story. Give her a spicy why-choose romance any day of the week, and she's a happy girl.

With four dark mafia romance books self-publishing in 2025, she is on her way to her life's goal of being a best-selling author. For more information on M.K. and her books, follow her online on Tik Tok and Facebook at authormkmanson. And on Instagram @authormkmanson1.

ELLEN CHRISTY

INTIMATE PORTRAITS
ELLENCHRISTY.COM

Before he stole her heart...
She reclaimed her power.

Ellen Christy Intimate Portraits
Elizabethtown's exclusive boudoir only
studio

Every dark romance has one undeniable truth:
POWER IS SEXIER WHEN IT'S YOURS.

At Ellen Christy Intimate Portraits, we specialize in
capturing the raw, unapologetic beauty of every woman
—through luxury boudoir experiences that feel like
stepping into your own seductive novel. Whether you're
the queenpin or the quiet force behind the empire, you
deserve to see yourself the way the world should:
confident, irresistible, unforgettable.

With over 20 custom-designed sets, all-female staff, and
handcrafted albums and keepsakes, our studio is a
sanctuary where you take back the narrative, frame by
stunning frame.

Because every femme fatale has a soft side worth
celebrating.

And every woman is the heroine of her own story.

Book your session. Rewrite your Chapter.

ellenchristy.com | @ellenchristyintimateportraits
Dare to see the woman he would burn the world for.

Visit Us: ellenchristy.com
Contact Us: christy@ellenchristy.com
2791 Shepherdsville Rd, Elizabethtown, KY
270-317-6960

www.ingramcontent.com/pod-product-compliance
Lightning Source LLC
Chambersburg PA
CBHW030630110726
47901CB00002B/397